Gillian White is a journa~~~~~~~~~~~~~~~~~~~~~~~~~~~~~~~~~.
She has four children.

Nasty Habits

GILLIAN WHITE

PHŒNIX

A PHOENIX PAPERBACK

First published in Great Britain by Random Century Group in 1991
This paperback edition published in 1995 by Phoenix,
a division of Orion Books Ltd,
Orion House, 5 Upper St Martin's Lane, London WC2H 9EA

A CIP catalogue record for this book is available from the
British Library.

ISBN: 1 85799 338 1

Printed and bound in Great Britain by
The Guernsey Press Co. Ltd, Guernsey, C.I.

Dedication

· ——— ·

For Ron — for all the love, help, patience, encouragement, fortitude, stamina, endurance, courage — how can he bear it all, he must be a martyr or something — etc etc etc. But most of all for making me laugh like he does. With love.

It must have watched him coming, he thought afterwards. Through the thin green curtain, it smiled its
rictus smile and it must have watched him coming
through eyes that were not there, smelled him through
a nose that was not there and listened to his faltering
footsteps through ears which had long ago shrivelled up
and rotted away. And he hadn't known . . . *he hadn't been
able to sense it . . .*

The tide was coming in. Fast. Putting Desmond in mind
of his mother's fox fur as the silver slid round a grey
shoulder of rock.

Desmond was a timid man and he nibbled a timid
biscuit. A custard cream. The last of the packet. He
crumpled the wrapping tight in his hand before stuffing
it back in his pocket. A timid, tidy, tortured man.

This was the first time Desmond Hartley had ever
been completely and utterly alone and free to go where
he chose whenever he wanted. Not a staggering achieve-
ment? Surely a fairly mundane circumstance for anyone
capable . . . anyone normal? But Desmond was becoming increasingly aware, and uneasy with the suspicion,
that he was not capable, or normal, and that if he wasn't
careful he would end up a lonely old man on a bar stool,
going home to the empty house that, even after her death,
would still smell of his mother, taste of his mother, *ooze
his mother.* Hot hair and slippers warming, Radox-scum
on the bath and the sticky buds of cheddar triangles in
ashtrays.

The hot sun burnt his neck. It turned the surface water
to mercury and made the deeper stuff a thick, steely
metallic. He sloshed past the crooked little, sea-battered

sign that said PRIVATE, up to his calves in water, up a creek that was hardly a creek, more of a cleft in the tall band of rocks that formed the high banks of the estuary. For he had seen, or thought he had seen, a North African Squacco heron in full breeding plumage. And if he could take a picture of that with his new camera he could send it up to *Bird World* and maybe get fifty quid for it.

Unaware, unknowing, he drew nearer.

Desmond had planned this holiday with the greatest of care, turning down the offer to go with Roger and the boys to the Algarve again. Desmond hated competition and deep inside he suspected this was because he was so competitive that he just couldn't bear to lose. Going to the Algarve with the boys was nothing but competition from the moment he stepped, heart beating, on to the aeroplane, to the moment he collapsed in an exhausted heap back at Heathrow . . . drinking, diving, tanning, bonking . . . he remembered the fortnight he'd spent at the Mirimar last year and quailed. He would have loved to have sat down and asked his friends – the young men with the bold, contemptuous eyes – if they really did enjoy themselves, or if they were just pretending. He was never honestly one of them, never felt genuinely included. He always ended up with the thin, fawn-coloured girl who looked like him, as though fawn went naturally with his own fiery copper.

Yes, he'd been quite determined to be alone, he'd hoped that being alone would help him feel less alone than he did around other people, so that was why he'd pretended an interest in ornithology and, so far, it was proving to be completely uncompetitive. He'd had trouble getting his way.

'Why do you want to go off on your own?' Enid had asked him, taking the under-interested line she used when she was intent on finding something out. She licked an envelope with care, and he watched how neatly she ran the tip of her tongue along it, devouring the gum. Her

2

eyes moved with her tongue, devouring also. Devouring lies, a favourite habit of hers, sniffing them out first, prising them out like a whelk with a pin, and savouring them, intrigued, before she swallowed. 'And since when have you been interested in birds? What are you up to, Desmond, that's what I'd really like to know.'

Desmond handled her carefully, for the club she wielded over his head was a powerful one, and spiked with his impotence to make her happy. 'I would have thought you would be pleased, Mum, that I've got a new interest. You don't approve of Roger or the others. And Devon's only three hours away. That means I can get back quickly if you need me.'

'Oh? And how will I know where you are if you're travelling about? How would I know where to phone you?'

And the unasked question – if you're going alone, Desmond, then why aren't you asking me to come with you? Would you rather be off on your own than with your own mother?

'I'll let you know where I am. I'll keep in touch.' His lips and eyes had moved smoothly over his lie, and he had felt, again, that ridiculous sense of shame as if he was up to something quite evil. Would his childish fear of her never leave him? For she made him feel that he wasn't just making excuses to be on his own, but was conniving and conspiring with intent to do something so wicked it must be on a par with murder, or blackmail, or probably something more distasteful than that, like rape, or fiddling with a child, or stealing a bag from the feeble hand of a pensioner. But he had lied, and appeared to convince her, although she had sniffed and tried to trick him into the truth in her various subtle ways. Poking about with the sharp pin that was always there, needle thin in her glances.

Once, at school when he was little, the humanities teacher had given every child in the class an egg. They had to paint a face on their egg and cover its head with a little scarf. They had to make it into a person, invent a personality. 'Now this egg is your baby,' said the teacher, Mrs Blaire. 'And so that you understand something of the responsibilities involved in the twenty-four-hour care of a child, I want you to keep it with you at all times until the lesson next week. If you have to leave it, then you must first find someone to baby sit.'

When he went home and told her, Enid took the whole exercise most seriously. She made sure that the egg sat on the table next to Desmond at breakfast, and when he went to bed she checked that it was on his bedside table. When he went out to Cubs one night, she had insisted on being responsible. 'Don't worry about it,' she told him. 'It will be quite safe with me.'

Desmond hadn't been worried. Not at all. It was only a silly old egg.

Over-zealous, Enid had taken it into the bathroom and set it on the side of the bath while she got in. When she stretched across for her plastic bath cap, the egg had toppled and fallen into the water, smashing in the process.

When Desmond came back from Cubs, she was upset beyond all reason.

As if she had lost a son!

She, of course, recovered, but Desmond felt he'd been floating formlessly in all that scummy water around the vast body of his mother for as long as he could remember. Even when she stood up to hoist herself out of the water he imagined himself, all the transparent, slimy strands of him, probably still stuck to her. Just a floating egg. With a bloody, half-fertilised eye.

Anyway, it was burdened by bird book, binoculars and a brand-new Minolta autofocus camera that he crossed the rocks in his near-fatal hour, an earnest, worthwhile look on his face. And that would possibly have been all right. The problem really lay in those

4

slippery, bright red plastic sandals that his mother had bought for him specially, and packed in a wad of tissue. You can't run over black, slip-sloppy seaweedy rocks, binoculars banging your chest and bird book clammy in sweat, screaming your head off in terror wearing sandals like that. You can't run like that over sheer, black rocks that are covered by seawater most of the time and expect to get away with it. Oh yes, Desmond realised that afterwards.

He had worn those sandals today because, even from this distance, he had a terror of betraying her, of letting her down. As if in some mystical fashion she would find out and know. He saw her there, at home, alone, crouched like an old fortune teller over her foggy blue ball. He shivered guiltily as he imagined her speculative gaze, and how it would fill with dangerous tears if she knew how he felt about those sandals. But it was because of his plastic sandals that he went down. Out cold for the count. And it was just lucky for him that he was spotted or the tide would have come in and swept him away and he would have become just one more pathetic statistic, one more rotten, bloated cadaver washed up in a month or six weeks' time, one more sight forever to be remembered by the unfortunate finder, some crab-seeking child, or fisherman, or lovers touching hands and maybe dreaming down by the water.

Every step was taking him nearer.

A fact which Desmond did not know but would be informed of afterwards was that, at low tide, when tourists swished up the estuary with their lilos and their beach bags and their non intrusively coloured National Trust rugs, this little spot was used as a lavatory. People imagined no one could see them there, hidden behind the swathing of green. Clammy fingers of trailing creeper, still wet from the last high tide, touched his shoulders. And he could see that the tide was a high one because of the blacker marks on the rocks between which he

5

paddled. It was lucky he did not know what he trod on. At least his unfortunate sandals were a protection from that.

But how could he leave his mother? She wasn't well. She had never been well. He loved her guiltily – and there's nothing like guilt for its durability – and, what's more, he was responsible for her and had been responsible for her for as long as he could remember. And the special illness that was hers was always crouched inside her, waiting to launch itself like those vicious plastic monsters they stick on the fronts of T-shirts. It always started in the same way, with a slow flow of despairing tears which ended, if he failed to respond correctly, in a tortured, howling anguish, an anguish that invariably destroyed him, not her. Never her. But in the face of it, with the memory of it, how could he possibly move out of the house he had lived in all his life, and go with Roger to Renfrew to start a new company up there? Roger was brave and eagerly embraced new experiences. Desmond was not, he was nervous of change. All this went through his head, so that his mind thrashed and twitched about like a trapped animal, hurrying him, making him clumsy as he swished along. He was not a failure, it wasn't like that at all. In five years he had paid off the mortgage on his mother's house, happy to relieve her, at last, of that burden. Desmond was a comfortably rich young man because he knew everything there was to know about computers . . . a subject in which, unfortunately, he had absolutely no interest at all, not now, not after an initial, fleeting one. Although he had an Apple at home, and a library full of his own games which proved very popular on the market.

He didn't sense it. And yet he was almost upon it.

At the far end of the creek, where the water was only just reaching, he climbed up the steep, slippery rocks, cursing his binoculars and wondering why, if he had chosen to be alone, it felt so much like failure. It gave

6

him the same dull pain as losing. People would think he had no friends. He ducked to avoid the sharp overhang which was craggy as the Red Indian's nose in the video game Gunfire One, and immediately smelt the dank, stale odour of static air. Ancient, muddy air. Similar to that in some old museums. He was aware of the incoming tide. He knew he did not have long. So he did not take the time that he might have to haul himself up over the lip of the shallow, dry cave and unfold himself to full height inside it. It took time for his eyes to accustom themselves to the darkness. The air was sour and heavy to breathe. Behind him the tide whispered urgently.

It must have watched him coming . . .

Erotic in a grisly way. Shockingly indecent in the way she drooped. Bone and shadow, trailing.

Talons for hands. And the black eye sockets stared out from a deep and deathly nowhere. The hole where the nose should be gaped open. And that leer, that frozen smile clamped on to him, locking him into the mocking joke of some ghoulish, graveyard nightmare.

Into the silence she seemed to shriek at him.

Instinct kept him still. For one second he experienced a strange and immense calm. There was no action he could take, no way he could combat this intensity of fear.

Then he heard himself pleading: 'Oh no, no, please . . .' but he didn't recognise his own voice and jumped as he wondered where the hollow sound came from.

Another appalling second went by and still Desmond wore no expression. He was a non person, staring at another non person. For it was years since the spectre he gazed upon could ever have been called a person. And yet she wore . . . and thick scarlet lipstick had been meticulously applied around the edges of the teeth.

Jesus Jesus Jesus. Was there a world out there or was this it now . . . just him and this? . . . to Desmond nothing had meaning. He backed away slowly as the reaction

7

came. It started at his feet and moved up his legs, between his thighs, flattening his stomach, squeezing his chest, throttling his neck, opening his mouth, widening his eyes. And when the reaction reached his brain, then it was that Desmond Hartley started to scream. Then it was that his body, all reaction now, took him like a startled crab, scuttling down over the rocks the way he had come, missing his step so that he fell, flat on his back on the black strings of slippery nodules and dark green fronds, and his head smashed on a sharp piece of rock as he went, and he lay there, supine, at the far end of the little creek. Out for the count. While the water that was far from clean at this stage wrapped foamy white fingers round his legs as they hung there loose as a sleeping child's.

And that might have been that, he was told afterwards. The end of the road, or up the creek without a paddle for Desmond Hartley. Curtains. Had not a yachtsman making his way to shore with his outboard craft just fifteen minutes later happened to look to his left and chanced to catch a flash of bright red, followed by the sight of a couple of thin white things dribbling down into the water which could have been somebody's legs. Without this miracle Desmond's mother would have been unable to welcome her travelling son with a cheery smile and the kettle on. She would have had to finish making the rug with the bambi on it alone. She would have had to let his room and buy small dinners for one, play patience instead of whist, stop peeling potatoes and cooking the endless baskets of chips which Desmond liked to have set on the table the instant he came home from work. Wouldn't she?

But the keen-eyed yachtsman did spot him. And Desmond, with his book and binoculars and Minolta autofocus, was rescued. Probably because of those sandals. And was taken to hospital very quickly indeed.

*

Throughout the night Nurse Mary Dobson kept popping in to keep an eye on her semi-comatose patient. He looked very young lying there, with his carrot hair and his freckled face and his hospital striped pyjamas buttoned right up to his chin. All men should wear striped pyjamas, thought Mary Dobson, frowning, as she thought about Giles and his disordered nude body, waiting for her in the flat they shared. It was easier to tuck them in and put them away tidily if they wore pyjamas. They were not so rudely *intrusive*, somehow.

She wiped his forehead and she listened to his mutterings . . . 'I saw it. It was there.'

'You've had a nasty bang on the back of your head,' said Mary Dobson, her fresh, puppy-soft face angelic in the night light. 'But you're going to be all right. The wound was quite superficial. It's just confused you for a bit. Can you hear me?' She didn't know his name or she would have called him Desmond. 'You are in hospital in Plymouth. My name is Nurse Dobson and you are going to be all right.'

The young man who looked like a silly boy tried to sit up.

Mary Dobson smiled in a motherly fashion as she pressed on his chest and he sank back again.

'But I saw it . . .'

'What did you see?' Patronising. She thought of Giles who would never go down like that. Nothing of Giles's would ever go down, even if you pressed it. But Mary Dobson was glad of Giles, happy to put up with Giles at the moment. It was comforting to have someone come and pick you up when your shift was over, reassuring to have someone big like Giles to walk home beside you. Since Nurse Vane went missing three weeks ago, they have been advised by the police to be escorted, just for a while. It had made everyone jittery. Even the male nurses and doctors had stopped giving lifts in their cars. When

9

the scare was over Nurse Dobson had already decided to ask Giles to go.

'I saw the nun. No . . . the skeleton. But she was a nun.' Desmond moved the back of his hand across his eyes. He was crying.

Mary leaned across for a hard, hospital tissue and gently wiped his eyes.

'Yes . . . well . . . it's easy to think you saw . . .'

'I did see,' said Desmond, coming to himself and recognising the helplessness of his position with all the frustration of a small boy back in bed with the measles and a sore throat. He forced back the smell of his mother's cool stick, the eau de cologne she had smoothed on his brow. It had made him a sissy. He'd hidden it . . . hated it . . . and then it had been: '*I'm picking up the phone now, Desmond,*' her voice had come clearly up from the hall. '*I'm dialling the number now, can you hear me? And when the inspector answers I'm going to have to tell him because a thief is a thief and will always be a thief, and it doesn't matter whether he steals from his mother in his own home or if he's robbing a bank. One theft leads to another. I'm doing this for your own good, Desmond, and if you don't tell me where you've hidden that eau de cologne then the inspector is going to have to come here and make you . . .*'

Desmond shivered.

'I know, I know,' said Nurse Dobson chirpily. 'And you can tell us all about it in the morning when you have had a good night's sleep.'

'I am not tired,' argued Desmond, taking in the stark hospital surroundings and, for the first time, feeling the weight of the oversized bandage wrapped round his head. He lifted his head and touched the back of it tentatively with his hand. 'I do not need sleep. I know what I saw and I demand to tell somebody about it. Right now.'

Nurse Dobson's expression changed. Her comfortable face tightened up like loose, pink denim pulled by a zip. She tucked a wisp of stray hair away under her cap, cross with it, as though its wiry escape had undermined her authority. 'Tonight you must sleep,' she said in her hospital voice which only ever excited Giles no matter how strictly she used it. 'Nobody is going to listen to you tonight. There isn't anyone here to listen but me for a start. No, in the morning the doctor will come . . .'

Desmond sat up, wincing softly, and saying as sensibly as he could: 'Listen. I have to speak to the police. I am not imagining things. I know I have had a knock on the head and I even remember falling. I can remember nothing since then but I can remember quite clearly what happened up until the time I fell. I went into a kind of cave and it was because of what I saw there that I came out so fast. It was because of what I saw that I fell. Now kindly call the police or bring me the telephone so that I can call them myself.'

He didn't tell Mary Dobson how, when Enid was out, he used to climb on to the telephone seat in the hall, feeling the scratchy material of it on his bare knees as he dialled nine nine nine with a chubby wet finger. He didn't tell her because he didn't like to remember those times himself, those guilty times when his childish tirade, warbling over a string of confessions, had gone on and on and on until the lady at the other end sighed and put the phone down. He didn't tell her about the secret, shameful pleasure those confessions used to bring him.

As cuttingly as she could, on the loose end of a scornful sigh, Nurse Dobson said: 'You saw a skeleton dressed as a nun?'

Desmond nodded and groaned.

'And you honestly want to telephone the police and tell them that? Knowing the effects concussion can have? Wouldn't you rather wait until morning when you have had a chance to clear your head? If it's a skeleton that you saw then it's not going to go anywhere now, is it?'

How was it that all women seemed to know, and use

the exact tone in which his mother talked to him? Men never did it . . .

Desmond closed his eyes to see if he could picture it once again. And there it was in terrible clarity. Lying, languidly one could say, across the shelf of rock at the back of the cave. One leg obscenely hanging open and on the ground like the models in porny pictures. Only covering the top half of the apparition had been a long black habit and veil . . . not over its face though, oh God not over its face. For its face was all teeth and eye sockets . . . there was nothing holy about that grin. Desmond gritted his own teeth, opened his eyes and sobbed: 'I'll leave it then if you think . . . I'll wait until morning. But Jesus Christ – how do you think I am going to sleep?'

Nurse Dobson had got her way. So she could say, quite briskly: 'Well we can't give you anything to help you to sleep, I'm afraid. Not in the state you are in. It would only confuse you further. So I suggest that I dim this light just a little bit more and that you just lie here and rest. You'll be surprised how easily sleep will come . . .'

And so it was that Desmond Hartley started to experience the worst and longest night of his life as he let his eyes follow the stark angles and lines of his bleak hospital room. He was forced to keep his eyes open because whenever he closed them he saw the spectre . . . the thing . . . and he tried to tell himself, over and over again he tried to tell himself it was something he had imagined, something his rock-hammered brain had conjured up of its own accord. But his imagination was one which had never worked like that. His brain was a logical, mathematical machine, never given to daydreams and images. No, he liked to keep himself busy in practical ways, he had never dared be a dreamer.

He had never been so relieved to see the light of dawn come through his window. He had never been so relieved to recognise that what he saw must be fact . . . because he could not have kept the illusion going so correctly, so unswervingly accurately, for the eight long hours he had lain there going over it.

Seated at the prow of the police launch Desmond could have been an explorer going up the Nile like in the game Snare that Crock. He would have liked to have had a jungle hat.

He feared that the inspector, an enormous man built like a wrestler, considered him a crank, just another attention-seeking tourist taking up more expensive police time. He had taken hours, sitting half dressed, on the edge of his hospital bed, trying to convince him. There were times when his fantasies . . . for how many times had he imagined this scene . . . threatened to drown him. He had to convince him . . . he had to prove himself right . . . otherwise the inspector might do things to him, *might close the door and hurt him.* And it isn't easy to be convincing with pyjama trousers on and bare feet. Desmond's abject vulnerability had made him shudder with agonised pleasure.

For the first and only time in his life he had told the police the truth.

Now they neared the place and Desmond shouted: 'Slow down, you're going to go past it . . .'

The inspector peered out under his flat cap; plain clothes made him more sinister. Apart from the cap the massive man was dressed for the office and he had the tired, appraising eyes of an office man, or an inquisitor. The sun glittered hard on the silver bands he used to hold up his sleeves. Desmond looked down and saw that the man's suit jacket, abandoned, was getting wet. Even when he stood tall, the huge man appeared to be seated, about to swivel round into attack. 'What, there? You could hardly get a boat in there. I'm surprised you ever found it. It's barely more than a crack in the rocks.' He spoke loudly to counter the throbbing engine and Desmond noticed that he had a pen behind his ear.

Actually Desmond was sweating with a fair amount of relief because he had begun to fear he might not find it, or might not recognise the place again because it was, with the tide in, almost obscured. The leafy green curtain hung down and the prow of the boat parted the tangle of fronds as it edged its way carefully between the narrow opening of rocks.

'It's only just above us now. We could almost sail straight into it,' said Desmond, leaning forward to see.

'Excuse me.'

Desmond sat back lamely as the inspector and two sergeants held the boat steady, tied it to a greasy green tree trunk, and clambered out past him. Desmond wanted to go with them. By seeing it again in the broad light of day, with strong people around him, maybe it would lose some of the preposterous proportions the nightmare sight had assumed in his head. But they did not signal for him to follow. It was obvious that he was supposed to stay where he was, just a member of the public now, uninvolved. But it was his skeleton, wasn't it? He had found it. He felt a twinge of annoyance along with a good deal of mounting apprehension. Maybe the nurse was right . . . maybe concussion . . .

They were inside the cave for no longer than a couple of minutes. But Desmond knew the body was there because of the way the inspector glanced at him . . . no mere attention seeker now . . . no, an important witness. Hah! But along with the triumph came the sneaking, shameful feeling of dismay that, now, this man might lose interest in him. There would be no inquisition. No punishment. Desmond blushed, quite unable to understand himself, frightened and ashamed, and turned away.

And it was with urgency that the powerful inspector spoke on his walkie-talkie. His voice, like the voices of many giant-sized men, was disappointingly high-pitched, almost womanly. And the two sergeants stayed deployed, outrageously out of keeping, at the mouth of the cave as the boat swished away, borne on the throaty rev from the engine.

They made their way back to the police Land-Rover with its waiting driver. It attracted little attention from late-arriving tourists heavy with their picnics and with their hot cars glinting. Some spread newspapers over the windscreens before they bobbed away between the sand dunes. The inspector, with spreading dark patches under his armpits, asked Desmond:

'And you say that the skeleton you saw was covered in the clothes of a nun?'

'Yes,' and Desmond tried to demonstrate to the policeman with his hands. 'The black material was draped down one side of her, like this. And there was what they call a wimple, don't they, well there was a wimple kind of sitting on her head.' He found himself clenching his teeth again. They ought to have let him have another look. He couldn't go through life with that awful picture scorched on his brain. 'Why?' he suddenly thought to ask. After all, he had tried to explain it now so many times.

'She, if it is a she, she's not dressed like a nun now,' said the man as he dourly opened the door for Desmond.

'What do you mean?' Desmond paused. There was no newspaper over the Land-Rover and the inside was stiflingly hot. And his head, which he had assured the doctor was fine, had begun to ache threateningly.

The inspector, so dark and swarthy he put Desmond in mind of Popeye's Pluto, gave an unpleasant laugh. 'Unless there were two skeletons and you only caught a glimpse of one of them.'

'Why?' Desmond wound his window down and winced as the pain took him round with the winder.

The inspector glanced at the driver and passed what Desmond imagined was a significant look. 'There is one skeleton in that cave, George,' he said as the Land-Rover moved away, edging its way through the crowds with

15

their shorts and their sandals, their lobster-red thighs and their melting ice creams. 'And that is well above the water line, quite dry, and it is covered with netting and feathers.'

They drove out on to the main road and Desmond welcomed the cooler air that wafted through the window.

'Young man,' said the inspector as he swivelled around expertly to face Desmond. Desmond did not like the way the man looked at him, definitely regarding him as some sort of odd-ball, 'Either you have your facts wrong or your brain has turned them around in a somewhat curious fashion somewhere in your head. For the relics you saw were certainly not those of a nun. The ones I saw were in scarlet . . . dressed as a whore.'

It was a challenge, aggressively put, and Desmond prickled with fear. Here he was, telling the truth, and yet they did not believe him. The situation was suddenly not very pleasant, not at all like his fantasies were.

Startlingly, Desmond made the connection. And he suddenly realised that this time, if he honestly wanted to find himself, he was going to have to deny his dark, quailing fantasies – *there must be no dark cell with high windows, no shackles, no chains* – and stand up against his aggressor. He must concentrate hard and keep him as Pluto, comic and ridiculous, in his head.

Or stay, slopping around in that tepid bath water, attached to his mother for ever.

A skeleton – well – how absolutely marvellous! And on Harry Featherstonehough's private bit! Wonderful!

News has reached the party on the verandah via the village grapevine. Nothing official yet, of course. Just juicy rumour.

Chelsea sits back and circles her glass with her long, piano-player's fingers. She has never touched a piano in her life save to play 'Chopsticks'. No, that was the description her mother, in an early rush of ambitious fondness, had once given her daughter's fingers.

How can people make you feel uneasy like this? Year after year after year? She has known them for fifteen years and yet they still manage to make her feel she is at the dentist's spitting into a basin.

Sod the lot of them.

They're not so different from anyone else! They love to think that they are. But my God – look how they love to get their tongues round a scandal!

Everyone gathered here tonight, with the exception, perhaps, of Rufus, despises Chelsea. And she knows it. They all wish she would go to bed so they can wallow in their memories. But Chelsea, sipping bacardi and coke through painted lips, knows it. She is well out of place and she knows it. They all suspect that Rufus married her for sex – she can imagine their very words – 'Well, what else has she got going for her, darling? Thick as a plank and so vulgar, hardly out of the top drawer. It has to be sex. Poor Rufus.'

Snobs.

Chelsea sits firm in her coveted niche and considers. Well, yes, that could well be true. Chelsea, at forty, is still coarsely beautiful in a red and black crimson way. With a figure that screams for attention from lorry drivers and navvies. She wears boob tubes and wickedly tight, often leopard-skin-patterned trousers. She still buys real fur. She is never without high heels. 'I feel naked without them.' And yes, sex is all she is good at, all she has ever been good at. She exudes it as she exudes her Panama Jack suntan oil, it beads her skin and bends the air in greasy sworls around her. If they asked her straight out Chelsea Pilkington wouldn't mind admitting it. She might have her traits but she's honest. And another thing . . . Chelsea, with the black Sea-Witched hair and the violet eyes, would rather not be here either.

And yet isn't this what it's all about? Isn't this what she's always wanted? God, isn't that so often the way – the Devil farts in your face, you get there and you wish you hadn't.

Chelsea comes from a family that had never coped very well with weekends, let alone a month doing nothing by the sea. They preferred to cuddle safely into the week with all its laws and structures. They covered their failure in a frenzy of gardening, a brisk spate of DIY or, if it was raining, the ultimate humiliation – an afternoon watching a film on TV. But the trouble was that every now and then they felt compelled to dip in a toe to test the waters. And this entailed bemusing, unhappy Saturdays in a car being miserable, searching for a private picnic place, with the car windows uncertainly neither very up nor very down, but usually just uncomfortably draughty.

Chelsea was not Chelsea then. She was June. June Dodds. The name change was the first positive action she took. God, those weekends. And Wilf, her father, forced out of his baggy cords and into his cotton twill with the matching beige airtex which helped to conceal his monstrous gut.

Chelsea's violet eyes, full of longing then, watched others having a wonderful time while she, spotty and

18

fractious, rode in the back of the old Ford Popular listening to Muriel and Wilf lamenting the world and their lack of position in it. She swore she would claw her way out, whatever it took. She swore, when her acne was gone, that she would discover that special picnic spot, find the people with the hampers and the bottles of wine and quails' eggs and laughter. She would say goodbye for ever to the sardine and cucumber sandwiches and the Thermos with rust on the bottom.

She found it. It's here. But the standards are worse here than ever they were at home. The only decent hamper they pack is once a year for Glyndebourne – and Chelsea is bored to tears there. And enjoyment, she's discovered, takes energy. The kind of energy that Wilf and Muriel, so busy with suspicion, never possessed, no never even dreamed of.

Chelsea found the energy lying flat on her back with her legs apart. It was the only energy, then, that Rufus seemed to require. Now he's changed. When they come to Tremity Cove he changes. Now he wants her to play badminton on the beach and swim from the catamaran.

Ugh.

Rufus says: 'Another drink, darling?'

Harriet says: 'Surely, haven't you had enough yet, Chelsea?' Harriet is edgy tonight. Harriet is not her amiable self at all. The skeleton find has upset her more than anyone else could possibly realise.

Ruth says: 'I'm surprised the children never found it . . . as it was on Harry's bit . . . and in a cave!'

'Ours are the only bits the children don't go to. They'd rather go further afield. You never think you'll find anything interesting on your own patch of land, do you?'

Simon says: 'For God's sake, it's too absurd. How long d'you think the damn thing has been there?'

Harriet says: 'Must we keep discussing it? I find it all incredibly unpleasant.'

Wendy says to Rufus: 'I'm surprised you haven't been

down to claim it, darling, you know how you adore bits of old bone. These gnats are awful. Why is it that they always go for me?'

Chelsea would hand over her insect cream but she knows Wendy is against that sort of thing and would, perversely, rather be bitten than use any brand made by anyone who conducts experiments on animals. Although Chelsea is sure the impressive list of companies which provide Wendy's enormous private income wouldn't bear close scrunity.

The nun, Helen, does not speak, but sits gazing religiously at the moon.

So it is no wonder poor Chelsea finds it hard to cope with this enforced summer holiday. In this house of skulls where shiny, broken skeletons are everywhere – on the bend of the stairs glowers a great ox head – on the bedroom mantelpieces sit the elongated, morose heads of sheep – they litter everywhere, even the kitchen shelves . . . from the tiny snouts of decayed fish to the massive, pocked heads of moorland bullocks. You even begin to suspect that you might find a vision in bone, staring from black eye sockets, hidden in your bed.

Rufus, who says they are artistic, collects them, has a passion for collecting strange things, things with which he is unfamiliar. They intrigue him. As if he needs to touch them in order to understand, needs to possess as if he cannot rely entirely on memory. Almost the first thing he showed Chelsea when he first brought her here was his childhood collection of shells. Which he kept, rather conveniently, in his bedroom. The second thing he showed her was his bed. A grim little bunkish affair tucked in a corner. They share that bedroom now, and a bed that is little better. And it is still a childish bedroom.

'Every specimen is perfect,' said Rufus, showing off,

fingering the smooth thigh bone of some seagoing creature with love. 'Perfection is the key. There's no satisfaction for me in acquiring anything that is even faintly flawed.'

Chelsea had once seen his anger as he discovered a chip in an otherwise perfect jawbone of an ass. It was a terrifying kind of anger – the anger of a baby or a hurt child ... flaring, vindictive, full of blame and unresponsive to sympathy or reasoning. He had destroyed the jawbone with quite unnecessary violence, crushed it with a mallet and a snarl on the work bench in the garage. Crushed it to smithereens. Chelsea had smiled ... all men are small boys at heart. But then she remembered looking at Gregor who had come into the room just then, and feeling a peculiar surge of relief at the knowledge that their child, their only son, was undoubtedly a totally perfect specimen of his kind. Chelsea never forgot that experience.

A house of skulls – the Pilkington holiday home. Yet not a home.

But, thinks Chelsea now, staring at the group who clink their glasses as if in a toast to the gathering darkness, he should not have collected the nun. There is no convenient place to put her for one, and for two, she does not shrink or mellow or harden to varnished perfection. Nor, it would seem, can poor Helen be thrown out when she is finished with.

But there – that is one of the traits of this family, they live in a dream world absolutely refusing to face situations as they really are or to think of the world as it really is. They still seem to believe, yes, even in middle age, that life is as marvellous as they would all like it to be. As it was in their childhoods.

And as if to prove it, whenever they come here to White Waves, they live life to the full. That's why the house is so damn uncomfortable. 'A house to be lived from, not in,' said the hardy Harriet Pilkington, matriarch, when

21

Chelsea last complained. As she waved a cheery goodbye and struck out with khaki shorts on muscular legs for yet another of her twenty-five-mile walks. And hell, she must be approaching eighty. And her legs are all muscly and bent like prostitutes' legs, or golfing women with plus fours on.

Nor is the house of skulls, so named by Chelsea, timeless as they imagine it is. The seaside hamlet of Tremity Cove was discovered by the Pilkington set in the thirties. They, and a close and carefully chosen group of friends, had erected their dwellings, had plonked them on the best spots when that sort of behaviour was environmentally acceptable, windblown spots with majestic views scorned by the locals. These decidedly weird, sea-sidey homes, half Victorian, half beach-hutty, dominate the humble local establishments. They wrinkle their noses at the bulging cottages of the ancient inhabitants, the odd, low-lying farm with its red-stone barn, the crumbling manors (old houses were not in vogue so much in those days). The locals dismissed the newcomers with just a few words: 'They've got so much money they don't know what to do with it.'

There was quite a bit of truth in that then.

There still is.

'I'll fetch some more ice,' says Simon.

'And another bottle of Perrier, it's on the floor in the pantry,' says Wendy, his wife, gesturing with a tired arm.

'Harry might not like the publicity,' muses Ruth.

'Is there such a thing as bad publicity then?' asks Simon, rising stiffly.

'There is when you're an MP,' says Wendy. 'Poor old Harry.'

'Why do we always call Harry old?' asks Joei, musing into his glass.

'Harry was even an old child,' says Rufus conversationally. 'I think it was the way he always liked to

22

take charge. And flap about blowing that whistle of his. He could never bear chaos. He used to clear his plate whenever he came to tea so he could get one of Nanny Weston's green stars.'

Joel is entranced by the memory. 'Oh, I remember those green stars! You got one for almost everything . . . a clean face, well-combed hair, eating fat . . . and when you got ten she gave you a treat . . .'

Here we go again, sighs Chelsea. Bored to death.

Harriet says nothing. The nun says nothing. Chelsea notices that her glass is empty.

Those white, wrought-iron chairs that Chelsea can just see, set between the low privet hedge, in the small garden bower, gaze out over the river as if they have been there, stuck in that same position, for fifty years. With the same pattern of daisies growing round them. It is dismaying. It is sinister. If there is nostalgia, then it is sick and suspect. And why do they, particularly Rufus, crave it with such shameless desperation? The reason, as Chelsea sees it, is that it gives them all membership of an exceedingly exclusive club. Understandable in childhood perhaps, but in adults rather distressing.

And how come they still need that sort of security anyway?

Chelsea, who loathes the monarchy, nevertheless compares herself to Princess Diana when forced to spend this annual month down at Tremity. Slap into all that tradition, the modes, innuendoes, habits of behaviour, memory swaps – a whole hateful month in somebody's else's holiday home. There is no real way of assimilating comfortably into this – it has to happen in early childhood. Although, admittedly, the other wives have managed.

But then they are not like Chelsea. They don't even bother to wax their legs or do under their arms. And they sunbathe with no clothes on, something Chelsea wouldn't dream of doing – well not in front of women, for goodness' sake.

Chelsea adjusts a painful sling-back and stares at all those great bare feet. She thinks that this place is all to do with broken dreams.

They sit with their drinks on the green blistered thirties balcony on this, yet another magical night, while a crescent moon hangs high in the sky. Yes, quite – a nursery moon. They sit with their thirties drinks and communicate – just – but each in his or her own world – a trap set by the stars on such a night as this one. They listen to the voices of their children as they play American football down on the dry river bed. Rufus will surely be thinking: thirty years ago and they could be our voices.

Well thirty-five, Rufus, actually.

'It's getting chilly,' says Chelsea. Some of them nod but nobody answers. Chelsea shivers. But she'll be damned if she'll go in and leave them.

She looks at Harriet. Three sons – Rufus, the eldest, Simon and Joel. They own the house now. Harriet has handed it over. Three sons with three wives, four children and a nun. And three wealthy cars in the rhododendron drive. Chelsea recognises her own son's voice coming up from below, gleeful as all the others. The night is still, but for a slight breeze that rattles the pine cones. Gregor – so named by Chelsea – plays with the others. He is one of them as she can never be. He loves coming here. And the loving of it grows as time goes on and he realises he shares a secret experience with his father. Chelsea is excluded from it and yet Chelsea understands it. Rufus has explained it often enough.

'It was freedom,' he told her earnestly, wanting her to know. 'Can you understand that? There was a kind of delicious freedom about it all that contrasted so dramatically with our well-ordered lives. All the individual adults merged into an unthreatening, contented group, and quite suddenly it semed to us that they ceased to care. We were free from authority ... even Nanny Weston stayed at home. We could be savages. Formal

24

clothing fell off us like bonds. Times of sleep and times of waking were no longer strictly adhered to. All of us, Chelsea, we seemed to fuse into a sea of sunshine, blinded by cobalt, as free and as strong as the swans whose wings sheer the water. And we were suddenly left with these glorious friendships, lots of space and lots of air. Our lives at home were stifling, the nursery or boarding school. The freedom we found here at Tremity was, for all of us, a kind of ecstasy.'

Wanker. Rufus was always so damn fanciful when he spoke of his childhood.

'So you keep coming back year after year, carefully choosing the same month. Along with the Wainwrights and the Harvey-Lees and the Featherstonehoughs, their children, their husbands and their wives. Clinging to your childhoods! And you think you are bestowing the same sort of experiences on your own children. But they're not you, Rufus. They are from a different generation. They don't need all this bloody Swallows and Amazons stuff.'

'You wouldn't think so by watching them,' Rufus had told her happily. And she felt mean then. And bitter. And wondered if her jealousy showed.

Chelsea finds the whole thing disturbing. Now she looks at Rufus, charming, treacherous. A man you can never be sure of. She glances at the nun uneasily. Out of her robes and yet still a nun – that shapeless, linen dress and those great Jesus sandals. They don't detract from what she is. They make her, in fact, more nun-like. Tall and thin and slow moving like something you might see in a tree in a wildlife programme, and the pudding-basin haircut over a face too old for it. And Chelsea sees how, under cover of darkness, the nun stares at Rufus. So secretive and sly. Yet surely, out of all of them, Chelsea ought to be sympathising with Helen. Surely, as a rank outsider, Helen must be feeling as out of place as Chelsea is?

3

No. The nun is used to spartan ways, to a basic existence and early mornings and brisk activities. The nun is more in tune here than Chelsea is.

But which is the nun and which is the whore as they sit here this evening, wrapped in their secretive thoughts?

The withdrawing sea gives a phosphorescence to the night. It reverberates, distantly thundering. The channel left behind in the centre of the river becomes just a streamer of silver rushing to catch up. From its privileged setting the house overlooks the mouth of the river. It stares down into the darkness from its place on high, while slanting shafts of night slide by the whispering pine trees. The trees breathe in turn, sighing and rattling their fir cones. Ice clinks in empty glasses. Rufus pours himself another. Chelsea watches his sinewy, golden-brown arm move out then in again. A scratchy gramophone should be playing somewhere from within the house, His Master's Voice playing, perhaps, 'Lazy River' or 'The Song of the Volga Boatmen'. They should be dancing to it on the top terrace lawn. That would be most appropriate. Chelsea draws deeply on her cigarette and blows out the smoke in a deliberately, well-directed O underneath all those disapproving, health-conscious noses.

While Helen watches her.

Helen watches her kick against the pricks.

Helen is the one who has to listen to Chelsea's complaints.

'Sod it, I might be common but I know what this is all about,' said Chelsea, catching Helen alone and wanting to get this off her chest. 'It's positively Blytonesque. This is all to do with untidily cut, thick-wedged sandwiches wrapped in greaseproof paper, shrimping nets, white floppy sunhats and sandy plimsolls, outworn, with their rubber toes cut out . . . that's what it's all about . . . nostalgia! And economy, economy is everything. Lots of busy pickling. Lots of bottling fruit and making jam. Last time I spoke to Wendy she told me it was the fun of picking the fruit, wandering along the dusty, summer lanes, she said, with a basket, pushing your hands through the prickles, squeezing up your eyes as you stretch for that impossible branch. That's what Wendy said to me when I last bothered to have a moan.'

And Helen hadn't argued. Helen had known exactly what Chelsea meant once it was pointed out to her. Helen needs to have things pointed out to her because otherwise she wouldn't notice anything around her. All Helen can see is Rufus.

But once Chelsea started to explain, Helen found it easy to understand. It was all quite true. Because the jam that was always made such a meal of, the jam which was such a tradition, was hardly ever eaten. It was left to rot in ageless jam-jars with string around the necks – last used for crabs – and grow mould, too thick for the most intrepid to pierce with a knife so that everyone had to resort to the golden syrup.

'And that doesn't sink into this hard, healthy bread like it sinks into Mother's Pride,' moaned Chelsea, spilling ash on the breakfast plate.

Yes. Bits of old bacon go crispy and blue at the back of the fridge and every one of those thick, arty mugs is chipped and cracked. Harriet loathes to replace anything. She doesn't quite say 'Make do and mend', but economy is everywhere. Economy dogs the place. There is even a smell of it . . . damp and rotten. It smells of damp wooden draining boards, and the old wooden trays have had their thin rims stuck down so many times with modelling glue that they sit unevenly angled on hard black beads of gummy solidity.

Helen hardly sees it.

27

Chelsea moans that there is always sand on the terracotta kitchen floor, and bathing costumes drying on the pulley over the Aga. 'I'd never dream of using these hard, grey blankets at home. Army blankets – they must be! When I first came here I even looked for the tattoo-coloured stamp, horrified. I wouldn't use them for the dog. And I wonder, Helen sweetie, does this attitude spring from a nanny upbringing – dear old Westy, that crumbly old crone – or the spartan experience of too much boarding school?'

Helen hadn't answered. Chelsea rarely required an answer. But Helen considers Chelsea quite prudish in her way.

'Economy! Huh! My mother could tell Harriet a thing or two about real economy.'

And it was true. Helen seemed to see it all, then, as if for the first time. The furniture was terrible. Just odds and ends picked up, nothing matching or even pretending to match. The curtains were second hand. None of them fitted. Books read on rainy days drooped listlessly open around the house. Getting damp. Rotting. Lawrence. Eliot. Shaw. While Chelsea read *Ambition* in a morning, knees to her chin, picking her teeth with a cocktail stick and refusing to join in any of what she calls 'their horrible activities'.

And it is true . . . the Pilkingtons have got it wrong. Helen turns her attention to the present for a moment and listens as Harriet interrupts the on-going skeleton discussion to chide Chelsea for feeding the cat. In the darkness the old woman's eyes seem pale and crested like the moon. Harriet is quiet, out of sorts tonight. But surely, at her age, that is her privilege. She is sharper than usual when she says: 'He's a ratter, not a pet. Don't mollycoddle him, Chelsea. He's an independent soul. He stalks the night.'

Chelsea, admonished, withdraws her bangled hand

with the crisp in it, but she and Helen are the only ones who seem to understand that the one-eyed, one-eared Merlin is no such creature. His scars result from cowardly flight, not from hunched-backed confrontations. He does not stalk, he slinks, mostly into next door's garden to eat from next door's cat bowl. Yet he is forced into being hardy and magical. He is forced to live up to his name. He is kept cruelly lean and prodded up trees in a rather macabre way.

Yes, what Chelsea says is quite true. That's how it is here. Everything is wrongly perceived by people with dreams but scant common sense.

'Sweetheart,' said Chelsea, scowling at the smoke that curled up her face, 'they've had it too easy.' That is how Chelsea put it.

The night grows chilly. The ancient Harriet, wrinkled and brown, with a straw hat crammed on her near-hairless head, who seems to shrink and go small when the cold comes, picks up some glasses and goes to bed. Muttering rather madly. She is not herself. Her three sons, Rufus, Simon and Joel, discuss their plans for the catamaran. The heady plans of schoolboys.

Vegetarian Wendy, Simon's wife, and the dewy-eyed, pale-haired lisping Ruth, are enjoying the peace. Wendy is dark and slender, with the *Country Life* surreal quality of a misted photograph. A brigadier's sensible-looking daughter, good on a horse. Her chestnut, shoulder-length bob is thick at the ends like King John's. Made of sterner stuff than Ruth, she speaks with a royal accent. It is hard to imagine Wendy in bed with anyone. She is too sensible. But it is most difficult of all to picture Wendy in bed with her husband because Simon has the soft, chubby face of a schoolboy, and Gabriel's heavenly curls. Simon plays golf for a living . . . and there is a golf ball on a divot of grass embroidered in glossy green on the pocket of his short-sleeved shirt, over his left nipple.

Wendy enjoys coming here. She is an active woman

29

who grew up in a Scottish castle and thus despises comforts. She won't stand nonsense.

Ruth, wife number three, shivers and pulls on her shapeless cardigan. All Ruth's clothes are like that, all of a childish pattern and brightly coloured or watery weak and they look as if she's grown up in them, just in the way she's grown up with her eager-to-please, little-girl smiles. She is a typical English rose, but bonier, and on the end of a long-suffering neck, her fair face either lifts or droops according to concentration, and her well-cut corn-coloured hair is petalled. That vague expression of suffering she often wears, that expression overridden at all times by a stoic smile makes her resemble a vicar's wife. Her soft grey eyes are at all times full of sympathy. She feels sorry for everyone, especially her husband, Joel, the youngest of Harriet's children who looks like the oldest, stoops like a professor, and conducts a well-known orchestra under a mass of lanky blond hair. Ruth will get up in a minute and put together a special late-night meal for the children. One of those quick, tasty suppers she throws together so effortlessly, smiling throughout to please everyone. A tasty midnight supper.

Ruth enjoys coming here. She thinks the sea air is good for Joel and she feels it is important for him to keep in touch with his family . . . to keep in touch with as much as he can . . .

It's all games.

Helen won't stir. She is practised in quietness. She can make herself hardly noticeable. Helen is happy sitting here just as long as Rufus is close. Just as long as she can hear his voice. Helen would keep up this vigil all day and all night if necessary. On her knees, if necessary. Never tired never cold never bored with the fire in her heart so burning. She never stops thanking God. She thought she had lost all reason for living. She had stepped out into a cold, dark void, empty and alone. And then, like a miracle, along had come Rufus. More forceful than God and not as forgiving. He with the silver-blond hair, the languid movements, the oh-so-knowing eyes, the long, artistic fingers.

His is the face of Christ. In gold. Just as sensitive but far more beautiful.

These people think they know. They know nothing. They think they can read people's eyes. They think they manage other people's lives, but they don't. They never reach below the surface.

Helen is excluded but she doesn't appear to mind. She's glad of it. It allows her to think her thoughts uninterrupted. She wishes that Chelsea was not staring at her with such bold, unfriendly eyes. Does she know what Helen knows? *How can she not know?* Helen sits on the balcony and watches the others. Her thoughts are covered by darkness. Her pale green eyes are as far away from them as stars, and anyone looking into them would believe that the light from those eyes went out a billion years ago.

But something fierce lives on under those lashes.

They'd thought they were watching suffering, all those viewers at home. But they'd missed out on the suffering, the real kind of suffering that happened before Rufus, with his cameras, came.

Was there a time before the cameras came? Sometimes it seems to Helen as if they have always been there. Watching. So has her whole life been a performance?

No, no, there were real times. She might not like to remember, but they were there, just behind her, and incredibly only two years ago. She'd been a different person then. She'd been a nun.

A nun who dropped to her knees with passion . . . she who in childhood had so wanted to be a saint in order to please her mother.

The ache round her brows had scratched hot as thorns. Her chin jutted out in angled resistance. Her fingers clenched as a shudder passed through her. 'Don't leave me. Don't go.' And her robes dripped over the side of the prie-dieu like anguish, spilling messily on to the floor.

For months she had felt her faith slipping, slipping away like a death. Stunned by the fear and the pain, she'd wanted to call 'Take me with you, take me with you', and go with it into the abyss, into the stone-cold tomb, and, with her hair, tend to its fatal wounds. She wanted to burn on top of the funeral pyre with her lost love. With her lover. Mourning.

And a great quiet filled the chapel as if there was a dying.

But it seemed that she must suffer alone. For she could not go. The world stayed starkly real around her, set in the stately arch of the ceiling, in the high greyness of the walls and in the cloying softness of the crimson curtain that never moved unless she stared so hard at it she sensed its breathing in sombre time to her own. And she was set as if she was part of the chapel, one of the sacred statues chiselled in stone. Yet warm and alive with a trickle of sweat going down her back. She could feel her body acutely . . . down to the thick grey-stockinged gauze of her toes, up through the sagging weight of her habit, the humble curve of her back, the numbness of her begging knees and the tight-fitting veil round her head. The rosary stung her fingers. The crucifix burned her chest. She was human, not stone. Human, and indulging in a stealthy, cunning occupation now, no longer blessed. Her desperate supplications were entirely for herself, no longer for others. Her prayers ceased to be prayers. They seemed to be turning into spells.

As each day passed she became more and more real. She could not make herself fade like her faith, no, no matter how many hours she prayed, no matter how long she spent on her knees in penance staring with burned-out eyes at the cross above the altar.

Because the answer that came so unfailingly back from

those crucified eyes was always the same: 'Bear it, my child. You must bear it.'

The penetration of the agony became something almost delicious. She opened her heart quite brazenly and abandoned herself to it.

She could only vaguely hear the bells. She was only just aware when others came in or out. Suddenly those grey-veiled women existed at the periphery of her lonely consciousness, like dense draughts passing in a darkened corridor, whereas before she had been one of them, and they had been her life. Like a flock of sparrows they had flown and swooped together at matins, in the refectory, across the courtyard swooping they went to their cells after vespers. Their communal timing over the years, over the thousands of prayers, had come together to create a black and white flight of perfection.

It is rare to see a sparrow fly off in another direction. Unless it is a decoy hunted by a hawk.

But there was no hawk. Helen was a victim of herself. Staring at the one on the cross. But she, unlike Him, would not see Heaven tomorrow. The nun would never see Heaven, for Sister Helen of the Seven Sorrows there was no benign Father waiting. For the breaking of her vows was a mortal sin.

She imagined she saw black sheets on her bed and that the crucifix above it turned into a faun, demonic, with a cape round his shoulders, and horns. She started to touch her body at night . . . intimately . . . the worst thing she could think of. She lay naked on her back with her legs spread . . . concealing nothing of herself. Waiting for something hairy and swarthy. Doing. Showing. Perhaps God would punish her, anything, give her a sign.

'Helen, my dear. Have you thought that you might be just trying a little too hard? Why don't you give it a rest for a bit, give it a chance? You're overwrought,' added Mother Superior, her rice-paper face conveying

33

the agony she felt towards this child of the convent she had known for so many years.

Helen sat forward in her chair, her eyes red-rimmed, her hands tight together. 'I don't feel as if I am making a decision, Mother. I feel as if somebody else is making it. It's a choice I want . . . . and it's a choice I feel I don't have.'

And another time . . . there were so many confrontations. 'Talk!' shouted Mother Superior, swishing and clanking backwards and forwards across the floor like a madwoman, wringing her hands. 'What good does talk ever do? I've never known talk change anyone's mind in my life. Pray, child! Pray!'

While Helen slumped before her, a sodden lump of squeezed-out clay. And my God, Helen had prayed.

Nothing.

So – one of the great outsiders, wanting to get in. Wanting to belong – is that what it is? And Chelsea says, cattily, that Rufus is always making films about people like that.

In spite of her innermost delvings, her torturous prayers, the agonised nights, the evasive answer had not come to Helen via Mother Superior, via God or anyone else.

All those wasted years!

So, six months later Sister Helen was released from her vows and was, unbeknown to herself and all thanks to Rufus, well on her way to becoming a TV star, and well on her way to discovering the source of an eighth sorrow.

4

So you can see that 'Hartley, Desmond' – which is how he introduces himself to the bemused publican across the road from White Waves – is way out of his depth in all this.

Confusion reigns from the start, because the publican, surely an amiable, friendly Devonian, refers to Desmond from that moment on, understandably, as 'Hartley my lover'. The use of the unfamiliar, followed so startlingly by the so very familiar, unnerves Desmond. And it is no good trying to explain.

He's had enough of trying to explain, cravenly, timorously, down at the station with Detective Inspector Ainsworth. In the little room with the Formica table which was splitting apart at the edges.

The landlord says his own name is Cope and Desmond assumes that this is his surname. Cope's face pleases Desmond. It is the grizzled, grey, unshaven face of a pirate and the eyes are a brilliant, shifty blue. His hair is wispy and thin like the way mould grows on a prune, it is the wild, white hair of Michael Foot and could be tied with a bow at the back. Cope tells Desmond that he is lucky to get a room at all because it is August and almost closing time. Two days on from his macabre find – the first night he spent in a hospital bed, the second in a guest house on a main road in the centre of Plymouth – and he is exhausted after a gruelling day of questions. And now Desmond is furious because of the way the police seem to be responding to the description he gave. Real-life interrogation, he was discovering, is nothing like the fantasy kind.

It was far more boring.

'What did you say she was wearing? Would you mind going through that again?' Their attitude suggested they considered he had experienced some kind of strange mental aberration. This caused him hot embarrassment. And in fantasy your inquisitors are supposed, let's face it, in some obscurish way, *to like you.*

'Where are you staying?'

Well, at that point Desmond did not know because he had planned a travelling holiday – deliberately to foil Enid – visiting all the likely spots where he might find the rare birds he pursued with such furious zest.

'Don't go far, will you? We're going to need you again.'

Desmond was finding real-life authority tedious. It is a good thing I am on holiday, he thought to himself, and not just down here for a few days. He wondered what would happen if he was due back to work on Monday. Would the police ring them up and make arrangements?

He decided to return to Tremity Cove for three reasons. Firstly, he had spotted the pub on his previous visit and thought it welcoming, with the higgledy-piggledy shape of it and the lantern swaying over the porch outside. The second reason was because this was where he had left his car. And the third reason was harder to define . . . for he could not let his experience go. He had to keep near it. He might even go for a second look if he can pluck up the courage. But even coming back to the cove was flying in the face of his own fear – getting back on the horse that has thrown you. For the sensible, no-nonsense Desmond had been appalled to find, twenty-four hours after the event, that in unguarded moments his hands still shook. And that did no good for the outward presentation of himself at all.

Desmond Hartley is in shock. And indignant. He is unused to being disbelieved by people other than his mother. Obviously what the left-wing papers say about the police is quite true, they are a thick and nearsighted lot. Because time and time again he had explained to them that what must have happened was that some-body must have gone, between tides, and changed the skeleton's clothes. But every time he suggested that, fiddling with an obnoxiously lukewarm cup of coffee, the massive Inspector Ainsworth had given him a wry, disbelieving look. And Desmond discovered there was no pleasure in it.

Because how can you fantasize, no matter how vaguely, about someone who is thicker than you? Well you can't.

'Well what do you think could have happened then?' was all Desmond could ask.

And he had the awful impression that they thought he had set the whole thing up! That they thought he was a practical joker with nothing better to do with his time. Where would he get a skeleton? And why would he bother to put it together and drape it over a ledge? Good God – why would anyone? Desmond had tried to control his shaking hands. He could see the inspector stared at them, too. There were cranks going about doing odder things than that, Desmond knew, but he was not that kind of person. Why didn't they ring his firm and find out? Or his mother for that matter? She'd tell them.

All they kept asking for was another description, and another, and every time he told it Desmond pic-tured it.

And when Desmond went to ring his mother, in a coin box on a loud and gusty corner, he found he could hardly get the money in the slot for shaking. But he must get it in. He must hear a friendly voice. He told her all about it, keeping his voice very level.

'Where are you, Desmond?' She sounded surprised to hear from him at all. And hurt. Her voice made her real, they communicated together through thin wires across a cold and vicious world. She used to

37

tell him they needed each other in order to survive it. Desmond pictured her, sitting heavily on the telephone seat which was still in the hall . . . you had to rest your back against the wooden staircase wall.

He was immediately sorry he'd felt the need to ring her.

'It doesn't matter where I am, Mum. I'm phoning to tell you I'm in a hell of a state here. It was a dreadful experience . . .'

'So when are you coming home?'

'I don't know when I'm coming home. I've got to stay around here.' It was so much easier to be firm from a distance. He knew that when the call was finished she would go and sit at the kitchen table . . . the kitchen where the pale bamboo twisted and trailed its way up the wallpaper to the ceiling and where the silk geranium still lived on the shelf above the sink next to the mirror . . . he had given it to her when he was six years old. He saw her sitting there, puffy eyed, her dull brown hair held back from her face by a piece of rayon scarf. He saw the folds of grief that waited, like blinds, to roll down her face from her forehead. And he heard that voice from the past: 'I can't go on. How can I go on? How can I possibly be expected to go on when I've got a child to bring up on my own and no man to bring the money in? When you've gone to sleep tonight I'm going to come back down to the kitchen and get that cushion and lay my head in that oven. Only then will I get the peace that I crave . . .'

So, of course, he hadn't gone to sleep, but kept creeping down . . . because what would he do if she did what she threatened? What would happen to him? He knew the answer, he'd been told it often enough. 'You'll be taken away to a children's home and I will have failed you, same as I've failed in everything else I've ever tried to do in my life . . .'

'No, don't say that, no . . .' His voice had seemed

38

very tiny. How could a voice as small as that get through?

So now he said again: 'I don't know when I'll be coming home, Mum.'

And she replied: 'Well, I'm all right. If you have to stay you have to stay. I'll be all right on my own. I'm getting used to it.'

He'd wanted consolation. He'd wanted tenderness. Well of course he did because he was her son. He wondered whether to disobey the police and tell her about the nun–whore mystery. And then he remembered how she never could keep anything to herself . . . not even the most personal thing . . . he'd even heard her chuckling to Freda Jones the neighbour about some marks she'd found in his bed! Suggesting . . . he hated it when women laughed dirtily like that, especially her. He had never been so mortified. He had never been able to look the po-faced Freda Jones in the eye again.

He tried once more. 'It was a terrible shock, Mum.'

'It must have been. And what did the doctor say again? Has he given you anything?'

'The concussion wasn't too bad. The shock was finding the thing.'

'Yes, that must have been nasty. Old bones . . .' And he knew, with a painful stab of awful certainty, that she was about to say that she would make old bones before long. And then wouldn't Desmond be sorry.

'A complete skeleton,' he said.

'Very nasty, Desmond.'

But he could tell she was already thinking about saying goodbye. About how she could do so in the worst way . . . so that he'd be left worrying about her and feeling bad inside. He wished he could say: 'Well, you've got your committees, you've got your needlework, your knitting, your flower arranging, your monthly theatre coach trips.' He wished he could say that, believe that, but the truth was that she didn't have anything like that. She had nothing. Nothing but him.

She gave up work when he left school and started earning, saying, and sounding like a tyrant as she cut herself off from the world and laid out his straitjacket for him to see: 'It's about time I sat back and put my feet up. After a lifetime at it.' And her voice held the kind of triumphant bitterness he had come to know so well.

The goodbye, as he'd known it would be, was awful. With him saying things like 'They shouldn't need me for long. After all, if there are suspicious circumstances, they must have happened a good many years ago.'

And her going all silent on him, and giving an occasional sniff as frantically he pushed more money in the slot.

Cope wears a red and white spotted handkerchief round his neck and Desmond pictures it tied round his head, and a patch over one eye. Cope wears a navy blue guernsey and walks with a rock. The jovial man shows Desmond up to a room which puts him in mind of the galley of a Tudor sailing ship. The wooden, low-beamed room slants quite sickeningly, and the window is no larger than a porthole. The watery blue of the wallpaper puts out a clammy aura of fog. He has to part the tightly strung curtains and bend to see out. All he can see, across the narrow road, is the high walls of a house and the sign, White Waves, to the side of a tall green gate. Beside his bed, inside the chipped and coffee-ringed walnut cabinet, Desmond is astonished to find a Gideon bible.

'Too late for a meal I'm afraid, Hartley my lover. But Nellie the wife might manage a round of sandwiches. You're in luck tonight, for without that last-minute cancellation we would have had nowhere to put you. The caravan leaks.' And Cope winks for no reason. Desmond assumes the man has a twitch.

Desmond drops the Adidas sports bag packed by Enid on the low double bed. He is having to pay for a double room, but there is no alternative and he doesn't mind. At least it has character, unlike the sterile room he slept in last night, a room he imagined was normally patronised by travelling salesmen. It is hard to imagine how small a single room at the Merry Fiddler would be. Desmond showers by standing in the flaky bottom of an iron bath and pulling plastic curtains of pale fishes round him. Even the bathroom is slanted. He dresses in the only clean, casual clothes he has with him ... green canvas trousers, a T-shirt and a lightweight jacket over the top. Green goes well with his red hair, Enid says. His eyelashes are hardly existent, and colourless. His eyes are almost blue. His violent red hair and the force of the freckles that cover his face compensate for his otherwise pastel self. Somewhere, in all the dramas of the last few days, he has lost his red sandals.

Downstairs again and the landlord pricks up his ears when he hears about Desmond's discovery. He narrows his eyes. ''Twas you found 'e then?'

The ancient beams are shiny and yellowed with nicotine. Someone has obviously attempted to start a collection of keys, but they run out halfway along the dark overhang of the bar. 'I wish that I hadn't,' says Desmond, picking at nuts and perched on a high bar stool. He eyes the landlord defensively. Does he consider Desmond a liar, too? There are no locals in here, only tourists, and they listen and pretend not to hear. Cope's teeth are strong enough and white enough to take a cutlass. Is Cope dressing for the visitors? Is his behaviour a performance for Desmond ... for all of them? Desmond wonders about that. He had been

41

advised by the police to say little. But he longs to tell this amiable man all about it, actor or not. He longs to tell someone. They have heard about the skeleton, they think they know more than he does about the skeleton, but nobody knows about the way the thing was clothed.

'Do they say how old it were?' Cope slips in and out of his accent with thoughtless indiscrimination in the same way that his face turns sly and back again.

Desmond shakes his head and takes a hungry bite from his round of crab which is smothered with salad they refer to as garnish on the menu.

'Man or woman?'

'Woman,' says Desmond definitely.

'Do they say how she died?'

Desmond can't answer this. He can feel the landlord's interest waning. He is moving away with his cloth over his shoulder where the bobbing parrot should be, collecting the glasses from the last orders. He goes to the vast fireplace to kick the last of the dying logs. They snuggle together protectively and wisp white smoke up the giant canopy. On the uneven walls hang yellow pictures of ships which all appear to be sinking, or in various stages of wreck. Desmond wonders why, if they want the place to be sea-oriented, they still call it the Merry Fiddler ... perhaps it is some strange quirk of Cope's. There is no sign, anywhere, of such a person, apart from the one that hangs over the door. Obviously this place is in the process of changing its image and they haven't got round to the name yet. Perhaps all these old beams and slanting floors are nothing but mock disguise ... not old at all ... but built not that long ago? Could that be?

''Twas in all the papers this morning.' The landlord pushes *The Western Morning News* along the bar towards Desmond. ''Twill be bigger news than merits because 'twas found on Feathers' land.'

'Feathers?'

'Harry Featherstonehough,' says the landlord in a mock-haughty voice. 'MP from somewhere up the line. Has a house down here with the rest of them.' And Cope sniffs while he rattles some ice cubes viciously. 'They don't mix.'

Desmond is trying to eat his sandwiches, sip his beer, read the paper and listen to the landlord at the same time. He frowns, and he feels as his mother must feel when she takes part in those gossipy conversations he so disapproves of. 'Who?'

'The posh set o' buggers who come here each summer . . . they own the four big houses overlooking the river. They own the one you can see from your window, White Waves. They come with their children and their visitors, my lover. They often come at Christmas. They don't bother to let them out . . . no need to do that . . . enough money without having to do that. Yes,' says Cope, with gloomy pleasure, 'there's still a lot of money about. You wouldn't think so but there is. They don't come in here. Not good enough for the likes of them. Pubs.' And then, as an afterthought, Cope adds: 'He were the one who did that programme about that nun. You must have seen it. Went on for weeks.'

Cope lights a cheroot and holds it daintily between two hefty fingers. After his energetic session of clearing up, two long threads of white hair veil the sides of his face softly with the smoke.

Nun? Desmond feels himself sweating anew. Desmond had seen the programme. He and Enid had watched it together. It was one of a series of programmes about people on the outside of society . . . you had to watch them trying to get back in. It was the sort of programme that made you feel comfortable about yourself, relieved, as if you had somehow succeeded by doing nothing. And the nun had captured imaginations, probably because she came across as so terribly ordinary, so hopelessly inadequate and so naive, gullible. And didn't they do several follow-ups?

Cope rings his bell again, narrowing his eyes towards the few remaining groups who linger in the murk of the candle-lit dining room, or ante room, behind the looped Victorian curtain. With a beating heart Desmond asks: 'Who made that programme?'

'Rufus Pilkington, one of them across the road. He is a director of some company that makes films for the telly. But he makes them himself, too. Very artistic is what Mister Pilkington thinks of himself, with his flashy wife. Oh, and the nun comes now, too. Loaded they are. All of that lot. We've known them since they were nippers. Always come here. Allus has. Shocked us rigid when Rufus married that one, parading about with her cheeks hanging out of her shorts. At least the others married their own kind.' And Cope puffs back two floating pieces of white hair.

Desmond is terribly excited. There are hard bits in the crab. They seem to be stuck to Desmond's throat. He swallows more beer to wash them down.

'All right, Hartley my lover?'

Desmond frowns, fearing that he might choke.

'The crab? All right for you was it?'

Desmond manages to nod. 'The crab was fine . . .'

'Only it's too late to be asking Nellie to do anything else . . .'

'The crab was fine.' Desmond's voice croaks as he tries to nod to Nellie the wife, peroxide and fluffy, as her terribly rouged face comes through the hatch, over the sets of salt and pepper, inquiring.

'She's got a bad hip,' says Cope, as if her sudden appearance requires an explanation no matter how irrelevant. 'She's had it from childhood.'

Desmond's eyes continue to water. He must tell the police about this! Surely, here in the village lies the answer to the puzzle. A whore and a nun . . . for

44

there can be no mistake. This will shake them! And all it took to find out was a visit to the local pub.

But wait a minute. Desmond is a stubborn man and not easily forgiving when crossed. He considers the police, particularly Detective Inspector Ainsworth, have, in all sorts of ways, let him down. With his bemused expression and his relentless questions, Ainsworth has insulted him. Desmond has got to stay around for the next few days so why doesn't he go along with the police and their patronising attitudes on the one hand, while with the other do some digging for himself? What harm would there be in that? And if he could find some answers, if it's all going to drop into his lap as easily as this, well why not?

It would certainly be one up on Ainsworth. It would prove something very important to Desmond, too.

Perhaps the whole thing was a practical joke, set up by the people at White Waves to catch a fool such as he! Perhaps it was something to do with a programme they were filming. But maybe not. The possibilities are endless.

Eager now, and wide awake, Desmond tries to press Cope for more useful information. But Cope is keen to turn off the lights and Desmond realises that he is the only customer left in the bar. Every now and then the room is swept by departing headlights. There is something depressing and lonely about the way the place has suddenly emptied. Because with the departing lights goes the cosiness, too. With the dipping of the coloured lanterns goes the atmosphere. Desmond almost expects to see Cope with his teeth out, hugging a hot-water bottle shaped as a teddy bear like the one Desmond uses at home. And Nellie his wife, in a fluffy blue dressing gown and mules. His fellow residents, if any there be, must be already in bed.

He has time. There's no hurry. He places his empty glass on a mat and sees his hand shake. Damn them if it was a joke! Desmond finds nothing to laugh at. And nor does he laugh in bed that night as the sight of the robed skeleton jerks in and out of his nightmares and he thinks he hears Cope laugh, a horrible, rasping sound, that tangles in shreds of torn rigging.

And his mother's voice, coming through the wind, accusing him: 'I love you, Desmond dear. And I need you. And I just think it's dreadfully cruel of you to be thinking of leaving me all alone and moving out. *At a time like this.*' He stares at her in his dream and notices, with a complete lack of horror, that she has no head.

And in the morning, to Desmond's embarrassment, he realises that he has made a large, worried hole in his bottom sheet.

5

A seaside dawn weighs whitely in from the ocean. It creeps over the sand dunes and their tough, stalky grasses with misty stealth, rises and takes in the river cliffs. It steams like a ball of twisting smoke over the water, channelled between the high pine-topped sides of the estuary.

The sun directs a fierce, early morning ray through Desmond Hartley's little porthole window at the Merry Fiddler and yet he sleeps on. He is exhausted.

Harriet has often said: 'Best time of day! What a shame you always miss it, Chelsea.' Chelsea, with her head well under the covers and old make-up streaking her face, is sound asleep this morning. As she is on most mornings until gone ten when she rises and comes downstairs in a cloud of coughing and cigarette smoke. Her silver mules make clacking sounds on the sandy, terracotta kitchen floor. But for now she dreams the dreams of a child . . . she curls up like a child . . . her thumb is near to her mouth.

The nun is flat on her back with her arms crossed over her chest and her eyes closed. Innocence – ah. There is little of childhood about the nun. And her dreams are not childlike. Something fires her. What is it?

Harriet Pilkington wakes up this morning with a weight on her heart that feels heavy as lead. She drags herself un-energetically out of bed, she who is normally so keen to get up and embrace the start of the day. She remembers the skeleton like you might a half-forgotten nightmare or an aching tooth, aware that it's there, conscious that it happened, but uncertain whether to delve any deeper or try to dismissively wave it away.

Waves of nausea pass through her bony frame as she steadies herself on the window sill.

Oh Hugo – how could you leave me with this? Didn't you know it was bound to come back? Why now? Why now? And anger makes quick her slapdash dressing, it quickens the hairbrush in her hand and it makes her discard the suggestion of make-up she might otherwise have put on. And then she droops and stares at herself, at her ancient self in the mirror. She pulls a swathe of grey hair from the brush and stares at it where it rests in her hand . . . duck-down . . . she cannot afford to be so brusque . . . she is half bald already.

Harriet's smile waits for a moment, and when it comes it is sad. Hugo used to say you would know you were too old when you were afraid to dance in case you fell over. Ah but you danced on to the bitter end, didn't you, Hugo? And me, well I am growing increasingly afraid, my dear, that I am going to trip.

Shortly after those first sun rays Harriet struts out, a short, slightly bent figure in a battered straw hat held together by air and habit. Tortured by insomnia, Harriet is always glad to see the dawn, never more so than this morning. She doubts if she's had any sleep. She hurries along, her khaki shorts well down over her knees, with a driver over one shoulder and a bag of old golf balls in a string bag over the other. She is off to knock the first balls of the morning out into the sea. As far as she can hit them with all her energy directed into her strong, nut-brown little hands.

Harriet is frightened.

But with the sun on her body, even this weak one, she can feel herself uncramping. She catches sight of her blue-veined legs and her gnarled and yellowing toenails. Damn it she is old, but not old in the way she imagines old. Old are the people who stand aggressively back, cowering into the hedges of country lanes, waving their sticks with a 'I haven't got much longer so why are you trying to knock me over?' look on their faces. Nearly eighty, but Harriet still drives – dangerously, they tell her. She longs to wind down her window, put two fingers up and shout: 'Stay on the road for God's sake . . . stay on the road and take your chances! It's a good feeling – it really is!'

But she doesn't. She dives off the rocks, alone, instead. For Harriet is not an aggressive person. In fact she despises aggression.

Harriet is frightened and she wants to grip the fear as she might place both hands on the shaft of her golf club and grip it, swing it, wallop it down with as much might as she can muster. Why can't you do that with fear . . . why is it so elusive? She takes the sandy, curling cliff path so that on the way to the dunes she will pass the Featherstonehoughs' house – Wild Horses; the Wainwrights' house – Hillside; and the Harvey-Lees' – Water's Edge. The names, Harriet muses, are surprisingly disappointing . . . she thinks of her own house – White Waves. Naming a holiday home is a little like allowing small children to name their pets. She supposes there are so many magnificent choices that in the end you panic and resort to the basics. In their own family they had gone through years of a cat called Kitty, another called Thomas, and a third . . . a wretched, motley creature called Pussy. Little children have disappointing imaginations. She has always adored her children, but she prefers them now they're grown up.

Her sandalled feet slap silently down the sandy path. She pauses to watch a pair of swans, their white wings surging them over the flat, silver-morning water. She thinks the sound is metallic, of wire springs twanging. Harriet is relieved to see Harry Featherstonehough already out in his garden. Always an early riser, even as a small child, she wants to talk to someone and Harry is a welcome sight.

Harry is amazingly active. He always was a busy boy.

Loved organising. Couldn't stand disorder. These days they would call him overactive and blame his behaviour on additives. Take him away to some clinic three days a week, sealing his fate for ever on paper.

'Harriet, darling, come and drink some fresh orange juice with me!' Harry flaps an early morning hand in the direction of Harriet's head over the hedge. He is in his silk dressing gown.

And Harriet wonders if Harry, at this hour, has laced it with anything else. He can be jolly naughty like that. If he's not careful the puffs on his face which are turning it flabby will fall into the folds of a persistent drinker. Sad, Harriet remembers the dimples. Tanned, he looks much better than he does in the winter, and the silvery streaks of hair at his temple give him an air of authority it would be well worth him cultivating and hanging on to.

Slip slop slip slop across the early morning dew comes Harry in his slippers. Under his paisley silk dressing gown Harry is wearing his shorts. He should not wear such wide-legged shorts. His testicles are always falling out and Jessica is always having to tell him. Harry is always the one who stands on that flat piece of ground in front of the Houses of Parliament wearing a perfect suit but his hair all messy, telling the cameras what he thinks. So dedicated is he that he even appears in the pouring rain under a black umbrella with his collar up. Harriet can't help it – but whenever she sees him she wants to laugh because she still regards him as the rather paunchy little boy who cried when he was not leader. Or couldn't get his own way. Or was out at cricket. Always an organiser, Harry was a Member of Parliament even as a small child, assuming responsibility for everybody else, only safe when he was directing proceedings. Harriet smiles to herself. Harry is everyone's safe older brother.

Harry is a proud man, and secretive . . . it is his way of maintaining power. He never discusses his problems . . . a little like Hugo . . . he maintains he doesn't have

50

any. Hard on himself, yet Harry has any amount of time for anyone else, especially his neurotic inadequate wife, Jessica. Bluff and dependable, he loves to look after people. He encourages Jessica in her self-indulgent nonsense while he protects himself with that shiny, florid veneer of hearty bonhomie, which Harriet so much admires.

Harriet doesn't realise that all her life she has done exactly the same thing herself.

Couldn't Harriet confide her fears to Harry? My goodness, certainly not! Talking to Harry about anything slightly doubtful would be most embarrassing . . . for them both. No, Harriet's secret isn't one that can easily be shared. A man who embraces old-fashioned values, his family and friends mean everything to him, he would fight to the death to protect them. And yet Harriet knows she cannot confide in him on an issue like this.

And it's funny, so responsible for everybody else and yet Harry would be the last man on earth to ask for help in times of trouble.

'Your feet are now almost directly over the tomb,' says Harry in his loud, speech-making voice. 'The empty tomb, since the police in their great wisdom have carted the body away.'

'They could hardly leave it down there, Harry. It's all rather horrible, really, isn't it?'

'The police were here all morning yesterday. Annoying Jessica. And I only hope they are going to leave us alone today. We can't give them any answers. We're the last people to help . . . incredible . . . having a skeleton not yards from your door and knowing nothing about it.'

'It's funny the children didn't stumble upon it.'

'The children are furious. The police wouldn't let them in when they went to view yesterday. Doing tests. And the press . . .' Harry sips his orange juice. Harriet stares at it but can't tell if it is laced or not. 'They wanted to see the

51

cave. Take pictures. Not on, really, I decided. RIP and all that.'

'I don't think it would have done any harm.' Harriet casts worried eyes down over the edge of the path, in the direction of the fabled cave. Oh God, Hugo ... you could have found somewhere safer! She tries to lighten her voice. 'Might have caused some unwelcome erosion.'

'They wouldn't have kept to the rabbit tracks ... bumbling fools.'

'There's nothing to stop them approaching it from the sea, I suppose. Nothing to stop them taking the same route that young man took.'

'I'm putting a wire fence up across the entrance to the creek.'

'To stop the press?' Harriet is surprised.

'If they get that far with their blasted cameras there's nothing to stop them swarming like flies over my house and garden,' says Harry. 'And my privacy, when I come down here, is precious, believe it or not.'

Harriet smiles because she feels she has to. Not because she feels like doing so. The dragging weight still lies in her chest and it seems that nothing on earth is going to disperse it. 'I didn't know you were such a private man at heart, Harry.'

'I don't particularly relish the prospect of every crank in the land knowing where I retreat to every summer. There's pictures of the front of the house in two of the tabloids this morning. With comments ... they've doubled the price of it. And anyway Jessica gets upset. She likes to feel safe lying around in the altogether. And there's nothing the fiends would like better during the silly season than a grainy picture of Jessica with her boobs hanging out. She's too old for that sort of thing ... how unspeakably boorish these people are. Jessica's going through a sticky patch at the moment, Harriet, as you well know. And anyway, that bit of creek is

52

unhealthy. People have started using it as a lavatory. Nobody takes any notice of the sign.' And Harry looks rightly peeved.

'Do you know any more? Have they told you who she was?'

'Nothing. I don't think they know themselves yet.'

Harriet shudders despite the sun. 'Perhaps the bones are ancient. Ancient and interesting.' There is no hope in her tone for Harriet knows very well who that skeleton was.

'No . . . not ancient. They know that much.'

'How frightfully disappointing.' Harriet's bag of balls is digging into her shoulder. This conversation is becoming absurd. This is not helping Harriet's state of mind at all.

'The press, of course, are convinced it was murder. Nothing better to do with themselves at this time of year but go round sniffing for scandal.' And Harry rubs his slipper over a ring of daisies in the guilty way he had when he was a child. But he's not guilty of anything. Harriet knows that . . . Harriet understands.

Oh yes, Harriet understands. She understands all these children who are not her children and yet she is so close to them that they could be.

Harriet is the last of the old set, and for that they all adore her. Everyone is dead. Hugo is dead. Hugo died five years ago. Every time a low-flying aeroplane passes over, every time she crouches and feels that sudden prickle of dread as if the world is going to end and she needs to know from which direction the menace is coming, every time this happens she thinks of Hugo. Such a gusty, loud, domineering man. The world went quiet when Hugo died. It took her a while to tune in to other sounds again. She's sat with him in the chapel of rest and wondered at his silence. She'd remained alert, sitting there with her hands crossed restfully on her knee, expecting him to rise up with a boom at any moment.

And yet Hugo had been a good man in spite of his problems. Caring. Adoring of his three sons. A decent father. And a loving husband. He had overshadowed her, her friends were always telling her that. And yet she'd been perfectly happy to be overshadowed.

Harriet moves on when she sees the curtains twitch at Jessica's window. She doesn't want to get caught up with her . . . long, involved discussions of illnesses and homoeopathic cures. Past the privet hedge of the garden of the Harvey-Lees she goes, and Harriet hears the sound of leather on willow. She smiles. She can see the ridge of a tent. Thomas and William have spent the night out and now they are up and playing. Oh dear God there is so much to protect. It's super, she thinks, as she has thought so many times in her life. It's super for the children. And she can't help feeling gratified and putting their undoubted successes in life down to the wonderful times they have had. The best of both worlds, really . . . quite an intensive childhood, never a moment's rest, and then, on the other hand, these idyllic long holidays full of blissful freedom.

But now a dark shadow is threatening to bring every-thing they so treasure crashing down on their heads . . . everything Harriet has worked for . . . all the family dreams . . .

Coming to Tremity had been her idea. She had come here with Hugo by accident, had taken the wrong turning on a driving holiday to the west country the year after they were married. Nineteen thirty-five. That's when they had discovered Tremity Cove. Together. In the Humber with the hood down and a tub of potted shrimps to share. She had taken one look at the river slipping out like cooling lava, the dunes, the sky, the trees. And she'd had the idea.

'Why don't we build a place, a retreat, where we can always come . . . and if ever we have children . . .'

'Here?'

She had stood, savouring the atmosphere, eyes closed, arms to her sides. 'I have a feeling it has to be here,' she had told him. He had come across the dusty road and taken her into his arms. When Harriet was in Hugo's arms there was nothing else in the world. He was so large he put out the sun. 'If that's what you want, old bean, then we shall do it,' he boomed. But it was only later, after the war was over, when the children came, that Hugo fully appreciated the idea. And having the others so close, that made a difference to Hugo. He had really been such a gregarious, such a sociable man.

She passes the Wainwrights' house, Hillside. She hears children's voices giggling. Girls' voices. A curlew rustles and remonstrates from its nest in the brambles. Harriet feels the sea breeze stronger on her face. Here in this place she feels at one with the world. Quite dizzy with the wonder of it all. She hears the waves lapping in, toppling and tumbling over and over one another as the tide comes in and the river bed gurgles full. So keen are her senses now that she thinks she hears fishes breathing and little crabs scuttling.

How wonderful it all is. And the girls and the boys all get on so spiffingly together. This is one of the things that Harriet adores about Tremity Cove and their holidays here. It is all so marvellously sexless.

As Harriet would so love to have been. Naughty old Hugo.

DAMN YOU HUGO AND YOUR BLOODY NASTY HABITS.

Harriet holds back her sobs. She must think of the good . . . She must . . . she must . . . for there is so much good in all this! They can swim together, camp together, make fires together, ramble together, fly kites together, all healthy, harmless activities, particularly as they all go to single-sex schools. That's why this holiday time is so important for a good, wholesome development.

And everyone fits in so brilliantly well. Harriet frowns as she strides out. She walks so fast that the wind dries her tears. And old people do tend to weep in the wind. Nearly there now. Everyone, except, of course, for the slatternly Chelsea.

6

No. None of her boys are like Hugo, thank God.

There is an island. Harriet is passing it now.

It can only be reached by foot at low water otherwise you need the dinghy. Branches hang off it. Tree roots are exposed and hung with seaweed like a mermaid's hair, clogged with mud and catching all sorts of weird shapes and tangles of driftwood. It is a very small island, hardly deserving of the name, and round, not more than twenty yards across. And still there are the signs of the wooden hut they built there, Rufus, Simon, Joel, Harry Featherstonehough, Toby and Alexander Wainwright, and Felix Harvey-Lees.

And it was here on this island, in the last childhood of summer, that the seven of them raped Nellie Mundy. It was the year the sickly Joel went to school. It was the year that Nanny Weston left Burford.

Oh Nellie was never one of them, and they never spoke of it afterwards. Indeed, sometimes they wonder to themselves if it was true or merely a dream, so little communicating was done after the event.

No, she was never one of them. She was a native, a village girl, long-limbed and sexless as a bean pod. Her father owned the village shop and her mother, Joan, was a cleaner. They had always known Nellie. She had always been there. She was thirteen and they were just a little older when it happened. They took off all her clothes despite her trembling protests and they looked at her before they touched her for they had never seen a girl so naked before. They joked a great deal, standing back and pulling at each other's arms, punching each other on the chests and laughing. Joel and Harry had a puppy fight on the sand while it was all going on.

'Take me back,' Nellie had said at first, a little stiffly, when she arrived and realised that the tide was coming in and the water was too deep and too fast, at this particular time, to swim to safety.

And it had been that appeal, that sense of danger where danger never was before she put it there with her voice, that had started them off. They thought later. Or something like that. It must have been. Because surely nobody had meant it to happen when they offered to scull her over . . . something she had always nagged at them to do in her high, wailing voice, and up until that day they had refused.

'Take me back!' And she had planted her legs in the wood-chipped sand, dug her bare toes into all the soft whiteness, and placed her wiry arms on her waist. The fronts of her arms were white to the brown on the backs. She wore a flimsy cotton skirt with buttons down the front, not shorts like the girls they played with. She wore a blouse, also buttoned, not a T-shirt. And under the thinness of the blouse you could see two small bumps in the front.

Breasts . . . even the word was plumply enticing. Yet nothing of Nellie Mundy was plump.

Someone said it . . . Rufus had read it in one of Harriet's books. He had thumbed and re-thumbed the dirty page. He had taken the book to bed and hidden it under his pillow. 'Budding breasts,' he told the others, and they shook and fell to the ground with laughter.

'Jelly on a plate,' roared Joel.

'Fish on a plate,' said Harry, looking oddly angry and flushing.

Nellie angled her head to one side and sneered. 'You are so childish! Take me home or I'll shout and my dad will hear me.'

'If you shout we will shut you up,' said Simon, as he would have spoken to any of his friends.

Nellie Mundy went to stand at the door of the ram-shackle hut, all her fleshiness making the nails look stark in the wooden struts. She stood there, arms akimbo, scowling at them, tracing patterns in the sand with her big toe. It was a surprisingly large big toe for the rest of her feet, with a grubby nail. For she lived out of doors in the summer as they did. And was forever following them round. And spying.

'Spy,' shouted Harry. 'I think you've been here before. In the winter. When we're in London!'

'Have not!'

'Prove it,' said Harry Featherstonehough, MP, who knew they should not be doing this but was too scared to back out.

'Why would we believe you anyway?' asked Joel. 'Give us one good reason why we would believe you.'

'I wouldn't be the slightest bit interested in coming here,' she looked around her, wrinkling her nose with the sunburn patches on it. 'I wouldn't want any of my friends to see it. Ugh! It smells. I bet you've been pissing on the sand and not in the water. I've seen you having your secret pissing competitions.'

There was anger then. A communal anger made fierce by the sun and directed at Nellie Mundy. She was not a nice child. She was not pretty, or clever, or attractive. She had nothing to offer . . . and her mother, Joan, they said, was lazy and untrustworthy. It was even rumoured that she had been known to steal things . . . like a canteen of fish knives and forks . . .

Joel said: 'You'd better take off your blouse and let us see what you've got.'

Nellie laughed, but coyly. In a way they hadn't heard a girl laugh before.

'So . . . and what if I do? What will you give me?'

'We might take you home,' said Rufus, looking vaguely off into the distance.

'Might? You'll have to take me home anyway. You

can't leave me here all night or they'll send search parties out. You'll have to take me home and you know it. I don't have to take off my blouse to get taken home.' And if she was younger, at this point Nellie might have put her tongue out. But she didn't.

Felix produced his bottle of ginger beer. 'But you'll take your blouse off for a swig of this.'

Nellie Mundy eyed the bottle and shrugged. 'Don't even like ginger beer,' she sniffed.

They were circled round her now, staring at her angrily. 'Take your knickers off then,' said Alexander Wainwright, his eyes coal black and comic tattoos, half peeled, all down his arm. 'I'll give you a ten-shilling note if you take off your knickers.'

Nellie looked round nervously. Badly tempted. This they saw and took note of.

'There's nobody here. No one can see us. No one can see the island, not even from the garden of our house.' And Rufus' voice was quick and severe, cajoling her, so much so that the others looked at him and Harry threw a stone as far as he could out into the rising water. He should stop them now – they'd listen to him. This was getting out of hand. The dinghy was tied to a stunted tree. It bobbed as the water ran under it and Nellie Mundy stared with her pale, round eyes as if she was working out whether she could reach it or not. This sign of intended flight was exciting. There was a splodge of jam – or was it wet sand? – on her bottom lip.

'We could take your clothes off. You couldn't say anything about it.' Rufus looked round at the others. 'If you told anybody we would say that you undressed yourself and that you let us do things to you. That's what we'd say if you said.' He looked at the others. 'Wouldn't we?' And his deep voice squeaked, quite out of his own control.

'Hah!' said Nellie. 'Why would they believe you and not me?'

'They just would,' said Rufus, moving his eyes away from the girl's.

Nellie seemed to think about this for a moment before she said: 'Well, I don't care anyway. I want to go home and if you don't take me now I'm going to yell anyway.'

So they had to act. Didn't they? She forced them to act. No one remembers who first stepped forward. It might have been all of them at once. But they put their hands on Nellie Mundy and it was easy to unbalance her. They did it quite gently, and lowered rather than pushed her, down on to the sand. They knelt above her. The sinking sun got in their eyes. Even Nellie, staring up at them, shaded her eyes against it.

'Take off her knickers.'

'You take them off.'

'Oh for goodness' sake I'll do it!' And Nellie Mundy, seemingly fed up with their fumbling incompetence, sat up and took her own knickers off. No eyes watched. And the knickers, well, nobody knew where to put them.

It didn't matter any more which of them spoke. They were one then. Closer than they had ever been except for the time Joel swam out too far and got caught in the current and all of them did what they had been warned never to do. They pushed out the raft to get him.

When Nellie was naked they knelt on her hands and legs to stop her from moving. She squirmed and she shifted. The sun made the sand very soft and hot. The sand got everywhere.

'Hairy . . . she's growing hair there.' Joel nudged Harry and they laughed just as if they were little boys.

They parted her legs and squinted up there between her legs for a long time before anyone touched her. Then it was Rufus. 'Fish,' he said, and they fell back on the sand. Nellie did not get up. She lay there. Some sand went into Rufus' eyes. He ground it out with the back of his hand. Then they all took a turn. 'I didn't know they were so big,' said Joel, measuring the girl. 'I thought it was just an inch long.'

'It has to be big,' said Harry.

They made Nellie Mundy bend her knees. They pushed with their fingers again while Rufus, with two hands, held her open.

Her growing breasts were not extraordinary nor much to linger over. They were lumpy and envelope shaped, like a purse. And the nipples, which they twiddled between their fingers, grew stiff like tiny cob nuts. Her skin was warm and yet it was dotted with goose bumps. She turned her face away from them and her long, pale hair, which had been in bunches, covered her cheek and got stuck to it in damp wisps.

'Lie her down again and hold her legs open, no, not like this, like that . . . like that . . .' And Rufus arranged his swimming towel over Nellie Mundy's face. In a special way. In a way that must be just right.

They watched as he finally found his way into her, pulled back, pushed in, pulled out. His face became redder, his exertions huge as he gritted his shell-white teeth and held his sweating face to the sun, eyes quite closed now. Sand tousled his eyebrows, they seemed tangled and spiked like the hair on his head . . . the golden hair on his head. His body was suntanned, lithe and thin. Small muscles worked on his glistening back. Then he came and flopped on the naked body beneath him. A body that felt smaller, frailer than his. Exhausted. Letting his breath go in gasps.

'Gosh! Bloody hell!' in the voice of his father. He threw himself down on the sand and landed with a whump. He forced his eyes to stare at the sun. He wanted to see how long he could hold it and not close them. He felt like the sun going down. Getting cold.

And then they all took their turns, with different people holding Nellie Mundy in different positions. Some succeeded, some did not. But they all tried. And they never noticed when the sun disappeared or when she cried or when Rufus had another turn but found that he couldn't do it again.

And every time the carefully placed towel came away from her face, Rufus put it back. Gently. Tenderly. And Nellie Mundy's eyes peered out from the slit in between it. She drew it over her mouth to protect it from flying sand.

Wait till we tell them at school, was the unspoken message then. And Erskine Major would have to believe them . . . for they had watched each other . . . they had witnesses. Proof! Then they shared the ginger beer. They let Nellie Mundy have the best bit. She drank the last quarter of the bottle. She never offered it back. She drank it all. But she buried its base thickly in the earth, grinding it in with a small, grubby hand, making the sand spiral up high around it before she said very firmly: 'Now, will you take me home?'

But there was no room in the dinghy. And they wanted to punish her more . . . for something between them, unspoken . . .

'We'll come back for you.' Their voices floated back over the black water.

But they didn't.

But it wasn't they, or anything that they did, that dislocated Nellie Mundy's hip. Although it could have been. No, it was the long swim back in the dark that caused it . . . and that was her fault. She should not have waited on the island for darkness to come. She should not have been so gullible as to believe them. But she was afraid of going back . . . she'd had errands to run that day and she had not run them. Whatever time she went home Nellie knew there'd be trouble. And it was dark when she finally realized the trick. But Nellie was a good, strong swimmer. She had swum to the island and back many times without anyone knowing it. But not in the dark. There was no moon that night. No warning

63

given . . . no time to avoid the fast-flowing basket of branches sweeping down into the sea. In the dark, in her panic, Nellie didn't see it. It crashed into her just as she was nearing the safety of the shore. If she had met with it earlier, it would have taken her out with it.

She was in pain . . . but for days she said little about it. She left it too late, the doctor said, and there would be permanent damage. Well, she knew her mother would want to know how it happened and what she had been doing and where she had been. And she knew that whatever she said she would be blamed. And smacked. For her mother, Joan, never believed her. And anyway, Nellie Mundy wasn't sure if it hadn't all been her fault. She had protested only mildly. For Nellie had believed she might be accepted. Might be allowed to be one of them. The envy of all her friends. Everyone in the world seemed to have a boyfriend but her.

There were no immediate consequences.

Nellie Mundy grew up hobbling slightly and later she married Kitch Cope the local publican. Who had not been a publican then. He had been a cowman at Allington's farm. They married and moved away and only came back five years ago. Publicans now, for they went on a course put on by the brewery when they were living in Hull.

·——7——·

Harriet had found those beastly magazines in Rufus'
room before he'd even introduced his family to his
fiancée.

Harriet never normally searched his room. She'd been
under his bed, laying down poison for the rats which had
invaded the house that year quite indiscriminately, taking advantage of the owner's absence and overrunning
the place. Harriet hadn't shown Hugo . . . well, hell's
bells, Hugo was bad enough without seeing sights like
that. And now, Harriet supposes, she has to admit that
Chelsea had been jolly brave in a way to expose herself
to strangers like that. A whole collection – under Rufus'
bed. And afterwards Harriet hadn't been able to prevent
herself from the awful thought that the girl in the glossy
pictures – she couldn't call them suggestive pictures
because there was nothing suggestive left – but the girl
could have been just another of Rufus' collections. Dead
under glass. Harriet had been reminded of the first time
she dissected a rat in the labs at Cheltenham. Held open
the raw flesh with tiny nails knocked into wood. No . . .
she never told Hugo. And she'd never told Rufus she'd
seen them.

But Harriet had had to swallow hard when Rufus
brought Chelsea to stay and she'd recognised the face.

Harriet holds up her chin so her face gets the sun. They'd
been appalled! They had never believed that dear Rufus
would go so far as to marry the girl, and where could he
possibly have found someone like that? Everyone developed
this rather awful, flirty relationship with her when she first
arrived, especially poor Hugo . . . never dreaming . . . so
it was hard, when she came into the family so irrevocably
firmly, to change to anything remotely respectful.

65

Harriet knows that Chelsea hates Tremity Cove and White Waves. Finds it all unspeakably boring, stultifying. No shops except for the little post office/grocer's. She supposes that Rufus really ought not to come, ought to take her to Greece or the Bahamas. But Rufus adores it so . . . and little Gregor . . . the image of Rufus . . . how dreadful if the boy should be deprived just because his mother is . . . well . . . a whore. That's what Hugo used to call her – Rufus' whore. Dreadful! But then Hugo could often be dreadful. Was renowned for being dreadful, in public, too, sometimes.

Harriet is surprised and discomfited to see the figure so still in the dunes. She likes to have this time in the morning alone. The solitude is precious to her. Harriet sighs but does not break her stride. She merely takes a slightly wider angle, one which will take her well round the figure that stands so silently, so still, staring back to the house . . . . her back to the sea.

Oh dear! Rufus and his collections! Such sad collections, too. Always dead things. Peculiar things. Unsavoury things. But always dead, thankfully, until this. Until the nun! This, Harriet thinks, as she strides along, is going beyond the pale. Someone should say something. Helen is an intruder, an outsider, more so than Chelsea who at least bears the family name. And yet last year Rufus had asked her: 'Would you mind, Harriet, only I do feel responsible.'

'Responsible, darling? You were only doing your job!'

'It'll only be this one time. I made a mistake. I suggested it and she jumped at the chance. I didn't honestly think she'd want to spend a month with us.'

'Well, if you've invited her I don't see how you can take the invitation back. But I wonder if it's wise, Rufus dear, I really do. What will she do all day? Pray I suppose.'

But Rufus had smiled. 'She doesn't pray any more. That's the point. She's stopped all that and she's empty inside. To her, the loss of religion was like a death. A

66

little like you when Hugo died. All empty inside. With a great big hole left to fill.'

Oh? Good Heavens. Naturally Harriet had raised her eyebrows, recognising the wheedle in Rufus' tone. The same wheedle he would use when he wanted to bring his collection of rotting starfish inside, when he'd asked if he could store his dead newts in the fridge. Why did he have to show off his collections? Why couldn't he just keep these things decently hidden?

And now the nun has been coming here two years running. Everyone can see how the nun feels about Rufus. Immature . . . so silly, thinks Harriet, dropping her golf balls in a good firm square of sand a hundred yards from the water's edge. Harriet supposes, as she takes her first swing of the morning, that the obsession will just fade away in time. Well, what's the point when there's nothing can be done with it? She hits the ball cleanly and firmly and lifts her head, following the whistle of the ball as it cuts the air and flies steadily out towards the ocean. Most satisfactory.

Worship – that's what has happened. Poor Helen has found something else to worship. Rotten luck really, for her. And where will it end? Harriet watches the far-away ball plop into the sea with great pleasure. Some of her worries . . . some of the torment she feels at the moment goes flying out with it. She wishes Hugo could have seen that one. Perhaps he can? She squeezes her eyes to the weakly sun and whispers: 'Did you see that one, Hugo?'

But how is Rufus dealing with it . . . that is the question. He is, in spite of his work, in spite of his father's influence, not all that clever with people. Always preferring his static collections, stroking his bits and pieces of bone with a soft, fond look in his eye. Such a splendidly beautiful golden boy. Such a beautiful man – even now at forty-five. And it's rare for a man to look good at forty-five. Women try. Men give up. Rufus, she has to admit although of course she's never shown it in any way, Rufus has always been her favourite son. The one who resented the intrusion when they invited friends down here for the weekends. Even people he knew and liked such as the Sweetings or the Lords. Always resenting 'outsiders' which is what he calls anyone without a house at Tremity Cove. Anyone who isn't as satisfied with his life, or as self-sufficient, as Rufus. He promises them something . . . but can he deliver? Is he willing to deliver? Is this subconscious behaviour of his an invitation, or, by his very nature, a threat? And it is for this very reason, Harriet supposes, as she bends to set up another ball on a handy-looking worm cast, it is for this very reason that these 'outsiders' are drawn to him.

Outsiders like Helen. And to some extent, Chelsea.

And how is Chelsea coping with it, Harriet asks herself as she turns her back to the nun and all that she stands for, to take a jolly good whop at the golf ball that shines blue-whitely in the sun before it takes a deep, dark dive into the eternal depths of the ocean.

Jolly good shot! Jolly good show! Perhaps, after all, she is wrong, perhaps everything will be all right.

Click . . . whirr . . . click . . . whirr . . . goes the shutter of Desmond Hartley's Minolta autofocus as he goes round the village of Tremity Cove taking photographs mindlessly. Later, at low tide, he is going to wander up the estuary and see how close he can get to the cave. He is determined to force himself. He imagines he takes the pictures for some mythical magazine who might, at some point, be interested enough to pay him for his results. Really, he takes them for his own satisfaction. He cannot come to terms with the state of his own fear. Well . . . he's not under threat is he? Nothing is going to do him harm. No one is going to come up behind him unexpectedly and pounce on him. He looks down fiercely at his hands. So why do they keep on trembling like that?

Desmond feels vaguely sick because of his hastily eaten breakfast. At home they have cornflakes and toast. But Cope's wife, Nellie, woke him up at eight o'clock with a tray . . . 'We'd rather serve them upstairs . . . saves messing up the dining room and Joyce the cleaner likes to make a start at eight because she's got other homes to do on a Friday apart from us.' So it seemed that there was no choice. And Desmond doesn't like tea first thing in the morning. His mother always brings him coffee. He misses her.

While he ate, a beam of sun played on his face, annoying and almost blinding him. Nellie had dragged the curtain back, stumping across the slanting room with her small roll, or limp. Her frizzy, peroxide hair was tied back with a bright blue ribbon. And her skirt, for a woman of her age, was surely far too short. Desmond saw the varicose veins at the backs of her knees and was put in mind of his mother. Who had the good sense never to wear a skirt like that. Yes, he misses her.

He thought he might stroll along the village street to the shop for a paper. He imagined he might return to the pub to read it. But the downstairs of the pub at that hour had been gustily unwelcoming . . . a fierce-looking woman manhandled a Hoover . . . the door stood open letting in draughts. Everywhere was the smell of polish. No sign of Cope, or any of Desmond's fellow residents. Perhaps they were upstairs preparing for the day . . . families with buckets and spades . . . preparing for the day. Desmond was suddenly struck by a pang of loneliness.

And so he went for his camera and, putting an air of whistling contentment on his face for it was important to Desmond that no one feel sorry for him, think him needy or lonely, he left the Merry Fiddler with a resolute step full of purpose, which slowed, and slowed, as he passed

69

the shop and recognised, by the limp grey blind, that it was shut and would not open until nine thirty. By then he was definitely drifting.

For Desmond felt uneasy with this. Desmond, from up the line, was used to shops opening, sometimes, at half past seven. Especially newsagents. Desmond, backtracking and making for the dunes, is lonely and disconcerted. Because you can get behind a newspaper very easily and make it seem as if you want to be there. Without that you are naked. He holds his camera up to his eye and clicks it.

The Pilkington set need never be lonely. Let's see – if every member of this select group decided to congregate for breakfast in the kitchen there would be twenty-four. Twelve from White Waves: four from Hillside: four from Water's Edge and four from Wild Horses.

They would fit. There is plenty of room to accommodate them all. The barn-like kitchen is large enough. The table is big enough. And two sets of church pews stretch down beside it, long enough easily to seat eleven quite comfortably upon each. The remaining two would take the ends. The pews are padded for comfort with faded garden cushions from an old hammock that rusted away ... fell apart from lack of enthusiasm and attention. Damp-smelling cushions with all the puff out of them. Eleven down the sides and two at each end. Who would the two be? Well ... Rufus and Harriet. And there are plenty of those pottery plates, and enough knives and forks lying around somewhere. And Ruth, her martyred face covered with well-meaning smiles, would knock something up if someone else would clear the table first.

But they do not congregate. Apart from the children they start their mornings quite separately. Now, as eight thirty approaches, the White Waves children rise, communally, having decided to spend last night sleeping on the floor in sleeping bags in Gregor's room. They make for the kitchen, cut slabs of bread, cover them with peanut butter, and with lemonade slopping over the edges of chunky mugs, they pad outside on to the grass for this the first meal of the day. The grass is cold on their feet. Little wet bits stick to their toes. They leave footprints. There they fall on a damp rug which someone has forgotten to bring in, wearing the crumpled shorts of last night. They lie on their backs and they eat.

There is Gregor, son of Rufus, golden, cool and confident as his father. The beautiful child is Amelia, daughter of Wendy and Simon, and there are Ferdi and Laurence, the pale twin sons of Joel and the stoic, supper-getting Ruth. They take no notice of the man who passes down the road so uncertainly with his camera. He looks like a boring old fart.

The boys treat Amelia like a girl but nobody is aware that they do. They show off when Amelia is there. They fight more often and more fiercely. For Amelia is extraordinarily petite and beautiful, in secret Gregor compares her to Tinkerbell, with whom, at four, he had a kind of infatuation. Amelia's blonde, curly hair falls prettily round her neck. Her eyes match the bluest of skies but her lashes are dark and cast cloud-like shadows. Amelia, being ten, knows this. The leaders shift daily according to activity, and she flirts with the leader of the day quite blatantly, once she's worked out who he is. Only none of them are aware that she does.

Now, on the rug, with the boys all lolling on their tummies, intoxicated by the promising sense of an early morning, Amelia sits cross legged before them, knowing they can see up her shorts. A certain distance only.

Gregor, Rufus' only child, and perfect, says: 'She's out there on the dunes. As usual.'

'Watching again,' says Ferdi, with a crust hanging out of his mouth which he tries to suck back like a strand of spaghetti. He tries to sigh but fails.

71

'She watches all the time. She's a watcher. She very rarely takes any action,' says Amelia, banging her knees together so that her calves flap. She leans to pick daisies, ready to make a daisy chain. But deciding she cannot be bothered she sprinkles her legs with the wet, white heads instead. Then brushes them off with a half smile.

'Your mother is going to go crazy when she realises what's going on.'

'There's nothing going on,' says Gregor. 'That's the whole point. But we've got to try and make it.'

'We don't have to,' argues Laurence, pulling fluff from the rug and twisting it painfully round his finger. His finger goes white at the end. Laurence stares at it. 'It's only a dare. We can, if we want, just refuse to do it.'

'It wouldn't work anyway,' says Amelia wisely, closing her eyes in the knowing way her mother does. 'Rufus is not interested. And who would be? I mean . . .'

'Still waters run deep,' says Laurence.

'I don't think Helen's very deep.'

'You can't tell. She's intelligent. She's a teacher.'

'Teachers aren't intelligent. Harriet says they're only there because they can't think of what else to do. She says teaching is a last-ditch resort. Especially in a school such as that!'

'I wouldn't like to have that nun teaching me. She's so dry and dull,' says Gregor.

'I'd like to see her get drunk,' says Ferdi, looking up the tempting tunnel of Amelia's shorts and hurrying his eyes away.

Laurence sees what his brother is doing and turns his back. Laurence thinks Amelia likes Ferdi better than him, and this thought, whenever he has it, hurts him. 'We could get her drunk. Easy.'

'Get her drunk and see what happens?'

'I bet she's never been drunk in her whole life.'

'She'll have only drunk communion wine.' Ferdi glugs noisily, making his throat go in and out and drying up

72

all his saliva. He puts his hands together and closes his eyes, kneeling up on the rug. He is the one who is always fooling around.

'Rufus collected communion wafers once,' says his son, Gregor, quite proudly. 'He was given a whole box of them and he put them in the cupboard under the stairs. It was definitely a collection.'

'Dead!' says Amelia, having listened to Chelsea talking. 'The dead body of Christ. Yes, Rufus would collect them. He likes anything dead.'

'Joel collects wine then.' Laurence tries to impress Amelia who says, cuttingly:

'Everyone collects wine. That's quite different. Wine is full of life.'

'Chelsea would go mad if she knew,' says Ferdi. He wants more bread but can't be bothered to go back indoors to get it. He wonders if he can bribe Laurence to go for him.

Gregor has started to become defensive when the others speak of Chelsea. He suspects that they talk about her behind his back. It is only this summer that he has become aware of the possibility and he finds it hard to handle. 'I don't see why she would,' is all he says. 'Why would she?' But he doesn't want them to think he is defending his mother.

All the children, apart from Gregor, are a little afraid of Chelsea. She does not treat them as the other mothers do, and she does not treat Gregor like a child. She talks to him, she talks to all of them as if they are adults and she swears using terrible words. She even asks them to oil her back if Rufus is not about. And they hate doing that . . . hate touching her back and having to push their fingers under her straps. Her skin sends off strange messages. When she asks, and Gregor is around, he does it for them, quickly, so they don't have to do it and he doesn't have to see that disgusted look on their faces.

But at least she doesn't show her bosoms like Ruth

and Wendy do. She keeps them covered all the time and makes them all the more fascinating for that. Ruth and Wendy even sometimes sunbathe without their pants on. When they were younger the children hadn't minded because they had been naked, too. Now they mind. Now they rarely go into that part of the garden.

'I think that's what we're going to have to do . . . get Helen drunk. Get them alone together and see what happens then. We'll have tried anyway. And maybe Rufus will kiss her. That would be our dare done then, and Thomas and William would have to do theirs.'

But that is an event scheduled for the barbecue this evening and there is the whole, delicious day to go yet. With their swimmers under their shorts they will go and collect Kate and Holly Wainwright from Hillside, Thomas and William Harvey-Lees from Water's Edge, and Archie and Jasper Featherstonehough from Wild Horses. They might go with Rufus and Simon to the chandler's in the town . . . they might be able to persuade either of the men to buy them those knives with the orange handles. They might go and watch the visitors arriving in the car park, see if there's anyone worth bothering with. They might play cricket on the beach. They might swim. They might get out the dinghy. They might finish up in the den up the creek. They might dive from the high rock where it's said to be too dangerous but they know it isn't – they swing out on vines. They might help with the painting of the catamaran. They might make a fire on the island. Or put bets on the fighting crabs they keep in specially constructed cages.

Probably they will see if they can outwit the police and get to the cave of the skeleton.

But for now they loll as children do, squinting over towards the dunes and the figure of Helen that follows Harriet back. At a distance. Carefully.

And they all feel quite surprised when Amelia says: 'I don't think Harriet likes Helen.'

Because they all realise something that they hadn't realised before. They realise that nobody really likes her . . . except perhaps Rufus in his funny, collector's way. Gregor has an extra thought . . . that nobody, particularly Harriet, likes his mother either. He recognises in a sudden, quite hurtful flash, that Harriet finds his mother distasteful.

They are gone when Harriet, followed five minutes later by Helen, comes into the garden. Some broken daisy heads and a long, chewed crust are all that they leave behind them.

8

Desmond Hartley feels relief when more people like himself start arriving in cars. For his morning had begun to
feel like a performance . . . here he is, supposed to be on
holiday and enjoying himself . . . but he cannot relate
to anyone else around him. There are either stooped,
suspicious women grumbling along the road with string
bags and accusing eyes, ancient men with knotted root
arms, over-bronzed to a dirty brown, also accusing . . . or
tourists who stand out blatantly obviously like himself.
Their shouts break the quiet. Desmond is uneasy with
the quiet. Where are the children? There are no resident
children. And what, he asks himself, would they look like
if there were? Smaller versions of the old people, all bent
and accusing?

Desmond asked Cope about this when he saw him
shifting barrels about, using his stomach for leverage
like a balloon-cheeked weightlifter as he staggered up
the dark basement steps and into the light with his
eyes screwed up. His wild hair wafted flamboyantly
round him.

'No, all elderly people now,' Cope grunted. He spat,
sensing criticism in Desmond's question. 'Last child we
had here went missing all of ten years back. Emily Jane
was standing at the bus stop just round the bend there
waiting for the school bus, and that's the last anyone
saw of her. But she were a right 'un underneath that
innocent tunic and blazer. Innocent as the day is long,
she looked. Bah! There was talk that she'd been taken
off but Emily Jane was always threatening to go and
find the bright lights. And as far as everyone reckons,
that's what she did. Yep. The last child went without
telling a soul where she was going, my lover. And no

one's heard from her since. Broke her mother's heart she did. They all go. The kids. They all go. Can't afford to stay now, can they? What with property prices like they are.' And Cope manhandled his barrel quite threateningly and went puffing off back down the steps to his cellar again.

Hell, it's not Desmond's fault that no one can afford to live here any more and that the whole place has turned into a kind of Disney World with underground services. There's no point in anyone looking at him like that. He experiences another sudden yearning for his mother, for home territory, for his street of uniform cherry trees and the brightly painted front doors. There's not much goes on there during the daytime, true, but at least the residents there don't huddle up together against commonly perceived outsiders. Time goes slowly here. Folk move slowly, grumble slowly, even the tourists scratch and stretch all the time as if they are just out of their beds. There is no sense of *purpose*. And there are more flies here than there are at home. Maybe he should have gone to the Algarve with the boys, at least he would have avoided the experience of his shocking find. And Enid would have found that sort of holiday easier to accept.

Thinking deep thoughts, Desmond wanders down the road and heads for the beach. When he had last mentioned moving out, the conversation had become hysterical, hectoring, and finally uncontrollable. Enid pounced on the word 'Renfrew' and tossed it in the air a dozen times before falling upon it and tearing it apart. 'So far! What are you trying to do to me, Desmond? How long have you been thinking about this? How long have you and that Roger been plotting and planning behind my back? There's something the matter with that boy, I've always said so. I've never liked him. He's trying to get his claws into you, that's what he's doing.'

'Mum, honestly, I don't know what you mean. I'm not standing here telling you I've decided anything, or that

I'm going at all. I'm trying to ask you what you think about it.'

'And what's wrong with the job you have already? They like you. They pay you well. You get six weeks holiday a year and you're safe! What do you know about running a company on your own? How do you think you are going to start? And where will you live? With Roger, I suppose. In some flat with that Roger.' And they both realised together, that her voice had risen to a scream.

The eyes that met his across that kitchen table were bright with madness, yes, he had recognised it, for the first time in his life, as a kind of madness. Desmond gathered up his anger, ashamed of it, appalled by his sudden lack of sensitivity and understanding. She was terrified of being left lonely. Well he could understand that, couldn't he? Christ! It wasn't the money. He had sworn he would always look after her in that way.

Enid had dragged her heavily depressed body across the room, had launched herself towards the Valium and the cold tap. Desmond, despairing, watched her, watched her filling the glass in that slapdash way she did, feeling limp and bruised like somebody who had just lost a great fight, and again he felt the ache of losing. But he had deliberately lost . . . hadn't he? He had deliberately lost, out of fear of winning! Out of what might happen to him if, for once in his life, he won against her.

His voice was soft when he said: 'I have to go some time, Mum. I need to go. I am twenty-five years old and I need a place of my own.'

'What's wrong with this one? I don't interfere, do I? I cook you the meals that you like, even if I don't like them myself. I keep asking you to bring visitors home, how can I help it if you've got no friends, if you decide not to.'

'I have got friends, Mum. But I just don't feel easy with them here.'

She looked scared, but strangely excited, as if, this

time, she was determined to carry this all the way to the bitter end. 'Because of me? Is that what you're saying? You don't feel easy because of me. You're ashamed of me, Desmond, aren't you? You got that job with that snooty firm and now you're ashamed of me! My God when I think of everything . . .'

'No! Don't say it Mum. Stop!'

And then, suddenly, it was as if she remembered – anger could not beat him, sadness could. She turned her words into sad stones of despair and threw them at him. They rebounded off him, and fell at his feet making walking impossible as they piled up on top of the thousands of others, making a mountain too big for him to climb. He could not pick them up and throw them back. For he feared that one, correctly aimed, might kill her.

'I have been a good mother to you. I have never hurt you, raised a hand against you . . .'

No, no, she hadn't done that. For that sort of violence she used the police, or the 'man in charge', the station master, the park keeper or the headmaster. Enid never actually informed on him, she just threatened she would. And in bed he cowered and fantasised. But his response was not to his fear, it was to the way she clutched and clawed at him with her loneliness and dissatisfaction, it was to her desperate suffering – and most of that, he knew, was on his account. Because he'd been born. Out of wedlock. In the days when 'women like me were nothing but outcasts. And yet I kept you, I could have given you away, they wanted me to, but I kept you. And look at me, Desmond! Look at me!'

And Desmond had looked. And had felt ashamed.

'What sort of life have I had? What sort of future have I got to look forward to?'

And Desmond had not been able to answer. But now he has this chance to go with Roger to Renfrew . . .

He follows the track round the point and starts up the

estuary. He walks quickly, trying to escape his fantasy – rising up to his full height, confronting Enid across that dire kitchen table, grabbing her by her hair and smashing her face down and down again until it is reduced to the bloody pulp of an overripe melon, until her head is no longer there, until all that misery he has caused is reduced to a mess he can gather up with a cloth and sweep away tidily into the bit bucket.

Meanwhile, just a little way further down the estuary, Harry Featherstonehough, maddened by his wife's increasingly neurotic ravings, half out of his mind with secret worries of his own, eyes Desmond's approach over a neat patch of privet, lines him up in the sights of his shotgun as Desmond moves slowly, almost dreamily, in the direction of the cave. Not intending to wing the blighter, just to scare him. These journalists have got to learn that no means no.

The smell of garlic sausages fills the air. Pungently. It trails down the village street – the locals raise their eyebrows and wrinkle their noses – and curls down the cliffs to the water. Across the road Cope clanks about with crates full of empties. He does not look like a pirate this morning. He looks like a down and out with that slovenly old jacket and those bagged, torn jeans. Coffee percolates in the White Waves kitchen. Actions, smells, atmosphere, Rufus is up and he creates all these. They hang about him. Rufus is up and at the barbecue. He has thrown all he needs into a box and trundled it round to the balcony where they sat, contemplating the moon, last night.

Glasses with ants in adorn the rickety iron table next to a half empty bottle of wine and the ever present Perrier water. Chelsea's bacardi bottle is almost empty and there is no coke left.

Here comes the nun. Dawdling.

'Morning.' Rufus shades his eyes against the early morning sunshine. 'You're out and about nice and early.'

He is dressed in gaudy, zig-zagged shorts and his feet slop in thinly thonged sandals. His chest is bare and looks goldenly vulnerable in the morning. Because it is holiday time his hair is longer than normal, almost as long as Gregor's. The nun doesn't speak and so Rufus says: 'Hungry? Want some breakfast?' And does he know that he speaks gently-fondly, as he might speak to a dog?

The nun shakes her head and smiles. Dreamily.

'Oh come on. Have something!'

Helen again shakes her head.

Rufus says: 'To please me?' And does he smile to himself? That's hard to tell because he is concentrating on laying out the sausages evenly so they will brown evenly. His eyes are troubled by the low-lying sun and the clouds of charcoal-smoke. He flaps his hand and steps back, pulling an anguished face. He frowns at the box behind him. 'You could fetch me some tomatoes if you're going that way. I've left them in the kitchen. And the bread needs slicing.'

Helen goes like a dog might go to fetch the paper for its master.

Helen bows her head and flows away, managing to keep her arms at her sides and not to search, nun-like, for those ample sleeves. But she has been unable to correct that scurrying, purposeful stride. The children at the school where she teaches, they laugh at her, she knows they do. And Helen, who had always imagined she loved children, has decided they are not at all innocent as Jesus supposed. They are cruel and vindictive.

Helen enjoys this part of the day. It is the only time she knows she will not meet Chelsea. And lower her eyes, hiding her secret. And feel, so strongly, the urge to cross herself. To protect herself from her own wicked

81

thoughts. Because she has become wicked. Oh yes, she certainly has.

Helen gets on reasonably well with the other wives. Well, Wendy is kind in an aloof, patronising sort of way, and Ruth is sweet and patient. They are gentle with her, they speak to her like the sisters did, with quiet respect, when necessary. They don't expect her to speak to them or listen to them as Chelsea does. Nor do they curse and swear in front of her, or drink too much, or smoke those horrible cigarettes, or lift up their feet to paint their toenails. Nor do they paint their faces, blacken their hair, or totter round in high-heeled shoes wiggling their behinds.

But it is Harriet Helen likes to talk to. Helen has spent long hours talking to Harriet, trying to explain how it was to Harriet, who seems to understand.

It was in May that she experienced those first flutterings of doubt. It was after Christmas that she 'came out'. Everywhere was so cold, so bleak. 'And the traffic,' she told Harriet, 'hurtling towards me on the roads. I thought the lorries were monsters coming to gobble me up. I found myself cowering from the traffic, naked except for my strange half-clothes, and nobody saw me. Nobody spoke to me. Only dogs came towards me and I didn't know how to deal with them.'

And Helen felt despair as she recounted it, as she remembered how the taxi had taken her from the convent to the rooms in the high street above the dry cleaner's. How she'd had to pass through the same door as Mr Jones and Miss Tyler, who also had rooms above the shop. Up those narrow, well-trodden stairs with the worn-out carpet stained with grease marks, a small landing, and there was her door, Number three. With a metal slot where she was meant to put a piece of card with her name on.

She hadn't dared do that. Well she hadn't felt it was her name.

She used to force herself to stare into the shared bathroom cabinet mirror, so long sometimes that the pale-faced Miss Tyler used to have to knock and call at the door, wanting to get in. Helen used to stare at the stranger's face she saw there and repeat her own name over and over, trying to bring the name and the face together, to get them to stick, but the surfaces were too uneven for a hold. They wouldn't join. She wept. She ran the hot tap, held her wrist underneath the scalding water until it burnt, trying to make herself feel real.

Nothing.

She grew fearful of going to the bathroom where the mirror waited with its impossible questions. She tried to avoid going in there. She started to use a saucepan instead of going to the lavatory, ashamed of the noise that she made when she used it, afraid that someone would hear and know. And then, once, she met Miss Tyler as she crept along the landing with the pan in her hand and a magazine over it. Miss Tyler had known what was in it . . . she must have known . . . she turned her face away and stood back to let Helen pass, and after that her glances had disgust in them.

The days had been long and empty. 'I sat in my room not daring to go out. I wasn't even sure how to manage the gas fire.' She had not confessed to Harriet how she used to screw up her eyes and stretch out her arms in order to stay as far from it as possible while she lit it. She hadn't explained how it didn't make the room warm, only touched a few feet around it, drying the air which already felt dead to Helen. She hadn't told Harriet how she'd lived in a chair with springs in the seat that hurt her in those few warm feet of space. Or how she slept in sheets until they were filthy before Rufus came along and showed her how to use the launderette. She had lived on fruit and bread and cheese which she went out to buy in the early mornings from a corner shop that opened sharp at seven. Often she was back in bed by eight. Lying there.

Flat on her back with her arms crossed over her chest, as she'd lain in bed for so many years.

Only crying. And not knowing what to do. Yearning to go back, to find safety and purpose, but knowing she could never do that.

And then came the letter. Her first and only letter apart from the cheques that came from the DHSS.

It was the letter from Rufus. The miracle. The sign from God. Helen has it still. She will never throw it away. She would never throw anything belonging to Rufus away. And she has quite a collection of things now . . . the odd sock . . . a photograph she'd eased from the family album . . . nail clippings . . . a five-pound note he'd once given her . . . the cork from a wine bottle left over from a meal they'd once had . . . like you might collect a lover's charms.

Helen picks up the basin of tomatoes and eagerly goes back to the garden where she knows Rufus is on his own and waiting for her. She doesn't like to have him out of her sights for a second. On the kitchen doorstep she pauses, holds the bowl to her nose and sniffs. Warm . . . soily smells, the skins are so smooth. She runs her finger over the roundness and imagines the skin on Rufus' back when it bends and tightens, hot from the sun, tight and firm and ripe for the killing . . . she picks up a tomato and reduces it easily to pulp in her fist.

Helen lost God but found the Devil.

And then Harry Featherstonehough, next door, squeezes his trigger.

9

Bang!

Cough cough. Puff puff. Clack clack. Here comes Chelsea, down the stairs in her slinky black Reger nightie, cigarette loose between sleepy fingers, scowling at the morning, at the mess in the kitchen, at the cat who she can tell has shat in one of the downstairs rooms and yet no one has bothered to clear it up.

And what was the noise? Harry shooting rabbits again? And where has everyone gone?

She gropes for the kettle. Messily she flings coffee and sugar into one of the only clean mugs still on the hook beside the sink. She clacks to the step and picks up the papers, holding her wrap together over a bulging cleavage: *The Times* for Rufus; *The Independent* for Simon and Wendy; *The Telegraph* for Harriet; *The Guardian* for Joel and Ruth. They are such poseurs, why can't they share a paper and be done with it? They're all grey and unreadable. They are all exactly the same. Chelsea sighs and scuffs about for *The Mail* and sits at the table with it spread out before her, waiting for the kettle to boil.

At least there is no one about. No one to be offended by her coughing or her smoking, her smudged black eyes and her disordered hair, no one to turn their nose up and look away. And Chelsea is annoyed this morning because she can't find her vibrator. She knows she had it last week, there, wrapped up in her underwear drawer. She'd shuffled across the bedroom this morning, vaguely eager, vaguely stirring – for mornings are the most convenient times when the early rising Rufus is up and gone – she'd damn near tipped the drawer upside down because she couldn't believe it. Had she gone mad? No, she distinctly remembered using it last week. For alone with her machine and her fantasies is the only way Chelsea has ever experienced any pleasure from sex. But who could have found it? And why would they have taken it? Bloody kids – there is a limit! And how can you ask 'Has anyone seen my vibrator?' Well, you can't, can you. For nobody knows she's got one. Certainly not Rufus.

Chelsea knows that her early morning sluttish behaviour is accepted here far more readily than it ever would have been at home with Wilf and Muriel. Then you had to dress before you came down. Then breakfast was always ready at a certain time – even on Sundays – flung together angrily by Muriel between bouts of early morning cleaning. Breakfast was often a shouty meal, taken in terse sentences between bursts of an on-and-off-going Hoover, winding your legs in and out of the travelling, cold rubber flex. Breakfast, thinks Chelsea, now, often smelled of over-filled Hoover bags.

And she would have been trapped in all that if Muriel had had her way. Why had Muriel, that most miserable, unhappy of women, wanted to visit her trials upon her only daughter? Why hadn't she encouraged Chelsea in her revolt instead of trying to squash it? Surely, a woman so dowdy and tight would be glad to feel that, even if she had failed to do so, her daughter was going to live?

Not so.

Muriel was quite ferocious in her attempts to keep her pure – to keep her at home. Miserable bag.

Chelsea gets up to pour the boiling water into her mug. She catches a glimpse of the sea, glinting like a low string of sequins in the distance. Ah – even she cannot deny it – there is perfection in this sort of life. The setting. The freedom. The lazy ease of it all. The way she has everyone scuttling about, afraid of her. All right, they might not approve of her, but she has a certain position here in spite of that fact. And in a funny sort of way she is fond of them all. In the strangest sort of way she feels quite protective of all of them. Well, they are all so naive and silly. So easily fooled. If only there was a bit more going on. If only there were some interesting people.

Young men. That's what Muriel used to call boy-friends. Even, sometimes, callers! Chelsea had practised on every young man she could lay her hands on – and she had quick, deft hands, they would have been wasted on the piano – as soon as she understood what sex was all about. As soon as she realised it could get her, if she used it correctly, anything she wanted. She learned, at first, by trial and error. There was such a thing as being too cheap, as being considered an easy lay. But there was a place for that, too, in Chelsea's scheme of things.

'Your mam's soft, June, she's always giving you money,' said Ann Gibson, Chelsea's best friend. With jealousy, as they lit their cigarettes behind the school wall and rolled their gymslips higher.

'My mam has never given me more than two and six on a Saturday in the whole of her life. She doesn't like me having money. Money means I can do as I like. And mam doesn't want that. No, I earn my money myself.'

'Oh?' And Ann hadn't believed her. 'How do you earn it? Where do you work? You never told me you'd got a holiday job?' And she thrust her hat into her satchel.

And Chelsea, June then, smiled to herself. Because if Ann, if the others didn't realise how easy it was to get money, then she wasn't going to be the one to enlighten them.

So Chelsea watched and Chelsea listened and Chelsea soon realised that sex could either buy you presents and freedom or snap closed on you like a metal-jawed trap. Sex was the thing that snared all of them in the end, even Muriel, she supposed. It was sex to begin with that had her crouched, here, in this miserable semi on a road the same as all other roads. Scrubbing and muttering. Cleaning, cleaning, cleaning as if she knew what had done it and was for ever trying to scrub out that primitive stain, remove every last trace of it. And the thought of having to lie on your back every night – for that's what Chelsea believed was what happened between married couples then – the thought of having to lie there waiting for paunchy Wilf in exchange for his meagre wage packet, was enough to make Chelsea want to vomit.

She knew she had to get out of this town. Nobody in it ever became anyone. There was something about the terrible smallness of the place that reduced the people in it. Even the goods on sale in the shops were hideously scruffy and second hand. The films that finally filtered through to the Odeon were over a year old and everyone who was anyone had stopped talking about them. The school was filled with second-hand teachers – even the children who did well ended up in dingy offices and met for lunch in department stores in the shabby town centre. The hairdressers, too, were in collusion and part of it. Chelsea looks back at old photographs, sometimes, and stares at the hairstyles that made up the lives of her neighbours and friends. How could anyone, seriously, get anywhere looking like that?

Tormented by all of it, Chelsea was vaguely aware that the sixties was going on somewhere. She saw girls with money, fingering fluorescent feathers in Biba. She saw them walking down Carnaby Street wearing mini skirts and white boots with tassles. She looked down at her own knee-length skirt. She pulled at her sexless, coral pink twin set, and she hated her mother and everyone who had conspired to trick her into believing that this was all there was.

Why didn't they all wake up and get out there and live?

Money and style. A coat of white leather. Sod it. Chelsea was determined, at twelve, to find a man who would give it to her. She knew what she had to exchange. It was all she had and all she would ever have. So she practised it in bicycle sheds and behind bus shelters. Whenever she got the chance. She perfected her art in subways and on the steps of private basements. Even on the flat roofs of some of the department stores in broad daylight . . . disturbed only by passing helicopters. And when they panted and reddened and grunted and heaved, she smiled down on their helplessly bobbing heads, feeling an awful urge to pat them and say there there. As her mother would have over a scraped knee and the suffering that throbbed hotly from it.

God – men were so needy!

Now Chelsea lights another cigarette and gazes round the morning-battered kitchen. Where is everybody? At least someone has washed up last night's meal. Here they are so casual. In her childhood, if a cup was left by the sink Muriel would take the gesture personally and go all tight. She used extra, unnecessary props in order to enhance her suffering, like antimacassars, tray cloths and table mats. She gasped when she saw them stained, rushed to push saucers underneath spills, bought bottles and bottles of Thawpit and rubbed at the marks with her hard little shiny hands.

At home in London Chelsea has a cleaner and a dishwasher. And it is the cleaner, a genuine gem, who packs up anything disgusting and sends it to the laundry. In London Chelsea leads a life of pure and total leisure, shopping and having lunch and going out to dinner parties and to the theatre. She doesn't have to look at this sort of mess and feel responsible for it. But when she sees it, as she does when she comes to Tremity Cove, it irritates and upsets her. She supposes she was born with something of Muriel inside her. This thought upsets her, so she moves on.

She moves on just as easily as she moved on when she was fourteen years old with a hundred pounds in her pocket. That was a sizeable sum in those days. There was no clear reason. She hadn't had a row or an argument on that day – well, not worse than on any other.

'You're a scrubber,' screamed her mother, slapping her daughter across the face. 'You're always at it . . . no more than a bitch on heat. That's what you are. And you disgust me! I cannot bear to think of you as my daughter!'

She'd been reading Chelsea's diary again. Chelsea, as usual, crossed her arms and her legs and smiled. But it wasn't that that decided her . . . this just happened to be a convenient day and she felt not a pang of remorse as she settled down on the train with her ticket and her magazine.

She made an extra five pounds bending forward over the toilet in the train.

London, on that drizzly wet day, welcomed Chelsea with open arms. A Salvation Army woman approached her at the station. Chelsea laughed and waved her away. There was one, short, disconcerting hour when, lost, she pushed her change into a gaming machine and looked out, frightened, at the city buzzing round her. One small hour when she felt like a terrified child and wanted a rag to suck. She wondered if she'd got it all wrong. If she might find herself without a bed for the night. And the rain it rained, and the puddles they shone with neon like petrol. Chelsea fed her money in and felt a sinking dread.

She came triumphantly out from the Golden Palace on the arm of her first friend. She hadn't taken long – that look of hers worked in London just as well as it worked at home. Men were, after all, pathetically all the same. And it was he, Gordon of all names, who had taken her and introduced her to the club where she found her first job. And after that Chelsea had never looked back.

She had money. She bought her clothes from Biba. She rode in beach buggies and Mini-mokes while the lights of the city played on her hair. 'Bitch! Prostitute!

Whore!' All those names her mother called her. Well –
as far as sex went – well, Chelsea never felt anything at
all when she screwed with such wanton indiscrimination.
She was innocent and whitely pure as driven snow . . .
untouched by it all as she displayed her feathers in the
most free and natural way . . . not a shred of desire was
necessary. Had ever been necessary.

And that was her strength.

And that remains her strength.

And so when Desmond is carried, unconscious, into
the kitchen and laid on the table, with his red hair
and his little-boy freckles . . . Chelsea takes hardly any
notice at all. All men bore her, especially little red-headed
men like this. She clutches her coffee and scoops up *The
Daily Mail*.

Why does the nun hold a bowl of tomatoes? It turns
the whole scenario into something even more ridiculous
than it ought to be.

'Get the children out of here,' cries Ruth, looking paler
than usual. This morning she surely must be a vicar's
wife in those shorts that look as if they've been made
out of some sort of hemp and that pale pink suntop that
was obviously designed for a five-year-old.

Wendy, her bob bobbing hard, obliges, ushering the
children out in her royal way. And, protesting, they
go, mumbling and insulted. Far too many things are
happening round here from which they are excluded.
They are not used to it. They do not like it. They will
get their own back tonight at the barbecue.

With a very pale face betraying her fears but her smile
still just detectable, Ruth goes to the sink and soaks a
teatowel in cold water. Wringing it out, she brings it
back and places it on the head of the young man.

Harry has followed the procession up the cliffs and
in through the kitchen door. 'Dear God I didn't mean
to bag the bugger . . . just to scare him off . . . Christ

91

I didn't think the sights were that far out.' Harry's eyes stare wildly . . . the eyes of a madman . . . or someone who has already had too much to drink this morning. His hands this morning could be card-playing hands the way they're shuffling and re-shuffling that invisible pack.

Rufus shakes his head and stares down at the unexpected visitor, calmly waiting for signs of life. 'We couldn't take him to Jessica's kitchen – it would finish her,' he says to nobody in particular.

'Calm down, Harry, calm down . . .' Simon, with his neatly cut hair awry, and his carefully monogrammed golfing T-shirt crumpled with sweat, bends down over the body and does expert things in his careful assessment of the nightmare situation. Simon would have been a doctor had he not been claimed by his passion for golf. He would not have made so much money but his income might have been more certain. 'It's shock,' he turns round and says in a voice designed for calm. 'It's shock! He's out for the count. He'll come round in a minute.' And then Simon smiles. 'This'll teach you, Harry. For God's sake, you can't go round taking pot shots at everything that moves . . . you're not a child any longer! Think what the publicity would have done! Hell . . . if you'd killed him it would have finished your career!'

Desmond Hartley opens his eyes and stares about him with painful intensity. He thinks he is in the presence of Elizabeth Taylor. Smoking, in a very revealing, half-opened dressing gown.

10

On his dizzy way up the stairs to rest Desmond passes the pictures. In the state he is in they seem even more bizarre than they do to the level headed. What sort of place is this, dear God? Where have I come to?

For Tremity Cove is the sort of place which inspires amateurs to paint. Visitors to White Waves grow edgier and edgier with the urge until Harriet points them in the direction of the roof-top studio where picture window, roof light, canvases, watercolours, and pastels and oils – mostly dried up over the years to agonized tubes with solid lids, the paint just a mess behind crusts – await their fumbling attentions.

And it is the state of the tools which gives the paintings that Desmond passes, which adorn and obscure most of the White Waves walls, such a curiously jerky similarity – splodge/spread, splodge/spread.

The need to paint here is almost manifested in a trembling, spotted quickly by Harriet who can recognise the signs. Enthralled by it all, off they go, paints and easels in their arms, to commune with the sea and the sky. Harriet cannot bear to throw any of their first attempts away. She says she respects people's souls too much. And she firmly believes that all painting and pottery comes from the soul of the artist no matter how mean or how humble.

And maybe she's right. There is an honesty about these beginners that gets lost in the sly skill of the practised artist. Once Harriet persuaded Hugo to paint, sat companionably by his side in a deckchair, mixing his colours for him. Perhaps she was eager to discover something about Hugo's soul. Perhaps she merely desired him to be still. He had produced a geometrical design of brown building blocks. So Harriet hadn't discovered

anything . . . or nothing she hadn't already suspected
. . . dear Hugo.

'Careful,' says Ruth to her patient. 'There's three stairs
here that you might miss they are so unexpected.'

Harriet follows the silent party up the stairs, and
shivers. For this is the young man who made the find
and, incredibly, Harry has tried to shoot him! Why has
she never considered the find of the skeleton other than
unfortunate coincidence? Why has she assumed that the
blackmailer stopped after Hugo's death?

Had he? Had he . . . or had the blackmailer, cleverer
than that, turned his attentions to somebody else . . .
somebody eminently upright and responsible . . . someone in a vulnerable position . . . someone who would
do anything, pay anything, to protect his family and
everyone else he held dear. Harry! If Harriet were a
blackmailer Harry would be the person she'd choose!
Oh God, Harry, what happened? Didn't you feel you
could come to me? Or one of my children? Why did
you feel you had to carry this alone? What happened?
Did you find yourself unable to pay?

Harriet's worst fears are coming true. The note she'd
found in Hugo's jacket pocket . . . she hadn't been spying
. . . far from it. But the note said more about Hugo's soul
than any painting could have done. There were things
about Hugo that Harriet did not want to know, things
she turned her back firmly on. She wishes she'd never
read the note . . .

'Turn right now . . . it's the African room . . . full of
things that Grandpa brought back from the Congo. You
might find it strange but it's a matter of getting used to
it. People who have stayed in here get to like it . . .
tend to prefer it.' Wendy speaks as she would speak to
a sorrowful child.

Desmond, holding his head, eyes drooped, obediently
follows instructions. He can't have imagined he saw
Elizabeth Taylor, can he? He was nervous enough, full

of apprehension as he approached the cave . . . the blast of the gun shot, the sensation of whistling shot had been, for him, the last straw. But his nerves are not so frayed that he could have imagined . . .

Sir, went the note in an ignorant hand, done with a hard black pencil on a sheet torn out from a wide-spaced, Woolworth pad, *The money for the maid is late in the paying. My warnings are not empty threats. You and yourn cannot destroy someone's life and get away with it, no, it dont matter how big you are.* There was no signature. And Harriet's hair had stood on end as she'd read it.

Harriet had taken the note straight to Hugo. 'What is this?' she'd demanded. She'd hated to touch it. There was something so dirty, so frightfully obscene about that limp piece of paper.

Hugo had tried to make out it was some sort of joke but Harriet wasn't standing for that. 'Tell me, Hugo! I insist that I know!'

And then he had changed his tune, become angry, and Harriet always found it hard to cope with Hugo's anger. He was such a large man, and so loud. 'I have buried this skeleton somewhere so deep it will fall out of nobody's cupboard! It is nothing to do with you, Harriet! And now I suggest that you follow my example and think no more about it!'

Unsatisfactory. Very. But Hugo could be very insistent when he wanted to be.

Harriet knows who the maid in the note was, too. Harriet shudders. It was her fault, her fault for not acquiescing to Hugo's demands . . . for refusing to be what Hugo wanted her to be . . . for being a prude . . . for thinking sex disgusting. Hugo had been driven . . . oh God . . . oh God . . . and someone had found him out. It must be something dreadful for Hugo to submit to blackmail . . . his wenching and whoring were well known . . . something had happened to the maid in the note and it was something much worse than the general run of things.

Harriet's thoughts churn in her head as she follows the invalid party. But the blackmailer hadn't stopped? Had he? Else why has the skeleton been found? But Harry, beaten by exorbitant demands, should have asked for help. After all, it is Hugo's crime . . . her crime . . . and to take a shot at this young man . . . as if such an extreme action as that would stop anything as dark, as poisonous as blackmail. The young man could only have been following instructions . . . some messenger . . .

At the door to the African room they pass one of the pictures by Rodney Caruthers, and even Harriet has to agree that they are almost too dreadful to behold. There was clearly something wrong with the man, an RAF pal of Hugo's whose visits were limited to hastily taken weekends. His memory might be obscure, but something of his is left behind in the startling obscenity of his pictures.

'He died in a Spitfire. Burned to death at the end of the war. How can I possibly throw his pictures away?' asks Harriet miserably when faced with the shocked glances of her friends. And every time she tells it she remembers the maid, and how she came down to the house unexpectedly to discover Hugo and Rodney what you'd have to call *in flagrante* . . . with the large woman in the black and white cap and apron, there on the floor in front of the fire and who was doing what to whom?

Harriet's voice had been cold. 'It was my intention that this home be used for our future children! For happy, wholesome family holidays. I imagined us playing Snap round that fire . . . I dreamed of us playing Ludo and Happy Families on this very rug! How could you, Hugo? How could you? Coming down here with your dubious friends and getting up to this sort of thing, telling me you're having a fishing weekend! And I believed you! I believed you!'

She pictures the scene vividly as she reminisces. The

ungainly maid, all fleshy and white, had stood up, trembling, in her suspenders and that terrible pinny covering nothing! She had held a cushion up to her face . . . for shame she had hidden it! Hugo had had the decency to look ashamed of himself but Rodney Caruthers had just smirked! She'd never liked the man. That some ghastly accident had occurred that weekend after she had gone, after she had stalked out into the night to return to London full of horror and loathing, Harriet had no doubt. Because after that, Hugo had changed. He'd stopped bothering her after that. It was all very strange.

But she still cannot get rid of the pictures. Because of the way that poor Rodney died.

Rodney Caruther's pictures shake Chelsea rigid. Helen quite likes them. She identifies with them. She understands the madness in them. Sometimes at night when everyone else is in bed, she comes to stand on the landing just to stare at them, feel them and absorb them, and then she paces restlessly up and down before them.

Harriet did not have to point Helen in the direction of the studio. Helen was already something of an artist when she first came to White Waves last year. She teaches art at that dreadful school – the job Rufus found her. She used to paint shy, watery seascapes. Now her pictures are frenzied and bold, in oils . . . similar to those on the stairs. Helen does not give her paintings to Harriet. There are none of hers on the walls. But there are some things that shouldn't be painted at all. Some things that are better left unsaid.

But how can Helen help it?

The letter that came through the box in her miserable flat, the letter was from Rufus, asking if she would be willing to take part in a documentary series he was interested in making for his film company which sold its work to the television. Getting the letter was, for

Helen, at first a terrible shock. She read and re-read the name, unable, for hours, to believe it. Unable to stop herself shaking. Rufus. Rufus. She started to speak to the letter and found that having it there was like having someone talk back to her. And its tone was gentle. It suggested some understanding of her predicament. It gave a telephone number that she should ring. It explained how he had been given her name following an advertisement he had put in the paper, and Helen suspected it was that Miss Tyler who gave it. No matter. That was unimportant. She went to bed with the letter under her pillow. In the day time she sat and held it in her lap as she sat in her chair. Pondering upon it.

Rufus Pilkington. She ran her finger over and over the name because it was in ink. And human as opposed to all those typed words. Green ink. Who would sign their name in green? Only someone so confident, so certain, that they dare choose such a colour and flourish the page with it like that. To Helen, whose own name at that time was such an anathema, whose slot on the door was still blank, who hadn't yet found the courage to print her name even in black . . . to Helen the green was astonishing.

He suggested a meeting – oh how easy that must have felt for him. He suggested they meet and talk.

It took Helen a week to find the confidence to ask Miss Tyler about using a telephone box, to gather the correct change together, to decide what she was going to say and how she was going to say it. As for the programme . . . well, she didn't get as far as to think about that. She didn't have a television. She'd never actually watched anything on it. It was the meeting, to her, that was all important. She knew, by then, that her life must change. She knew she couldn't go on like this. She knew that something must happen so she knew she had to make that telephone call.

She knew that at last her prayers had been answered and that she must follow the sign from God.

With her heart fluttering like a bird in her chest Helen had braved the mid-morning high street racket. Up until then, except for her quick, early morning sorties, she had merely watched it going on through her net curtains. She braved the men with pneumatic drills who turned and stared at her as she went by. She braved the red-faced greengrocer man who called out 'Good morning' and then banged a packing case down on the pavement and cursed when she did not answer. She braved the strange old woman with the tartan trolley who grubbed about in the litter bin, twisting her face and spitting, and who wore three coats on top of each other. She braved all this to get to the telephone box, and then she stood there, breathless, trembling, the precious letter fluttering and trying to tug away from her every time a lorry went past.

She expected to hear the voice of the name on the letter. So when a woman answered the phone Helen was perplexed. 'I want to speak to Rufus Pilkington,' she said. 'I've had a letter from him asking me to telephone.'

'Mr Pilkington is out just now. Can his secretary help you?'

Helen didn't know what to say. She didn't know the answer.

'Let me put you through,' said the receptionist, taking the decision herself because she was too busy to deal with long pauses. 'Hold on just a moment.'

And then Helen heard music. Strange, restful music, and she thought something must have gone wrong with the phone so she stood there, bending, in the see-through booth and shook the receiver, feeling ridiculous, until she heard a voice again.

'Mr Pilkington's secretary, can I help you?'

And then, for the first time, Helen said it – her name.

And then, quite miraculously, it was all all right. And the secretary called Pat was telling her not to worry, that they would send a taxi to fetch her a week on Monday, that the taxi would take her to the hotel and after the meeting the taxi would take her back home again. 'It will be quite informal,' said Pat, so Helen wondered what this meant, what she was trying to tell her. Was there something special she ought to be wearing for the occasion? 'And you will like Rufus,' said Pat chattily. 'He will put you at ease very quickly.'

Will he? Well! Helen had stood with her back against the booth, shaking from head to toe. She'd done it! And as a result something was going to happen. At last she was going to meet him!

She saw the woman with the trolley approaching and pulled herself together with several quick swallows and a straightening of the back. She pushed herself off from the support of the phone booth before the woman got too close, she didn't want to be tainted, and went back to her room again, clutching the letter in her hand as if it was a life raft and she had to hang on to it or die. And it had felt like that. Just like that.

Rufus is saying: 'Harry is a damn fool. That could have been nasty. As it is, the likelihood of that young man suing is something not to be overlooked.'

'Thank God he didn't touch him,' says Wendy, brewing one of her herbal teas. She pointedly takes Chelsea's ashtray and empties it, almost shuddering as the ash and two dog ends slip into the bin. Into the clean ashtray Chelsea immediately stubs out her third, dragging it this way and that, torturing it.

'He must be a somewhat nervous character to go out for the count when he hears a gun shot.'

'What was he doing there in the first place? Harry says that when he pulled the trigger he was halfway up the creek and heading for the cave. Harry thought he was someone from *The Sun* . . . he thought that by warning one the others would leave him alone.'

'Nevertheless, what a bloody stupid thing for Harry to go and do. Good grief . . . one has to wonder.'

'Harry is under a great deal of pressure just now,' says Harriet, ashen-faced, close to tears. *Oh the fool oh the fool!*

'We will have to try and persuade that young man . . . what's his name . . .'

'Desmond . . .'

'Then we will have to try and persuade young Desmond to accept our apologies and take this no further,' says Rufus. 'It could be extremely embarrassing for Harry. Poor Jessica.'

Poor Jessica. Hah! Chelsea cannot imagine how anyone can be so weak and watery as Jessica lets herself be. She's sure it's a ploy to get Harry's attention. All that manufactured illness, all those migraines – psychosomatic – hypochondriac. She says so.

'We cannot all be as robustly hearty as you, my love,' says Rufus, and cups her chin in his hand. As he cupped it when she first met him. At the hotel . . . to which she was summoned by letter.

A letter signed in green ink.

To Chelsea's bare bed-sit where she lived had come the letter. On headed, magazine notepaper, signed with an emerald flourish. Inviting her to dinner at the Ritz! Asking her to ring and confirm. Breathlessly excited, immediately Chelsea had done so. They would send a taxi to fetch her. And she would be escorted home. It sounded so respectable on the telephone . . . proper office and secretary and everything like that. Chelsea was impressed.

She posed for pictures for the girly magazine *Madame*, of which Rufus was joint proprietor. She rubbed her nipples to make them sit up . . . she parted her legs and shaved off her pubes. She flopped and she stretched and she leered. She climbed and she postured and she pouted.

And when she met Rufus she realised that he was a monied young man with places to go . . . he was aiming to be a film director. He was co-director of *Madame* with a couple of old university friends while he waited for his star to rise.

Funnily enough, she hadn't had to work hard to catch him. He told her quite matter of factly: 'I have been waiting for someone exactly like you.'

'But there must be thousands like me,' Chelsea had said, open mouthed.

'No, actually, there aren't,' said Rufus. 'You are, my love, quite unique. You are the perfect whore.'

'You should know,' said Chelsea.

'Oh I do,' said Rufus.

And he took her home to meet Mater and Pater, just as if she was as good as anyone else. And Chelsea is a good wife. She never strays. Well, why would she? No man has ever satisfied her so, hell, what would she do that for?

11

Chelsea takes Desmond a tray at lunch time because
there is nobody else around. They are all outside, being
active. Even their caring is not quite genuine. It doesn't
last long and they don't approve of illness. Especially
Harriet who has always frowned on it. Wendy despises it,
Ruth is frightened of it. The men do not consider it their
business. Whereas Muriel, Chelsea's mother, delighted
in it. It was her main topic of conversation . . . the gory
details of hysterectomies enthralled her and she used to
watch a vividly truthful programme about operations on
the TV. Avidly. All Chelsea had to do to gain attention
from her mother was to feign a pain. And then she
was kept home from school, brought boiled eggs with
soldiers, and her hot-water bottle was constantly filled
and refilled. There was always a fire kept on in her room
at those times, and Chelsea remembers the singeing smell
of it, the dry-mouthed air of it, the sparking bars of it, and
that fire was her image of mother love. Together with the
sterile surfaces of a sick room, frequently wiped with a
damp cloth.

But the Pilkingtons and their friends do not care.
Their concerns are to do with whether or not Desmond
will sue.

By now she is out of her dressing gown and in
her livid Gambian toga. Her lustrously black hair is
brushed back from a face which is tanned, and her
violet eyes are streaked with effective green shadow.
So she matches well with Hugo's African room, for
her features and cheekbones go well with the ancestral
mask that hangs over the bed. A mask that Desmond
has been stretching his neck out to look at . . . for
a power comes from it and he would prefer to be

able to stare at it rather than have it hanging above him.

'How are you feeling now?'

'I feel very silly, sitting in bed like this. You should have called me down. I am not an invalid. I do not need a tray. Everyone seems to be conspiring to turn me into an invalid this holiday. Normally,' and he says this because he does not want this woman to think him a wimp, 'normally I am never ill.'

'Sometimes it's nice to be cosseted,' says Chelsea, endeavouring to be sympathetic.

And Desmond thinks to himself: I was right. I did see Elizabeth Taylor.

'Harry thought you were somebody from *The Sun*. That's why he shot at you.'

Desmond inspects the contents of the tray. Healthy food. Some kind of asparagus quiche and some beany looking salad. With a piece of rough, brown bread. The sort of food he is always asking his mother to buy . . . but she insists on sticking to chips . . . convinced that it's all he will eat, just because that's all he would eat when he was little. There is grapefruit juice in the glass. He sips and it is refreshing. Just right, for he is feeling dry inside, and wretched. He sees his hands shake and he tucks them under the hard, grey blanket which covers him.

His smile is a shaky one. 'Does this person, does Harry always take pot shots at people he doesn't like?'

'Harriet says that Harry is under pressure just now. And his wife is a nag.' Chelsea, having dealt with that one, lights a cigarette and tips Desmond's bread off the side plate which she proceeds to use as an ashtray. Desmond, who's always hated smoking, and whose mother never stops, nevertheless admires the slovenly gesture. It fits with the woman who does it. And the woman who does it fascinates him. He has never met a woman like this before.

'Don't just sit there staring at it. Eat it,' says Chelsea,

blowing the smoke away from the invalid through thickly lipsticked scarlet.

Desmond has to obey. 'I'll get up after I've had this,' he tells her. Reassuring. Wanting to sound like a man – not a child. He can smell her. She smells of roses. Her skin shines with oil. When she moves she moves like oil. Even under that vast cotton garment he can see how freely her body slides.

What sort of man, thinks Desmond to himself, as he picks up the slice of quiche between his fingers before he notices the knife and fork provided . . . what sort of man would attract such a woman as this? She is quite the opposite from the girls his mother finds for him . . . or Roger. For they are neat and stylish . . . always in fashion . . . but clean-living creatures, like himself. With high-powered jobs and silvery laughter. They like to pay their own way. They make him feel small. They drive Golf GTIs, while he defiantly sticks to his white Cavalier with its CB aerial. By living at home Desmond need never invite them back. If he moved out and bought a flat they would come to it . . . Roger would bring them. They would comment on his furniture, his pictures, his decorations while he was forced to keep a brilliantly interested look on his face and listen to their chidings. They would see what he kept in his fridge and in his wardrobe. He would be exposed. His lack of image would be revealed for all the world to see.

But Desmond's fantasies are not of these creatures . . . Desmond does not like the thin, the neat or the clean. He dreams of nuzzling into pendulous breasts, of being ridden by women with buttocks he can grip in his hands, of smelling the pink-sweat of exhaustion, the sweat of feline energy. He dreams of being a quivering tool in somebody's hands. Equality in bed – or worse, masterfulness, which, when the bottom line comes, is all that any of these girls want, quite frankly disgusts him.

105

The last woman he made love to had gone to shower before bed, had showered afterwards and applied some sort of douche. Desmond has sometimes played with the idea of going with a prostitute. Of paying to be degraded ... My God if Desmond's mother knew of his dreams. Pricks, to Enid, wiggle about under brown macintoshes and are just something extra to ring the police about. She had sex once, she said she'd been enveigled into it, 'And look what happened to me. Punishment, Desmond.' She'd puffed dangerously at her cigarette, gone to pick up his photograph, delivered a lungful of smoke on the glass and repeated the cloudy word: 'Punishment.'

Sometimes he thinks, uneasily, because of the way that he sometimes catches her looking at him, that she sees straight into his mind.

He stares at Chelsea's scarlet nails and imagines them clawing the skin on his back. My God, thinks Desmond, toying with a flopping piece of quiche, you'd have to be a real man to get to bed with Chelsea.

And then Chelsea smiles. Just slightly. Just mildly. And when she smiles her eyes close and she bites the edge of her lip. *As if she knows* ...

Of course she knows. She has this effect on every man she meets. Let alone one so helpless and in bed. Let alone one to whom she sits so close.

'They are worried that you are going to take poor Harry to the cleaners. You could, you know ... you could drag him through the courts ... tarnish his reputation for ever ... maybe even destroy his career ...'

Chelsea doesn't sound even mildly concerned by the prospect. Desmond asks: 'Why would I do that?'

'For money, of course. Hell, you could have died from the shock. Mind you, Harry would deny it. Harry would say you stepped in the way, that he was shooting at rabbits.'

'I would not normally have been so badly affected,'

says Desmond quickly. 'It's just that, at that particular time, my nerves were on edge anyway.'

'You went out for the count, sweetie,' says Chelsea, slightly reproving. 'You had to be carried all the way here.'

'All I had on my mind when that shot whizzed past my ears was that skeleton grinning at me, was the terrible costume she wore . . . I thought if I went back and sat for a while in the empty cave . . . you know, sat there by myself for a while . . .'

'You found it then?' Chelsea says casually, patting the ash off the end of her cigarette.

'I found it.' Desmond's red hair is ruffled. It stands up at the back of his head like a child's. His pale eyes gaze from his mass of freckles at Chelsea, they narrow slightly as, once again, he remembers what he saw. Desmond forces himself to laugh. 'And I am not supposed to say what it wore.'

'But you can tell me,' says Chelsea, crossing one leg easily over the other with a fleshily sheeting sound.

'Well,' says Desmond, wanting to please her, and wanting to prove there was some good reason behind his craven behaviour. 'You're not going to believe this, but when I found it, the thing was robed like a nun.'

'A nun?' Chelsea puts her hand to her heart and laughs nervously.

Desmond nods, bemused. 'But that's the problem. When I took the police there the next day they said it was covered in netting and feathers. They don't believe me. I'm sure they think I'm playing some joke.'

'A rather odd joke, surely.'

Desmond feels ridiculously shy. 'That's what they think. And I even began to wonder myself. I mean, why would anyone go there in the night and change the clothes?'

'I wonder who she was,' says Chelsea. 'Dying there in a cave like that. All alone. Unmourned.' And Desmond watches, greatly disturbed, as she traces a pathway down the bare inside of her arm with a long finger as if to emphasise life.

A habit over a skeleton. Cloth on bone. Life given to death. Chelsea is thinking of Helen. Of the first time she saw Helen. On the television.

The camera had travelled the convent walls like an animal sniffing ivy. There was no sound of breathing, but in living rooms up and down the land people imagined they could hear breathing, particularly when those quick shots snuffled their way through the arched windows and finally, slowly, came to rest on the medieval door.

A door suggestively scarred and heavily bolted.

Then came the chord.

In fact, Rufus told her, the door did not belong to the convent. Theirs was an unprepossessing one, a Victorian repro badly painted and with none of the original glass inside. No, said Rufus. For a door more in keeping the film crew had travelled to the church called St Botolph's which was over one hundred miles away, paying the incumbent seventy-five pounds for the privilege, a sum which was greatly appreciated and went to boost the churchyard clearance fund.

Oh yes, Chelsea watched and realised that a great deal of professional care had gone into developing the opening shots of the Convent of the Assumption. It was a first-class job – first-class photography, cunning lighting, might win a prize. The effects put together made the perfectly innocuous Victorian building look weirdly out of perspective, and shuttered where it wasn't shuttered, gabled where it wasn't gabled. It wore the shabby air of neglect of an American horror hotel on some soulless, godforsaken beach. And it made it seem as if it was on a hill whereas it was, in fact, low in a dip. Strange little winds played with the weathervane, and mists seemed to come up directly from the cellars, sending a dampness spiralling round it.

'It's chilling,' said producer Mike Morgan when he was first shown it. 'Was it really as bad as that, Rufus?'

Because one could imagine the shadows behind the windows were bewildered nuns peering out, and certainly the impression given was one of prisoners inside, fingers round grilles, plucking and calling. And the introductory music they chose was the song of a lone Irish nun called Bernadette. She sang 'One Day at a Time' in a voice so effectively simple and lost it brought lumps to people's throats. It left an impression so hesitantly sad, so desperately hopeless, that viewers who did not know it picked it up and went round whistling it for weeks afterwards.

Coming Out shot to the top of the ratings along with the soap *A Girl Called Dancey* and the game show *Take A Chance*. Everyone, including the viewers, was extremely happy with those opening sequences. But was Helen? Had anyone asked the nun? Had they, as they so often did, had they just naturally assumed?

For Helen wasn't a one to talk back. She still isn't.

An adventure! How would she cope? How would anyone cope, in this day and age, with such a change? And did you ever see such a sad, such an irreversible goodbye?

Chelsea had viewed in her smart London home, much happier there than she is at Tremity. 'There's something horrible about the way they watch. Something not quite nice, but I can't put my finger on it,' she'd said to nine-year-old Gregor. He sat drawing crisp outlines on a faultless page of geometry. On the floor beside him his bulging satchel was leathery-worn like a Bible. 'I don't think they see the nun as real, you know,' she went on. 'I think they imagine the whole thing's being done by an actress. Do they care what happens to her? Do they really care? Do they secretly want her to come to grief so that they can feel superior? All that terrible truth and goodness!'

'Well, do you care?' asked Gregor directly, rather rudely. 'Did Daddy care when he made it?'

Gregor was growing distressingly more like his father by the day – not just in looks but in arrogance as well. Tall and elegant, and those long eyelashes shaded his cheeks and made him look almost feminine. And from where his mother looked at him his neck was long and slender like a girl's. A golden boy, just like Rufus.

Yes, Chelsea had shaken her head and thought that Gregor was becoming much too like Rufus. Argumentative instead of conversational. He was beginning to make her feel flippant and stupid in just the same way. Because to be perfectly truthful, what did Chelsea care what they thought of the nun, or what became of her afterwards?

What did anyone care, for that matter?

But then, as if to make up, her son smiled, surprisingly sweetly, into his mother's eyes.

Chelsea had turned back to the television. She had settled down into her chair and turned the sound up, her long nails red on the black remote control. Rufus was late. Rufus had said he'd be back by ten. She worried about Rufus being out late in some of the places he worked. Only last week a Metropolitan policewoman had been bludgeoned to death and thrown into the Thames and the news was still all about it. 'She put up a desperate struggle for life,' said the policeman in charge of the case. 'The murderer must have gone home in a mess. Someone must know who did it. Someone must be protecting him.'

How appalling, thought Chelsea.

Chelsea had watched, stroking the side of her face as she thought. Rufus was clever. Oh, they hadn't left the heroine out. Helen was in the opening sequence, too. Not her face. They didn't want to give too much away. The whole point was to make people want to see what her face looked like and keep watching. So they didn't want to show her face at this stage, but after the building hypnotically faded the camera concentrated instead on her walking feet, clad in such sensible brogues, up the short calves and the unfashionable seams in her stockings, up the thick, tweed skirt and, almost straight away, a quick flick to the dowdy mac, the heavy bag and the rain-hood.

Truly an abandoned soul.

But there was something else . . . there was something else . . .

Chelsea felt uncomfortable. And she hated to feel uncomfortable, especially when she didn't know why.

No, they hadn't left Helen out. But they hadn't put much of her in there, either. And that's what seemed to happen all the way through. They had merely pencilled her in. Suddenly realising this, Chelsea had turned round in her chair and said quickly in case she might forget it: 'Look! What does she stand for? What does she think? All we ever see is her response to external situations . . . her response to the camera . . . to Rufus! She's almost blank! All she is is a kind of frame.'

At the end of the opening sequence the nun walked down the drive. A reconstruction, of course. They'd put a kind of halo round her head. It looked as though she carried a flickering candle. But it could have been anyone . . . any middle-aged woman, fascinatingly uninteresting, walking down a conifer drive, crunching the misty gravel as she turned her back on the building and made for the rather brighter, more cheerful effects beyond the gate and into the world beyond.

And the overwhelming message that came from that place was 'Welcome'.

But that was nearly two years ago.

Now Chelsea looks at Desmond's eyes . . . at the way they are staring at her with something akin to wonder

111

in them, and something bleak, too, and black ... a yearning. For Desmond something unobtainable, on a pedestal, created to satisfy his own needs.

Desmond's eyes.

Helen's eyes. Helen's eyes looking at Rufus? Are they the same? Is it the same look?

Lust? The nun has been invited to fall in love with Rufus ... but not the real woman, oh no. The image, the image Rufus had created for the screen. The perfect image of unsullied womanhood, virginity.

Why? Why would Rufus do that?

Just another perfect specimen? For Rufus, that specimen had to be obtainable. With the greatest of pleasure, taking all the time he needed, Rufus would admire and he would consider and he would speculate. But there was no doubt about what would happen in the end. There would come a time when Rufus would have to possess it. And there is only one way to possess a woman.

Chelsea shivers. She stares up at the African mask and suddenly goes very cold. She hates that honest stare, so severe, the unforgiving eyes of a dark prophetess. She shakes her head ... she shakes off the shocking feeling she cannot deal with. If the nun is part of Rufus' collection, could it be that she, Chelsea, is just one more?

A nun and a whore?

What the hell is this all about? Has Rufus started collecting people? Rufus has often called her his perfect whore ... but that is an anachronism, isn't it, for there can be no such thing. Chelsea could never be a perfect anything, could she? She dismisses the idea with ease. No! She's never been part of his terrible collections! The very thought is absurd! She smiles at the foolishness that has made her entertain, however briefly, such a bizarre idea.

She suspects that there have been others ... she's happy with that so long as he is discreet and he keeps his hands off her friends. But a nun?

112

Collecting people? HE HAS! So! That's what this is all about! My God!

Chelsea shivers indignantly. Takes a deep, last drag at her cigarette before she stubs it out. If Rufus can go to bed with a nun then Chelsea can have some fun also. She'll teach the bastard a lesson, collecting bones is one thing, spreading them ghoulishly round the house as he does. But going to bed with a nun . . . well, frankly, that's sick! And Chelsea will teach him a lesson he won't forget. Two can play those games.

Chelsea regards Desmond, as he sits there in bed, with a half-closed, speculative eye.

12

'By the way,' says Chelsea, passing Harriet later that
afternoon with a couple of iced drinks in her hands
and having absolutely no idea of the relevance of her
casually spoken words, 'that skeleton was not just any
old skeleton. When Desmond found it it was dressed
as a nun! But when the police arrived someone had
changed its clothes. It was dressed like a stripper, in
feathers and net!'

Chelsea was never one for keeping secrets. She considered the keeping of secrets absurd. And merely imagined
Harriet would appreciate that little snippet of information after her solitary morning in the dunes; and it was
a way of breaking the silence which so often existed
between them.

Harriet was towelling her legs dry in the kitchen when
Chelsea went by. Chelsea did not pause to discover the
effect of her words but tapped on out of the door, eager
to get back to Desmond. Who was not the bore she imagined him to be, but was quite charming and entertaining
really . . . he comes from the kind of world Chelsea comes
from. They bemoan their lot together. And Chelsea can
tell him all about the people here . . . their friends . . .
'You'll meet them all tonight at the barbecue,' she said.
'Sweetie, you won't believe it!'

'Am I invited?' Desmond cannot believe his luck. He
cannot believe that he is sitting here on a sunbed next
to a woman like this. Chatting as easily as this . . .
as if he's always known her. And only half an hour
ago she'd oiled his back for him. Not quickly to get
it over with, finishing with a quick slap and a wiping of
hands on the grass. No, not at all like that, seductively,
salaciously, expertly, with her fingers tickling his waist

as they moved just a fraction under his waist band. And then he had felt her hands on his legs. He'd bitten his lip, hard, as he lay there stretched out like a sacrifice. As he'd felt those cool hands travel up his calves, past his knees, and on and up, until they reached the legs of the shorts she'd lent him, push up and stop, push up and stop. Lingering there suggestively. Her fingers were so firm they must have left marks behind them. White marks. Claw marks. Desmond had clenched his teeth then, and squeezed his eyes closed. But he does not understand that Chelsea has a way – she has no need to touch them – of making all men feel like this.

Chelsea sees his reaction and smiles to herself. He is a mouse and she is the cat. However, she is becoming quite fond of Desmond, in an unexpected, quite unique kind of way. He is sweet and uncomplicated. Desmond belongs to her in a way that nothing else does at Tremity. She understands him, in a way that she does not really understand very much at all about Tremity. Never will.

So she hurried on out of the kitchen to return to her guest and had failed to see the controlled way Harriet straightened up, forgetting about her sandy legs, forgetting about putting a water bowl down for the cat, forgetting about hanging her costume on the pulley to dry or about organising a collection of wood for the barbecue. And if Chelsea had seen then she probably wouldn't have noticed, not being the most sensitive of souls, but being, rather, a creature of the moment, a woman of pleasure.

Harriet's face is a mask. So. A nun and a stripper! Hugo! Hugo's expression as he begged her. 'Put them on, old girl . . . for me . . . just the once . . .'

Herself blushing a deep beetroot red. Herself, all those years ago. Why, Harriet had hardly been more than a gel. 'Hugo! What can you mean? You can't want me to dress like this . . .'

And all those other unspeakable costumes . . . the nurse, the schoolgirl, the maid, the policewoman, the waitress, the schoolmarm . . . Oh God oh God oh God. 'No, Hugo, please don't make me do that. What can you be thinking of? What is the matter with me? Aren't I enough as I am?' And she'd looked down at her cotton nightdress, fresh and sprigged and cleanly smelling of laundry. She always had a bath before she got into bed and she wished Hugo would just sometimes do the same. For her sake. But no. He used to boom: 'What's wrong with the good honest smell of manly sweat?'

'Well nothing, Hugo, but the smell of talcum powder can be more pleasant sometimes . . .'

She had been a fair wife. Every time Hugo wanted . . . Hugo wanted . . . that . . . she accommodated him. Well of course she did, dutifully and fastidiously. What could Hugo possibly be wanting with those obscene black suspenders . . . those knickers with the missing gusset . . . those bras with the holes at the ends? All in black or crimson silk. She couldn't have guessed Hugo was that sort of man before she married him. He'd been such an energetic, outdoor man, with healthy appetites, revelling in his hunting and his polo. He had a rowing blue for Oxford.

It was not until after they were married that she'd begun to listen to the outrageous rumours . . . there were even suggestions in the newspapers, the sort of newspapers she never read. She never allowed them into the house. Odious rumours put about by Hugo's enemies. Of clubs that he went to and people he was friends with. Harriet knew that Hugo only went to one club and that was Brocks. Very respectable. And she liked the friends he brought home . . . the only friend she hadn't liked was Rodney Caruthers. Rodney Caruthers used to eye her in an uncomfortable way . . . hot, pulsing eyes without lids, like the eyes he painted in his grotesque pictures.

The man had been mad. In some ways it was a relief when he died. Some people are evil, thought Harriet then, and you know it when you meet them.

'But Hugo – a nun? That's hideous!'

'I'll leave it on the bed while I go and shower for you . . . put some talcum powder behind my ears. While you decide.'

Oh God, she had fingered the stiff, serge material with ripples of loathing passing through her. And all that starched whiteness. That's why she'd always been so repelled by Helen . . . the thought of anyone wearing such things . . . that voluminous habit spread on the clean, pink covers of her bed! Those filthy grey stockings. With the innocent light of her bedside lamp shining on them, shining through the mesh! How could Rufus have possibly wanted to collect a nun?

And when Hugo had returned, looking so horribly hopeful, he'd almost been a little boy looking for a sweet or a baby searching for a nipple . . . horrid! Oh God. 'Hugo, where do you get all these costumes from?' Because Harriet couldn't imagine!

Hugo had had the decency to blush. 'There are places,' he said. Then brightening as if he was telling a lie: 'Dressing-up shops, they hire them out for fancy dress parties.'

'Well what must they think of you, Hugo, going in and out all the time for costumes like this? I don't know why you keep bringing them home. You know how I hate it! I do hope you don't use your own name.' And then she had sat on the bed, and drooped, and wept. And she had finally agreed to wear the headdress and nothing else, but loathing herself and Hugo and everything that was to do with these sordid, disgusting acts. Seeing Hugo as a man she no longer knew . . . some demon under an awful spell, made horrible by desire, not caring that he embarrassed her, humiliated her so!

And the schoolgirl! She had agreed to wear the panama

117

and nothing else. But that had been bad enough. Because what did it all mean anyway? That Hugo secretly wanted to . . . to . . . to . . . to do things to a child?

And then she had come upon him with Rodney Caruthers – that terrible man – and the maid. Here, at White Waves, at this most innocent of places. On the rug by the fire . . . and the costume, Harriet was certain, was the same one he had made her wear, though she'd only agreed to the little white cap and the high-heeled shoes. Oh my God.

She'd been so shocked after that appalling incident that, for a while, she'd locked her door and made him sleep on the bed in his dressing room, not allowing him into the bedroom until he promised to behave. And then Rufus was born and things began to get better. His attitude had changed, too, after that incident with the maid. He came home later in the evenings, sometimes spending whole nights away. And he showed Harriet more respect, acted more gently towards her. He stopped telling dirty jokes at the dinner table. Perhaps he was ashamed of his indecent behaviour, afraid that she might divorce him – she had the grounds, didn't she? Not that she ever would have done that. Harriet loved Hugo, desperately, deeply loved him. She loved him so much she was prepared to forgive him for what she saw were his sexual perversions. Perhaps all men had them? But no . . . her own sons were never like that. Collecting dirty magazines was a different matter – a phase to be gone through. And Rufus marrying a girl like Chelsea? Well . . . that might be, but Harriet is certain Rufus doesn't get up to things like that.

But Hugo did.

And Chelsea would.

Chelsea would do anything . . . Harriet has seen Chelsea do anything, spread over two pages of the magazine *Madame*. Chelsea is entirely without shame.

Chelsea knows about the nun. Chelsea knows about the tart.

How does Chelsea know? How does Chelsea know . . . Hugo is the only one who could have told her! And does she also know that the skeleton is the body of the maid? For who else can it possibly be?

'Did you pay her, Hugo? Was she expensive . . . your little bit of weekend fun?'

Hugo had turned on her then. Harriet had never seen such a look in his eyes. It was a vicious look . . . she had almost imagined he hated her then. 'It is far better that you don't know, Harriet. Bury it. Bury it as I have done. We will not speak of it again.'

Bury it? And Harriet had been only too pleased to bury it. But when she'd found the blackmail note that whole, horrible, terrible time had flooded back to her. And because Hugo paid, because, like a dirty dog caught out in some terrible, filthy crime, he had submitted, Harriet knew that Hugo had chosen his words with care. That maid had been destroyed, as the scrap of paper suggested. By Hugo. And by that dreadful man Rodney Caruthers.

So Harriet was married to a murderer?

Oh good heavens no. Harriet considered that it was probably all an accident. That drink and passion and shame had combined to cause some awful disaster. Some disaster that, naturally, Hugo had been unable to speak of. He had disposed of the body . . . somehow.

Only now it had been found. After Hugo's death the blackmailer had, as Harriet would have done herself, chosen the stalwart Harry Featherstonehough as Hugo's most likely replacement. Harry, as an MP, had a reputation to protect. He was a family man and devoted to all his friends. And he was prosperous . . . or had been . . . oh dear. Unable to pay, and the blackmailer had decided to change again . . . to turn his attentions to Harriet! That young man, Chelsea's friend Desmond, had called the police to the skeleton, had told stories about a nun and a stripper . . . prompted by Chelsea.

Harry, knowing who the young man was, had foolishly tried to finish him off in a silly, ill-conceived act of desperation. Chelsea is the blackmailer! Chelsea, the only person who could possibly know about Hugo's nasty little habits, has masterminded the whole affair.

Harriet goes to the window and peers out. Sees Desmond and Chelsea laughing together out there on the lawn. Chelsea? Who Hugo had flirted with in such a shameful manner when first Rufus brought her to the house. Chelsea . . . who had responded, shamelessly, artfully . . . running her fingers over the back of Hugo's chair. Harriet remembers how Hugo used to reach round and catch her wrist, laughingly. It was a game that they played together! Harriet remembers – she even used to laugh at them herself, a little self-consciously because it was not a nice game. But what else could you do? They seemed to get on so well together, Hugo and Chelsea. One Christmas, Chelsea, kneeling under the Christmas tree, had been dragged up by Hugo, mistletoe between his teeth like a brigand. He had pulled Chelsea on to his knee, and she had sat there like a child feeding grapes into his mouth while he lurched and chomped at the hanging bunch, greedy like a crocodile. Harriet shudders. Hugo even took it upon himself to take his daughter-in-law in hand . . . to 'educate the wench', he called it, escorting her to the theatre and to art galleries, to the ballet and to the opera. Rufus had never minded.

Hugo called Chelsea 'Rufus' whore' in front of her face and Chelsea giggled but never objected! She almost appeared to like it, to take the insult as a compliment!

Harriet paces backwards and forwards across the sandy floor, to the table and back to the sink, and back to the table again. Her face is a tightly drawn picture of anguish. All this, all this going on in front of her nose and yet she had never suspected. Had Rufus? Had Rufus known and not minded? Surely not.

Hugo, the idiot, must have played his dressing-up games with Chelsea. Chelsea would have been only too happy to oblige. In which room? In whose house? He must have confided in her . . . trusted her . . . told her what happened to the maid and where they put her after the accident. Hugo could be so gullible sometimes, such an appalling judge of character. The blackmailer has to be Chelsea. Sly, acquisitive, immoral Chelsea, who cares not a jot about Tremity Cove or about anybody's reputation. Who is sending Harriet the starkest message she possibly can, a message wrapped up in black serge and crimson netting. A message that could not possibly be meant for anyone else.

Pay or I tell. Pay or the world will know. Your children will lose all that they have. Your reputation is lost. Pay . . . whatever I ask you must pay. And Harriet chills as she hears Chelsea's throaty, dirty laughter coming in through the kitchen window as she plays with the sort of man women like Chelsea can wrap round their little fingers.

Oh no, you little minx. Oh no. You have had your way with Hugo. You have had your way with poor Harry. You are leading Rufus a merry dance. But I am made of sterner stuff. You will not have your way with me.

13

Ruth loves painting, too. Ruth paints lots of pictures of her children sitting on straw chairs. Straw features highly somewhere in Ruth's subconscious and Chelsea supposes she is a country woman at heart, or maybe there's something biblical about it. But because Ferdi and Laurence refuse to sit still, Ruth always has to imagine them.

'Use stronger colours, dear,' Harriet advises. 'Look! You can hardly see the twins! They have disappeared, almost entirely, into that fussy background.'

Joel and Ruth are both pale people who meld into backgrounds. The only time Joel comes to life is when, in stiff collar and tails, he taps his music stand, commands silences, breathless hushes and atmospheres, wields his baton and leaps into an inspired frenzy of energetic posturing. He can go on for hours like that. They call him brilliant, and he looks like a brilliant man, often stalking round the garden, heron-like, stooped and nodding his head in time to some entirely memorised, often obscure, symphony. But very often Joel is merely rehearsing an angry conversation which he wishes he'd had the nerve to induce. He comes to White Waves every summer because he dare not say no in the face of the fervour of his two older brothers of whom he is afraid.

And his wife, the fair-featured, swan-necked Ruth, who smiles like a vicar's wife and prefers life's simple things, would never say no to anyone. Except, on rare occasions when she absolutely must, to her freckled twin sons Ferdi and Laurence. But even then she feels uneasy.

Joel, of all of them, does not look back on a childhood of sublime perfection. For he, by the nature of his calling, is a sensitive man, and sometimes looks back with a fair amount of unease. He winces and ponders on all the harm they must have done. A man who likes to confess, he has told Ruth all about it.

But he left out the rape of Nellie Mundy. He thinks Ruth would probably leave him if he told her about Nellie Mundy. And then what would he do? A vague, bewildered, disorganised man, he depends on Ruth for his welfare. If it wasn't for Ruth, Joel believes, he might get knocked over crossing a road, or die from a head cold, or fade away to nothing from starvation. Food, and the remembering to eat it, is not one of Joel's priorities in life. Which is why he resents being the one delegated to organise the barbecue food this afternoon. And it's far too hot to be thinking about food.

He had made his confession years ago to get it out of the way. And, to Ruth, sitting there listening so quietly, it sounded like a plea.

'In those days it seemed that, to Rufus, anyone who wasn't "one of us" was fair game. And Harry, the biggest, always went along with Rufus so there was little anyone else could have done.' This is how Joel started to explain to Ruth.

And Ruth's reaction was a sensible one which is what Joel wanted. 'Why didn't you go off by yourself?' she said. 'I think you protest too much. You did have a choice in the matter, Joel. You can't blame your actions on everyone else.' Ruth does darning. Ruth looks as if she has never committed a sin in her life and Joel often muses on the fact that she probably hasn't. She has a particularly direct sin-less stare. And yet, as is the way with introverted, quiet people, you're never quite sure what she's thinking.

'Rufus plays with people's lives,' added Joel, limply, on the night they discussed it. 'He plays games for a living, but the awful thing is that he sets it up so

123

that he always wins. If Rufus can't win, he doesn't play.'

'A bit like Gregor,' said Ruth as she sat in a pool of lamplight beside their Hampstead false-flame fire trying to thread a needle.

Joel hadn't noticed Gregor. He prefers not to notice the children, even his own. They are loud and tuneless. He cannot stand it when they go and bang on the piano. They can play nicely, so why do they need to show off like they do?

'You're too intense,' said Ruth. 'You should try to relax more. I wish you had a hobby.'

'Perhaps I should collect things, like Rufus,' said Joel, with a bitter flavour in his mouth.

'And I wish you were not always comparing yourself to Rufus,' Ruth added. 'I wouldn't have married you if you were like Rufus. I wouldn't love you like I do if you were anything like Rufus.'

And Joel had to be satisfied with that. He was Harriet's baby and he has never quite come to terms with the fact that he should have been Harriet's favourite but wasn't. It had always been Rufus. When Ruth said that about loving him best, it was the nearest she had ever come to bad-mouthing anyone.

He had confessed, that night, about Beany Widgeon. 'I don't think that was his name but that's what we always called him. He was just a tramp. He didn't bother anyone. But Rufus seemed to detest him! Everything he stood for. Calling him a mutant human being – grotesque – absurd – an abomination – a threat to the species. I'm sure nobody else felt that way about Widgeon, but we all went along with Rufus and called out names after Widgeon whenever he went by.'

'How unnecessarily cruel,' said Ruth, snapping her eyes when she snapped the wool. 'Poor old man.'

'He didn't hang around for long, not after one summer. And he never came again after that. He used to be a regular caller. I even asked after him at the shop, once, but they said they hadn't seen him after that summer either.'

'I shouldn't think that tramps stick to much of a routine.'

'Widgeon did. Beany Widgeon had been coming to Tremity for years. He was a sort of scruffy old landmark . . . came at hay-making time. I think the locals regarded him as a kind of fertility symbol, you know, like the last sheaf and all that. But Rufus didn't see him that way at all. Rufus called him a lamentable man. Rufus called Widgeon a walking catastrophe.'

'And was he?' asked Ruth with mild interest while she inserted her darning mushroom.

'He was just a bit of a piss artist,' said Joel. 'But he didn't steal the shears. He might have done, I suppose, given the opportunity. The fact that everyone locked their garden sheds when they spotted him staggering down the lane made it impossible for him to do so. Anyway, that's beside the point. And frankly, Ruth, I feel bloody uncomfortable sometimes when I think what happened to Widgeon.'

Ruth's smile was understanding. Her rebuke was only slight. She stroked the elbow of a child's red jumper when she said: 'Children behave in ways they often regret. You can't spend your life regretting every childhood misde-meanour you ever committed. You were probably too young to understand.'

'I was twelve. Simon was fourteen and Rufus was sixteen. And I did understand what was happening, Ruth. I remember it so horribly clearly. Nanny Weston had just left because it was the year I first went away to school. My asthma was better and she wasn't needed at home any more. Rufus, when she went, was completely gutted. Even though, since going to school, he had only been with her at holiday times. I suppose, of all of us, being the eldest, having had her from being a baby, he was the one who missed her most. And Rufus was always the special child.'

'Rufus, being beautiful, is easy to love,' said Ruth. 'On a rather superficial level of course.'

Joel was careful with his hands. He was never extravagant with them. He did not gesticulate when he spoke because he was used to dramatic responses to his gestures. He rarely required dramatic responses in real life, just understanding ones. His hands were neatly on his knees when he said: 'Westy adored Rufus. He was the only one ever to achieve ten green stars. Everyone, even children who came for the day, even children who came for tea, they used to try for a green star. It was something Simon and I both strived for . . . it became a quite serious contest between us . . . to fill that chart before the end of the month and get the mysterious "treat". One star was no good. You had to get ten, you see. But no, that only happened to Rufus. And then Westy left. That summer it seemed that Rufus was determined to get his own back on someone and it didn't seem to matter much who it was. Everyone was afraid of Rufus in that mood.' Joel had pondered uneasily. 'And I suppose we still are in a way.'

Ruth had stroked his hair and kissed him softly on the forehead.

'We told Widgeon he could have the shears. We stood at the gate and handed them over and Rufus said Hugo had finished with them. I remember the smile that crossed that old man's face as he took them, goddammit. The man believed he'd arrived in Paradise. They were very good shears. And Rufus said later: 'It's the smile of the wretched, the leer of the drunk. Joel, the man was out of his skull. It wasn't the sight of the shears that made him smile, it was the thought of the two days' worth of booze he could exchange for them.'

'We were all there, the whole group of us. But Rufus told Widgeon they'd fetch ten bob at the farm sale that afternoon. He told Widgeon to take them along and see what Nathan Pengelly made of them . . . Pengelly of all people! Why the hell did Rufus have to pick Pengelly?'

'Who was Pengelly?' Ruth broke a thread between her teeth. To Joel this violence that crossed her face looked like a horrible leer.

He stammered a little as he went on. 'Stalwart citizen, yeoman farmer, man of God, fanatic,' said Joel. 'I can see why Rufus chose him if it was a laugh he was after. Pengelly must have been the funniest man Rufus could think of. And the awful thing is that I thought it was bloody funny, too, at the time.'

'Joel, you were twelve years old!'

Joel smacked his forehead hard as he remembered. For him this was an extraordinary gesture. 'They came and asked Hugo if he'd given Widgeon the shears. Pengelly stood up on the auction block and damned old Widgeon to eternal fire. He threatened Hell and damnation. Everyone was there. Hell, Ruth, the whole village turned up, and those from the villages round about. All the people Widgeon depended on for his pathetic living. We sat on a hay cart and listened. We laughed, for God's sake. We fell about. And Widgeon started to cry before he started running. That old man, running like that, tears streaming down his filthy face, as if all the hounds of Hell were after him.

'He leapt the gate,' said Joel disgustedly. 'And I often wonder what we must have done to him by going to find him later that night with the drum and the cymbal and Hugo's damn hunting horn. By that bloody tape recording with the hunt baying on it. We could have left him. We'd had our fun. But no, that was not enough for Rufus. Why did we always have to go on and on like that? Why could we never leave anything alone?'

Ruth looked up, alerted by the threatened sob in Joel's voice. 'I'm surprised that nobody stopped you. That nobody heard you and sent you back home. You must have made a racket in a sleepy village like Tremity.'

Joel closed his eyes to bring the incident closer. He reclaimed his wild-feeling hands and replaced them on his knee. 'No, it was out by the dunes. Widgeon used to sleep under an upturned rowing boat . . . that was his home when he came to Tremity. We knew he'd arrived because of his little fire – a thin spiral of smoke from that bloody pathetic fire. He kept it going all night. No one could hear us because of the distance, and because of the waves. The sound of the waves muffles everything. But we crept up behind Widgeon, me and Simon and Rufus, Harry, Toby, Alexander and Felix. So pleased with ourselves! I banged the drum because I was the youngest.' Joel mused: 'That was the first musical instrument I ever played . . . the first time I played with anyone else. Toby blew the horn. Felix banged the cymbal. And Rufus, of course, set up the tape recorder with the howling hounds baying on it. He must have planned it all, Ruth . . . to have made that recording! He must have known in advance exactly what he was going to do!'

Ruth tutted and stared, expressionless, into the fire. Quite still.

'That old man got up. We crouched. He couldn't see us. But we could see him if we peeped round the reeds. His eyes were the eyes of a lunatic! Staring, out on sticks. His hair stood on end. He didn't stop to pick up his things but he covered his ears with his hands and he staggered off into the darkness. Then we crept forward and plundered his things! Oh God . . . we who had so much! We rooted through his abysmal belongings as if there was anything there we might want! Rufus found an old mouth organ . . . that was all there was worth taking. And after Rufus had burned Widgeon's clothes, he threw sand on the fire. I remember saying: "There's no need to do that. Widgeon will need his fire when he comes back. That's how he cooks." And Rufus kicked Widgeon's old kettle and gave me such a cynical look and said with certainty: "He won't be coming back."

'"What? Not ever?"'

'And Rufus said: "No, Joel. Not ever. We don't want people like that at Tremity. They are dirty and they smell . . . they are inadequate. They don't have thoughts like you or I. They don't have the same feelings, either."

'So I asked him how he could possibly know that – not being in Widgeon's head. I was already feeling bad about what we had done. And Rufus said: "No wonder you don't get your stars. Don't you ever listen to anything Westy says?"'

'It was just one rather unfortunate incident,' said Ruth tiredly, pulling her cardigan round her, for the tale was a chilling one. 'You are making a mountain out of a molehill. Widgeon probably found a home elsewhere. He must have had hundreds of places to go.'

'It wasn't just one incident,' said Joel, annoyed with her placid forgiveness. It was punishment he was after. That's why he'd recounted the tale. If he could be, at dear last, punished for it, maybe the sin would not feel so heavy. 'We were always doing things like that. Every year something happened. Every year we went along with Rufus and Harry. We seemed to turn into fiends every summer like that. At home it was safer. At home everything was so different. At home the adults took charge.'

'Well it isn't like that any longer,' said Ruth placatingly. 'Rufus has calmed down into the perfect father and family man. In spite of what everyone said at the time, Chelsea has had a calming effect on him.'

'Rufus was always calm . . . that's the point!'

Now Joel and Ruth are in the kitchen packing up boxfuls of food . . . sausages . . . chops . . . spare ribs . . . Ruth is whipping up barbecue sauces and washing the salad,

129

quite able to do three or four things at a time. She can think that way. She is a contented person. And good. She doesn't have to see out through dark thoughts or complicated wonderings. When she looks at an onion that's what she sees . . . an onion. When she goes to the sink she knows what she's gone for. She doesn't have to stop and frown while she works backwards in her head. Ruth is a most efficient woman. She can do the work and direct Joel at the same time. Whereas Joel only comes into his own in front of an orchestra.

Ruth has sent off the children to collect a pile of firewood and take it down to the beach.

'I didn't expect Helen to be here for a second year running,' says Joel absentmindedly, buttering a loaf of bread. 'What about booze?'

Ruth shakes more patience on to her face, more pepper in the sauce. 'The Wainwrights are doing the booze. Just concentrate on the bread . . . oh look . . . you're missing pieces. And you need to get more butter out.'

'I don't know what Rufus is playing at, getting in so deeply like this.'

'Is he in deeply?'

'I think he is.'

'Deeply into what?'

'I don't know what – Helen?' Joel stuffs one pile of buttered bread into a bag of greaseproof paper.

'Oh not like that, Joel,' says Ruth, gently chastising, moving over. 'He's just being kind, that's all.'

'She's not one of us, is she?'

Ruth's laugh is relaxed. 'Now you sound just like Rufus,' she says. 'She's a nun. Of course she's not one of us, you silly old dear!'

14

A motionless gull sits on the sign of the Merry Fiddler, quite still for a while, and then it lifts its tail. A yellowy-white wink closes the sly, enamelled eye but the merry fiddler, he plays on.

Normally the noisiest place in the village, this afternoon all is quiet at the pub because Cope and Nellie like to take an afternoon rest. All the residents are out. Because it is hot, and the thick walls of the reconditioned pub absorb the heat of the day, Cope and Nellie lie on top of their eiderdown, a cooling draught wafting through the open window like a child blowing kisses. Cope's chin sags stupidly open, and his rasping snores can be heard from outside in the silent street.

Just occasionally Nellie slips into the wrong position and winces slightly, easing off the damaged hip, rolling forward a little. But it doesn't bother her really. She's lived with it so many years now she's used to it. She never complains. She doesn't blame it on anyone but herself . . . she'd been brought up to do that. The nobs across the road . . . she knows they do not recognise her. Why would they? They come from another world. They must surely have long ago forgotten the existence of the girl Nellie Mundy.

So has Nellie. She has little enough of childhood left about her.

Every now and again a late car passes, and a blast of tape-recorded music rips the still summer air like a bursting paper bag. And the dry road gives a tired puff, a sandy sigh as if it, too, is exhausted by the heat and would like to go somewhere and rest. Away from all the hot rubber.

*

The heat is too much for Harriet. She and Simon are playing eighteen holes on the neighbouring golf course. But Harriet, paling and wiping her forehead, realises she should not have agreed to this. She pulls her straw hat further over her face and says, as they pass the shelter on the tenth: 'Let's rest a while, Simon. Just until this heat dies down. I think the full eighteen holes is getting a little too much for me.'

The blue of the sky is broken only by tiny clouds like powder puffs. The smell of silage is pungent and yellow, the sea is the hard blue of foil wrapping paper, and, twinkling brilliantly, folds and unfolds. 'Nonsense, Mother,' says angelic-faced Simon, short sleeves stuck to the pudgy tops of his arms, shirt stuck to his back. Every now and again he pulls it loose by his collar. His cap is settled high on his head, exposing moist, damp curls under the pointed, businesslike peak. 'You're fitter than anyone else I know.' Simon is used to playing to a crowd but he is quite satisfied to exchange that for his mother. She used to play from scratch in her day. She can still pass on a trusty tip or two. He goes to sit beside her, but fidgets. He cannot bear to hold a golf club in his hand and not be using it. Now he swings his four iron idly this way and that, torturing a patch of dried grasses. He plays with his ball in his free hand, throwing it up and down and watching it. They can see the roof of White Waves from here. They can see the catamaran very small and insignificant, very white, on the water below them. Harry, Joel and Rufus are working on the boat.

'Simon?'

'Yes.'

Harriet is finding it very hard to carry her burden alone. She must be getting old, getting afraid to dance. 'I have been wondering, just lately, about Harry.' Maybe her sons do know something about it. It is up to her to find out.

'Oh?' Simon is not quite listening. He is reliving the

last American Open, and fretting over the putt that put him in fourth position. Here, at this local golf club he is treated like a star. He is the biggest name they are ever likely to see. Designer sports clothes with his name on them hang on the rail in the professional's shop, crisp, pressed and covered in crinkling polythene. They hold the Simon Pilkington annual trophy . . . contributed by Simon who also supplies the runners-up prizes and the special tea as well. Reverent hands are raised in waves as groups pass by him, wondering, no doubt, what he is doing sitting down, and why he isn't swinging as he usually is on any piece of spare ground. At least there are no autograph hunters out and about today.

'I was wondering – keep this between us of course – but I was wondering about Harry's financial state of affairs.'

'What on earth made you wonder about that?' Simon is, quite naturally, amazed.

Harriet frowns like a wizened elf. And Simon is shocked by the age she wears today. 'Just the odd suggestion . . .'

Simon laughs. 'I am absolutely certain you have nothing to worry about on that score. Harry's all right. Harry's doing fine. If Harry was short, Harry would say.'

'Would he?' Harriet stares directly at her second son. She's so proud of him! She remembers the times they brought the boys here, she and Hugo . . . Simon had been the only one to show any real interest. Rufus always got angry and stalked back to the clubhouse sulking if he didn't come up to scratch. And Joel, well Joel, even as a boy, never seemed to be really aware of anything other than concentrating on getting his breath. He couldn't even hit the ball if it was teed up two inches in front of him. But Simon – well Simon was a born golfer. He was soon beating Hugo . . . and that took some doing.

Hugo had a massive swing. Hugo was massive in so many ways.

'You really are worried, Harriet, aren't you?'

'I think that skeleton find unnerved me more than I like to admit.'

'That doesn't sound like you.'

'And oh . . . having Helen around all the time . . . she's always there! If I wasn't such a down to earth person I could even imagine she was watching us now!'

Simon says: 'She does seem to give that impression, yes. She is a bit iffy like that. Perhaps we'll ask Rufus to give next year a miss. I mean, he's always the one to go spare if any of us invite strangers.'

'Chelsea seems to have taken up with that young man Desmond. I find that strange, don't you? She doesn't normally show much interest in anyone else.'

'Mother, you are in a peculiar way! You sound upset by all of it! You're normally so relaxed and happy when we come here. What has got into you today?'

'I just don't know, Simon.' Harriet blows out all the spare air and lets her shoulders slump, easing the tension out of her. And then she smiles and flaps her score card. 'It's hot. Perhaps the heat has got to me. And I'm getting old, I suppose.'

'We're all doing that,' says Simon.

'Sometimes,' says Harriet, quite out of character, 'I find myself imagining things.'

Simon is not happy with this conversation. But he has to ask: 'What sort of things?'

Harriet looks at her son, hard, as if she's considering whether to say . . . and then she changes her mind to: 'Silly really. But I think Chelsea has met that young man somewhere before. I do not think he is quite the stranger he makes himself out to be.'

Simon's golfing shoes make his feet look very large on the ends of his Bermuda-shorted legs. They are a shiny mixture of white and beige. He stares at them.

Hard. Gold hairs spiral from the knee he strokes. He is a golden brown all over, like his brother, Rufus. What is his mother suggesting? Why is she talking to him seriously like this?

'I don't know what makes you say that. Who could he be, Mother? Where would Chelsea have met him?' He sounds as if he is humouring Harriet. He pulls himself up as he realises.

'He could be somebody from her past.'

'He is half her age.'

'Yes, I suppose he is. I am getting very bad on ages.' And then she suddenly turns and says: 'Do you miss your father, Simon?'

'Of course I do. We all miss Hugo dreadfully. Why on earth do you ask? Why do you have to ask? Surely you know that?'

Harriet muses on the automatic, rather glib answer. 'He was not always the most . . . the most . . . cautious of men.'

'What are you saying, Mother?'

Harriet smiles. 'Hugo was a very human person.'

'Well thank God he was . . .'

'No! Simon. He was not always the person we might like to think that he was. He might not have been the man we quite remember him as.'

'Well I remember him. And what I remember of him, I liked. I admired. I loved. Very much.'

They do not often talk of Hugo like this. Perhaps, after all, Harriet has been overdoing it. It is hard, because of her active life-style, to remember how old she is. Perhaps they should all get together and have a talk, as other families do about their dependants. Simon feels a slight, uncomfortable embarrassment. But he knows this is important, for Harriet's sake.

'What if something came out? Something that made you see your father in quite a different light? How would you feel then?'

135

'People are perceived in various ways. My perception of my father could not be changed by anyone else's opinion now. Not now he is dead. He was Hugo. He is Hugo. He will always be Hugo and as far as I'm concerned that's that.'

'He had many enemies in his life.'

'He was a bold man. He put his head above the parapet. He was bound to be shot at. Mother,' and Simon's voice turns gentle. 'What is all this about?'

And to Simon's horror Harriet bursts into uncontrollable tears. There. Quite openly. In the middle of the golf course. And Simon does not know what to do or how to comfort her. So he gets up and shields her from the people . . . from the sun.

Chelsea, from her sunbed in the garden, watches Helen watch Rufus.

'She stalks him all the time,' she confides, giggling, to Desmond.

'What does Rufus think about that?' asks Desmond, seeing the nun settle herself on the rocks not far from the busy men on the catamaran. He sees the nun open her sketchpad and begin to draw.

Chelsea sighs. 'I'm not sure what Rufus thinks about that,' she confesses. 'I'm never sure what Rufus thinks about anything.'

'Bit of a dark horse is he?'

'I suppose you could call him that, yes.'

And secretly Desmond admires Rufus . . . for being a dark horse . . . for being a film director . . . for possessing one such as Chelsea . . . for being rich . . . for owning this holiday house . . . for the way he looks and the way he acts and . . . oh there are so many things for Desmond to admire about Rufus.

Desmond is fairly bewildered, at the moment, by all of this. By the way these people live, and relate, and take so much for granted. No wonder they are despised

136

by fellows like Cope. He has asked Chelsea about the
skeleton . . . about the nun and the whore and the
possibility of the children playing jokes.

'They would have said,' said Chelsea positively.

'Then who could have done that?' Desmond wants to
clear the matter up. It worries him.

'No one from here,' says Chelsea. 'I can't imagine
any one of us scuttling down the bank to the cave and
exchanging one set of clothes for another. Everyone here
is far too busy for that. Why? Can you? Who do you
think it is?'

Desmond shakes his head. He is lying on a red
and white striped sunbed not inches from Chelsea's.
If anything, his is a little lower than hers. He wears
a pair of Rufus' shorts, more expensive, he is certain,
than any complete outfit he has ever owned in his life.
Compared to Chelsea's his limbs are white and forlorn.
And he'd thought he'd been quite brown! She is lying
on her stomach with her bikini top undone. He keeps
squinting over, hoping, when she rises up, that he might
see something. But no. Her arms get in the way. The
bikini pants are tiny. His eyes are drawn. He is wearing
himself out lying here doing nothing. He thinks that his
eyes have gone dry.

He has never felt anything like this before in his life.
It feels as if some other person has got inside him. He
likes it. Enid seems very distant, and he feels extraordinarily free, like that bird perched on top of that still
pine tree.

'Some sinister yokel . . . bonkers . . . the lot of them,'
Chelsea dismisses the subject.

'You don't take anything very seriously, do you?'

Chelsea looks at him sharply, stung by the criticism.
But she doesn't quite raise her head high enough.
Desmond sees nothing. 'Why do you say that?'

'Well, if my mother had found a skeleton in her coal
shed she would put herself to bed for a week. And after

137

that she would hold coffee mornings every day just so that she could discuss it . . . my mother's life would be totally transformed by such a macabre find. You lot . . . you just carry on with your lives as if nothing particularly extraordinary has happened. As if it's merely slightly distasteful.'

Chelsea is not interested in Desmond's mother, and her expression tells him so. 'Extraordinary things are always happening,' says Chelsea. 'Far more extraordinary things than that. We did discuss it at first. At length. But really, it's nothing to do with us, is it, so why should we be interested?'

So that answer makes Desmond feel very dull and boring. For, he supposes, he and his kind are always interested in things that are nothing to do with them . . . other people's excitements, other people's little tragedies. He can't accuse his mother for ever, he's always reading the problem pages in her magazines to see if he can find himself there. And yes, he suspects that's because his own life is so dull and boring. He gets up, goes to work, sees the same people every day. And everyone is pursuing the same objectives . . . the getting of money . . . the acquiring of goods . . . the setting up of an image. Desmond is worried about his image because he fears he hasn't got one. To be quite truthful he still doesn't honestly know whether he really does prefer chips or asparagus quiche. Scornful of image, yet Desmond is desperate to find one. Most of the people he knows are exhausting themselves with all of it. But these people, thinks Desmond a little bitterly, these people need not waste time on any of that. They've got it all. So what are they striving for? What games do they play? Do they invent their own . . . or are there any real challenges left?

Chelsea is looking at him as if he is a challenge. And Desmond certainly likes that. He loves it. Heat sweeps him from head to toe. All over. *Does she really want him*

. . . in that way? Desmond is incredulous. Why does she? What has he got to offer a woman like this? But there is little doubt about it . . . her eyes are giving him only one message, and even Desmond, from what he considers to be his dismally uninteresting side of the tracks, even Desmond cannot mistake that message.

No one would. Not even his rather strange friend Roger.

15

Oh yes the nun is used to spartan ways and a hardy existence. She was born into them. Life at White Waves suits Helen very well, when she bothers to notice it. For her the barn-like house assumes cottage proportions. The food they eat is luxurious. Their conversation enthralling. Their sense of humour bizarre. The nun is an institutional person and unfamiliar with family life. And as for Rufus . . . cool, compelling, sardonic, confident Rufus . . . well . . . there was no one like Rufus at the convent. Although he has Father O'Malley's eyes.

Of course she watches him. She watches him whenever the opportunity to do so presents itself. And what does that make her?

She is drawing a picture of the cliffs today, but not as anyone else would see them if they looked over from where she sits gazing intently out over the red and blue afternoon. Helen does not go in for analysing her feelings, but if she did she might wonder why she sees the cliffs as black and purple and menacing. The yachts that pass up and down before them are merely drifting shadows of light. When she comes to add colour to the scene perhaps her mood will have changed and she will feel able to add some other, lighter shades. Perhaps not. This feeling she has is not a happy feeling. Passion is not pleasant. Passion is the colour of bruises, black and purple, emerald and crimson. Helen knows all about that. Helen is learning fast.

All these silly people! Behind her, in the garden, Chelsea and Desmond sunbathe and flirt. Helen has never seen Chelsea flirt before . . . not with someone she actually knows. She's normally cool around visitors. A little lower down, in a protected patch of grass surrounded by privet which they pretentiously call 'the bower', Wendy the brigadier's daughter is taking a nap in the nude. Helen was careful to avert her eyes as she passed on her way down to this, a darker place. Helen knows that Rufus can see her. All the men on the boat, as they work there desultorily in the sunshine, can see her. She waved when she took up her position and they all waved back. And made some comment. Oh she saw that, too, but she was too far away to hear what they said.

The cup which my Father hath given me, shall I not drink it?

At the hotel where Helen had gone, in such trepidation, to meet Rufus, he had presented her with a contract. She should take it away and get it looked at, he explained. Helen hadn't bothered. After all, what option did she have? Three programmes of an hour each . . . but to get those programmes would entail months of filming. Filming? Who would be there?

'Just my sound man, my camera man and me.'

'I am very dull. I stay in my room. I have few opinions and little to talk about.'

'You will talk about life, the world and experiences as you see them. That will not make for dull viewing. I promise you.'

'But what will I have to do?'

'Don't worry about that. We'll sort out what you have to do at the time. Most of the work will be done without you around anyway.'

He made it sound so simple. He paid for Helen's first meal out, for her only decent meal, actually, since coming out. She had been overawed by the palatial splendour of the hotel . . . the cutlery . . . the rich food. And the three different kinds of wine. The warmth and the silence in the hotel contrasted significantly with the cold, gusty weather outside. She was treated with respect because she was with Rufus and this was a unique experience

141

for Helen. People's eyes did not slide off her. And when he'd helped her into the taxi which would take her home, 'helped' was the operative word. Her head was reeling with sounds and images and she remembered Mother Superior's advice: 'Don't drink if you don't want to.'

And Rufus himself? While he talked, handling her firmly, precisely with what she considered was probably expertise, she fiddled with a lemon slice, her teeth in her lip, and watched him . . . the way his hair caught in the light and assumed a golden wreath around him, the way his eyes followed her movements, boring through her, a piercing blue.

Whom have I in Heaven but thee: and there is none upon earth that I desire in comparison to thee.

I am an oddity, she thought. I am peculiar. He is tolerating me. But she knew that at last she was finished with crying.

Her own, slower eyes followed his finger movements as they picked up a glass or played with a spoon. And the way he sat back every now and then, in his chair, as if to sum up the situation. Or to see if she had.

'You haven't much of an appetite, have you?' he said, smiling, expressing an empathy with his victim.

She had tried to make herself look good for the occasion. She had gone into one of a chain of shops which she knew sold simple, tasteful clothes. There were wooden floors, jugs of flowers, chintzy curtains, and everyone else on earth but Helen knows the assistants there are always impossibly rude.

No one had approached her. She had been allowed to inspect the dresses at leisure, giving careful consideration to every one. But when she'd been in the shop for about half an hour a young girl with a very white collar and blue and white spots on her dress came over and said: 'Can I help you? Was there something special?' And the girl had looked Helen up and down with bold, appraising eyes, wanting to dismiss her but, because of her position, unable to do so. 'What size are you?'

'Size?'

'Yes, twelve, fourteen . . . so what size are you?' There was an angry impatience in the girl's voice which she didn't bother to conceal.

Helen thought: She will think I have come out of prison. So Helen said firmly: 'Twelve.' And before she knew it she was thrust into a changing room smelling of scent and sweat and heaving with half-dressed women and surrounded by mirrors. She'd blushed. At the convent it was indecent to expose any part of yourself to anyone else. The nuns were not even meant to look at themselves. They wore thin white shifts in the bath for modesty's sake. There were no mirrors. But now she found the sight of such huge amounts of exposed flesh both shameful and compelling. Her heart thumped in her chest as carefully she tried her own dress on, facing the wall, shrugging and contorting and easing her shoulders into it without letting anything show. She was clearly not a twelve. Perhaps she was a fourteen? The girl obliged her by bringing a fourteen to try. Sulkily, suggesting that Helen should not have messed her about in the first place.

Helen was shocked by the sight of herself in all those mirrors. She could see what she looked like from the back. But how did she look to anyone else? Did she appear normal? Were people staring at her out of the corners of their eyes and thinking how awful, how peculiar she looked?

She checked with care. But nobody was taking the slightest notice. All the eyes that stared with such frighteningly frank assessments were directed at their own images. Not Helen's.

She dared to pause and stare. What did she see? A tall, thin shallow woman with frightened shoulders . . . but it

143

was the expression on the face that really shocked her. For her mouth, far from trembling, was smiling. And her eyes were not staring out of deep black holes, but were calm and affable as everyone else's. I really am here, she said to herself. And I really do look like everyone else.

She hadn't dared ask to try anything else so she'd bought the dress. A simple blue one ... blue, surely the saddest colour in the world and so many people's favourite ... they called the dress a shirtwaister. And she'd worn it for the meeting with Rufus. The thickness of the hotel carpet set her teeth on edge. She had kept her arms tight to her sides. She had tried to breathe very slowly. And walk very carefully. Had she amused him? And had he smiled? It was hard to tell. With Rufus it was always hard to tell if he was smiling or not.

Sitting so near him. When Helen felt he was disconcerted by her stares she moved her gaze away. But it was hard to take her eyes off him. Very hard. She wanted to see inside, to see further than her eyes would take her. But of course she couldn't do that.

He'd asked her some simple questions then. 'When did you take your final vows? How old were you then? Why did you decide to become a nun? What did your family think about it? Were you encouraged? Or dissuaded? When did you first feel you had made the wrong decision? Was there always a doubt?'

Helen picked up a red anemone, fingering the cool stem. A bead of water dropped on the cloth and stayed there, fat and solid like a tear. 'I was brought up in the strictest of church traditions. I was brought up by the Sisters of Mercy.'

'You were an orphan?'

The truth of her life was quite simple but it did not feel simple to tell. In the short time it took, Helen felt all the cold and the fear and the anger and the loneliness and the confusion and the always questioning why. She looked back on something akin to death. She looked across the

144

table and saw Rufus and in the aura of energy round him Helen saw life. 'No. I was not an orphan. But I was sent to the sisters as a small baby by a mother who could not keep me. However, I was not abandoned. My mother kept up her visits.'

'Was it expected, then, that you should become a nun?'

Oh Mumma I am bleeding:

> *I desire grace and mercy of our Lord Jesus Christ,*
> *to devote myself to his service*
> *in this Community*
> *in poverty, chastity and obedience,*
> *for the rest of my life in this world,*
> *and I pray you in the name of God*
> *to admit me to profession*
> *in this Community of the Sisters of Mercy.*

Helen was unused to talking about herself. She found it hard to counter the learned responses of self-negation. 'I think it was a way of expressing gratitude. Yes. For the upbringing I had received. It was not something that was demanded of us. Quite the reverse. But it was accepted with joy if one of the girls was chosen.'

Oh Mumma help me:

> *Do you understand that profession binds you in life long covenant?*
> *Do you understand that this involves a life of sacrifice?*
> *Will you diligently follow our Lord Jesus Christ?*
> *Will you strive to live in love and gentleness, humility and patience with all your sisters, in obedience to the Rule of this Community, and in the Spirit of the blessed Virgin Mary?*

I will.

*

145

'You have always lived in an institution?' Rufus had not concealed his curiosity. She began to feel this exposure was worse than taking off her dress in that stinking changing room. She was afraid he was after some precious part of her body she did not want to reveal. She slid her eyes round the room in the way she had slid her narrow shoulders under her dress, but there was no escape. The nun had no alternative.

'Yes. Yes. I suppose I have.'

The illusion was one of silence then, although the hotel dining room buzzed with life behind them. Other people's quiet talk fizzed round Helen's ears. Waiters shook burnished pans and blue flames leapt in the air. And the swing door which parted the room from the kitchen shushed with a kick and shushed back again.

And Helen knew that Rufus was pleased to think her so unworldly. And that the simple dress she had chosen probably added to the image. And when he poured more wine in her glass she knew it was in order to get her to speak. She accepted it. And drank it. Needing all the help she could get.

Rufus made notes. This, too, was disconcerting. She had not imagined her words could ever assume this sort of importance.

And then, two weeks later, he had come to her flat. And although she tried very hard there was no way Helen could conceal the lonely despair that was her life. For it had seeped into the very walls of the place . . . in the unmatching bits and pieces of crockery . . . the two second-hand wooden-armed chairs . . . the burn-stained coffee table . . . the threadbare carpet with a worn-out pattern that resembled the shape of a man lying down. How many hours had she sat and looked at it . . . the worn place that had two balloons for hands and a nose like a pebble? The room was unlived in as Helen imagined her body unlived in.

But there and waiting, should anyone feel like doing it up.

And Rufus saw the tiny bedroom through the door that did not fit, so you could never close it. The peeling linoleum on the kitchen floor and the smell of death that seeped from under it. The steam marks the kettle had made over the years on the wallpaper that resembled strips of pine, turning the brown to a stricken yellow.

Yes, Rufus had seen all this. And not commented. With lowered eyes, ashamed of it all, she had told him: 'This is the place they found for me. I am lucky to have it. I do try and clean it with the carpet sweeper they provide. I have spent hours trying to clean it. It is clean. It's just that it always looks dirty.'

'There are places like that. But that smell . . . it smells as if there's a dead rat somewhere behind the plaster.'

This was the smell that Helen had come to associate with the outside world.

And he had gone into the bedroom and seen her washing draped over the horse where there was never any heat and so it never got properly dry. Sometimes when she got into bed – she often spent whole days there – sometimes the sheets were wet and it was the warmth of her body that dried them.

'Is there nowhere provided for you to dry your stuff?'

Helen had shaken her head. 'Nobody has said.'

'What about a launderette?'

Helen had shaken her head again because she had never heard of a launderette.

So this was the first excursion Rufus had organised. He had introduced her to Keith Kierey the camera man . . . Ron Redfern who recorded the sound. And they were dry, wry men who smoked cigarettes and Ron chewed gum also. They were young and gloomy and wore jeans and baggy sweaters with jackets over the top. They sighed a great deal and imagined the world was against them. But it was Rufus who always spoke to her when she

147

had to talk to the cameras. It was Rufus' questions she had to answer. And she was amazed, when she saw the playbacks, that Rufus' voice had disappeared so that it looked as if she was talking to herself. Even when she went along the road with her big blue bag full of washing .. well, Rufus had talked to her then, but he was out of the shot and his voice was not there. It made it seem that she'd been wanting to tell people how she was feeling. She hadn't. She'd merely been answering, as best she could, Rufus' questions.

In the launderette they stood back and left her. She had to tackle those throbbing, yawning machines alone. Laminate and chrome and bubbles of blue. A money machine and white powder flecked with the colour of poison. A hard-faced woman with hair like a loaf who was picking her nails and only wanting to see what the camera was doing . . . only wanting to ask what this was all about.

Helen was ashamed of her washing. Why would people want to see her vest and her stockings, her blouse and her pillow cases? Why couldn't she scrunch them up and throw them in and slam the door?

'Do it slowly so we can see you.'

So, obedient as always, she'd taken the laundry out again, stuffed it back in the bag, and then brought out each piece singly, one at a time. She hadn't looked at the camera. It was easy to forget the camera was there . . . it was easy to forget that the boom that followed her was anything to do with sound. They were unfamiliar . . . but then everything was unfamiliar. She dealt with the filming as she dealt with the rest of her life then, with resignation and caution.

She'd made a fool of herself in front of the change machine. Rufus hadn't helped her. Rufus had stood back and let them film it all.

'Daft 'aporth,' said the launderette woman with great impatience. 'Come 'ere . . . anyone'd think you'd spent the whole of your life in a vacuum. What's the matter with you? Stick it in there . . . not there . . . that's where the money comes out. You can see it is . . . look! By the shelf. It's not hard, dear.'

So Helen hadn't dared ask her how to use the washing machine and Rufus hadn't demonstrated. She'd followed the instructions and after that it was all quite easy. They'd wanted to film her sitting down on the shiny, plastic benches the colour of skin – here and there people had picked strips off, it was red, like blood underneath – while others, more worldly than she, came and went and sometimes greeted her.

Rufus had asked her questions as she sat there. He had squatted on his knees bringing a microphone backwards and forwards as if it were something they were sharing. Helen had once seen two children enjoying an ice cream with their tongues like that. And she'd answered, and all the while her eyes had followed her washing as it swished round and round, all the fat heads and thin tails of it, venomous stripes soaking in white, and that is what Helen's head had felt like. Because of all the noise in the place.

While heavy traffic thundered by on the road outside.

There had been many strange outings then. To the post office, to the supermarket, to open a bank account, a disco, a packed lunch-time pub, the cinema, a trip on the tube, to Oxford Street . . . places you found in children's books . . . or places they went to through the round window on *Playschool*, a programme she sometimes watched on her newly hired television. Gently introducing the unfamiliar to the inadequate. Although there was no gentleness in the way Rufus did it.

'Just be yourself dear,' he used to say as she fought for breath, closed her eyes and attempted to answer his questions. On and on and on went the questions.

149

'*Tell us what you see, Helen! Tell us how you are feeling!*'

And sometimes: '*It's ten thirty. Tell us what you would be doing if you were back in the convent now.*'

And when she'd seen herself she hadn't identified at all with the person on the pavement with the black mac and the rain-hood. For that person, incredibly, looked the same as all the other people who had passed her with hardly a glance.

What had Helen expected to see? She'd expected to see a woman with her head on fire and the rest of her just a smoking, charred carcass. She'd expected to see yellow eyes with purple lids and a fathomless mouth like a gaping well. She'd expected to hear a voice that was a thin white bitter smoke trailing up into a sky that went nowhere.

But the woman with the mac on had even smiled sometimes as she told her lies in answer to Rufus' questions. They didn't sound like lies. They sounded like the words everyone else was speaking. And she realised that everyone else was speaking for somebody else as though they had cameras on them too, and microphones clipped to their chests. Just as Helen was speaking for Rufus.

Really, there was nobody there. Everyone was, like her, just an answer for someone else.

Helen raises her brush, rinses it, licks it, and mixes the colour of sky. Out there on the river Rufus is kneeling over the side of the catamaran. His reflection is pure blue in the water.

Hear, O daughter, consider and incline your ear; forget your own people and your father's house. The King desires your beauty: he is your Lord therefore bow down before him.

Helen brings down her brush and daubs the page with a dirty crimson.

16

Then there had been the magazines. So impossible did Helen find it to answer the questions put by all those smart people that she wrote down her life on a Smith's pad and learned it off by heart. With quotes. She wrote down her life and her feelings and her responses because she couldn't reveal the real ones. But these people, they all wanted something and they were all coming to get it.

And all the time Rufus stayed by her side, encouraging and helping her. They went on the radio together and whenever Helen couldn't answer, Rufus answered for her. And that was all right. That was better, in fact. Because Rufus made her sound very firm. Very real.

So drawn were the public to Rufus' image of the lonely nun that she began to get offers of help from the strangest people, people she'd never heard of. One offered her the use of a hut in Cyprus, down a track between orange groves. 'You will never have to see anyone if you don't want to,' this letter had said. 'You will never have to go out if you don't want to, either. All your needs can be delivered to your door by donkey.'

Rufus told Helen that she certainly did not need that. 'That's retreat,' he told her. 'And what we are trying to do is advance.'

And then that moody Mr Jones asked her into his flat for a coffee and told her: 'Call me Jim.' And Miss Tyler stopped shouting through the bathroom door and started to smile when they met.

What would Helen do when all this died down? When she was left alone in her flat again to pass the desolate days in bed or sitting on that wretched chair?

'We must find you a job,' said Rufus in his usual,

positive way. 'What are you good at? What do you enjoy doing best?'

Helen had raised her eyebrows and stared at him out of habit, quietly waiting for him to answer his own question.

'Do you know?' asked Rufus. So Helen knew that he really did want an answer.

Then Helen fetched her Smith's pad and shyly showed him the sketches she'd done. 'I always liked to draw and paint.'

'These are very good!' Rufus seemed amazed. 'These are outstandingly good! Have you ever tried to do anything with them?'

Well of course she had not. How could she?

'Give me a week or two,' said Rufus. 'I've got some ideas and we'll see what we can do.'

Rufus bought her paints and an easel and told her to get a collection together . . . 'So I can show it to someone I know.'

Helen was no longer lonely. Or miserable. Or needing anything else. Never before had she possessed anything so utterly wonderful. Never before had she had the time to indulge, properly, in this most passionate thing. She rarely went to bed any more. Because she discovered that painting by night is quite different from painting by day . . . and she liked both effects. So she could choose whether to stay up or go to bed. She had to accommodate Rufus, of course, and the terrible interviews. But she knew that she could always return to her room and her painting . . . and it was like having somebody there . . . waiting for her. Of her own.

The school he found was inside a Borstal, completely enclosed by grey walls. There was wire on top as well as glass, and big iron gates strung with mesh, that stayed closed.

'Don't be put off,' said Rufus, watching her carefully,

with his camera man, Keith, panning behind him, and his sound man posturing in front. 'They find it hard to get qualified teachers. They were thrilled when they saw your work. It will take time to get used to the new environment of course, but in some ways it will be familiar to you. After all, these pupils are imprisoned as you were. They never go out.'

It was not even slightly the same. Helen was as unfamiliar here as she had ever been anywhere. And more threatened. And more humiliated. And the cameras whirred and they loved it. And the public cheered and demanded more.

Sometimes, as he sat there at the back of the classroom with bars on the windows, Helen looked over and thought she saw Rufus smiling. But she could never be sure.

The mornings were always the same. There were only ever six or seven who came to the classes. And they were not there to do art. Helen didn't know what they were there for because they would not listen to her. Or do as she asked. Or put the paints away or clean up afterwards.

And the language was foul . . . especially on the days the cameras came.

In the eyes of her pupils Helen saw all the hostility she'd only felt emanating from the rest of the world. Here she could see it . . . here she could feel it . . . and sometimes, in their pictures, it showed itself, too. And Helen looked away, not in disgust, but in fear, because she recognized something in those violently raw shapes and colours, something that was buried deeply inside herself and denied.

And then there was always: 'Miss . . . Miss . . . Janice Chard has cut her wrists again, Miss . . .'

At first Helen had panicked . . . had rushed about, calling for help. For the blood that dripped down the slope of the desk had looked black as ink as it trickled on the floor, the livid cut on the tiny wrist like a baby bird's mouth, gaping. It was cruel to fill it with cotton wool. That was not what the gashes called for.

Gradually she had become used to it. 'You have to look at it and see whether the artery has actually been severed or not,' said flint-eyed Sister Jenkins. 'The same goes for overdoses or anything else like that. It happens all the time here . . . if we reacted hysterically to everything that goes on here the emergency ward at St Clare's would be more overstretched than it already is.'

'But what should I do?' begged Helen. The mess, apart from anything else, was gory and nauseating. She was aware that Rufus watched her, aware that she was near to exposing herself for the cameras in the way that they wanted. She calmed herself.

'Depends who it is,' said Sister Jenkins sternly. 'If you can, make the girl clear up her own mess herself. Same with vomit. Once they've vomited you know they're going to stay in the land of the living. There's a sink in the room, there's cloths, there's Dettol, get them to clear their own messes up!'

So . . . 'Miss! Miss! Janice Chard has cut her fucking wrists again, Miss!'

And Helen sat back in her chair, head drooped, eyes closed, as she said: 'Tell Janice to come here and show her '(fucking)' wrists to me.'

'She won't fucking come, Miss! And she's gone all fucking pale.'

She didn't want to see. She couldn't bear to see. She used to look out of the window and dream her dreams as the white snow fell and she was brought, out of total silence, lewd pictures which she wasn't supposed to know the meaning of. She used to wrap her arms round herself when desks flew and curses screamed and hair was torn and noses were bloodied.

'They are animals, some of them,' said Sister Jenkins resignedly. 'I've been in this job for forty years now and so I ought to know. For some are born without souls and for these there is no redemption.'

Ah yes, Helen could agree with that.

'And there is such a thing as evil,' said Sister Jenkins. 'There are evil people, and here in St Saviour's, we take our share of evil with every shuttle that comes to our door from the courts. You can see it getting out in its leather skirts and its crew-cut hair. It's there behind the blacking that covers their eyes. Unfortunately.'

But the slashed wrists called like children call. And the pale, drugged faces of the overdoses seemed needing a very childish pillow, even a breast to lean against, thought Helen, yet giving nothing away.

Once Megan McAllistair, of whom Helen was most frightened, brought her a picture . . . well . . . the innocence in it brought tears to Helen's eyes. She looked at the painting and she looked into the eyes of the girl . . . cold, bleak eyes, veiled and threatening. What should she say? Would she mar it for the girl by saying there was any good in it? By giving it the stamp of approval? But then why had Megan brought it to her? Wasn't she wanting some response?

'It's lovely, Megan. I have never seen you do a painting like this before.' Helen was careful, keeping emotion right out.

Later, the fire bells went off because Megan sat at the back of the room with a pile of matches beside her, trying to burn the picture and succeeding in causing quite a nasty burn to herself in the process.

'No, we have not called the brigade out,' said Sister Jenkins impatiently when Helen rang for help. 'The fire is out and no harm has been done. A little bit of buttermilk spread on that burn and it will heal in time.' Sister Jenkins turned to Megan, collapsed like a curled-up black spider. Cornered there with her singeing picture. 'Painful is it, Megan? Does it hurt? Well, perhaps you'll learn not to behave so stupidly

155

in future. Fire does hurt, Megan. Fire can be most painful.'

So can telling the truth.

On her way out of the room, Sister Jenkins had turned to Helen and muttered: 'You should have been able to stop that, Helen. None of the girls should have matches. What were you doing that you didn't see Megan McAllistair grubbing about on the floor trying to start that fire?'

What were you doing encouraging her to expose herself like that?

Helen hadn't been able to answer because she'd felt fairly chastised. She had been gazing out of the window mulling over the beauty of the picture, mulling over the fact that such good can come from such wickedness . . . for everybody knew and it was no secret that the fifteen-year-old Megan McAllistair, Irish, had calculatingly and cold-bloodedly killed her newborn baby in a churchyard. For shame of her motherhood being found out.

Now there's lots of wickedness somewhere in that.

Rufus said: 'You are seeing life in the raw. You might not be enjoying it but it makes for useful education.'

Helen wasn't sure if she wanted this sort of education. The cameras stopped filming if they were present on those more terrible days. 'The viewers wouldn't like it,' said Rufus simply. 'They'd stop watching. Apart from the fact that by being there we are probably exacerbating the situation.'

But Helen had the strangest feeling that Rufus was seeing if she would become *contaminated, if she could be touched*.

So there was St Saviour's on the one hand, and her quiet flat on the other. And somewhere in between there was always Rufus . . . in the background or masterminding the scene. He would take her out to dinner occasionally. Sometimes she was recognised in the street and children would come shyly up and ask for her autograph. She went on the local television magazine programme where she was asked, rather oddly, about men.

'I know very little of men.'

But still the young man interviewer had gone on . . . and on . . . while Helen said very little. But thought a great deal. About why people wanted to know about her. Particularly this side of her. About why they were always trying to frighten her . . . or shock her . . . or goad her into a violent response. Even anger. Just like the girls she taught every day tried to goad her. But Helen would not anger. She spoke very quietly and carefully, remembering what she had written on her pad and trying to stick to that so that one day she wouldn't say one thing and the next day another. Which is what would have happened had she spoken for herself.

The filming soon finished. The series was over and done. And last summer Rufus had asked if she'd like to spend August with him and his family. Well of course she would. She didn't need to refer to her pad to find a response to that.

Chelsea had surprised her . . . although she knew all about Chelsea by then. She had plied Rufus with so many questions about himself, that in the end, quite shamefacedly, he had presented her with a scrapbook. 'Just a few little things about myself and the things I have done. As you seem so interested. It might be worthwhile for you to keep a diary of events in your own life . . . with a few articles . . . these things are interesting to look back on.'

Helen had cherished that scrapbook, had read it from cover to cover so that not one detail escaped her, had even run her fingers over the faded pictures of Rufus in Chester making a documentary about children in care; of Rufus being interviewed for the *Bolton Echo* when he went to investigate unemployment there; of Rufus in Minehead with an actor with Aids; Rufus making a

157

film about the police in Liverpool. At the back were all the reviews. And they were mostly good ones. There were lots of pictures of Chelsea . . . you could see what sort of woman she was . . . and there were lots of little Chelseas at St Saviour's.

Uncharted territory. Should Helen make a scrapbook of her own life? If so, where should she start?

Surely her life had just begun the second she opened that letter. The second she unfolded the neat piece of paper and had seen *the name*, the name that was far more familiar to her than her own, there, in green, at the bottom of the page. That was when her eyes first opened and her mouth first nuzzled for sustenance. That was the second her scrapbook would have had to begin.

Any other pictures, put there by accident, would have to be ripped out or have a black line scored through. Because nothing else, to Helen, was real before that.

But she chose not to keep a scrapbook. Instead, she kept her journal safe in her dreams.

And she watches.

But it is not love that fires pale Helen's eyes. It is pure, undiluted, demonic hatred . . . passionate nonetheless . . . and it looks the same as love as it stares from that star cold place.

17

Contrary to what one might expect, Chelsea is not
repelled by Desmond's somewhat concave chest or the
muddy red hairs on his toes. Quite the opposite. Something childlike echoes off the hollow boniness of him.
Desmond is not a manly person and this appeals to
Chelsea. He is gentle, warm and sincere. Oh she's had
wimps in her time, yes, she's had wimps and brawny
men, fleshy and stringy men, but that was all a very
long time ago, before she was married to Rufus.

Chelsea has lost her vibrator. And Chelsea is very
bored.

And Chelsea is deeply disturbed about Rufus and what
he intends to do with that nun. Well, hell, for God's sake
. . . so Rufus screws his nun and what does that make
her? Never a person to care what other people say, yet
Chelsea is discomfited when she imagines the jibes of
her friends. 'What on earth happened, darling . . . perhaps you were not on your knees enough.' And so on.

She will look ridiculous.

Will a little jealousy dissuade him? Rufus has never
had to cope with jealousy. Let's see what it can do. So
Chelsea holds nothing back.

Desmond lies beside her and thinks that his time
has come. Well, naturally he does. She's been sending
him come and get me messages all afternoon. Once he
feared he'd got too much sun and started to worry about
sunstroke. At a time like this! But Chelsea had gone off
to find him a sunhat and then he'd felt all right.

When Ruth had come out into the garden and, from
the step, waved an imaginary glass in the air and acted
the drinking of it, Desmond had been most relieved.
For he felt parched and had not liked to ask Chelsea

to wait on him. However, picking it up from the grass and manoeuvring the glass to his lips had been tricky. It took three attempts to get it there without shaking, and then he gulped it too loudly, like a thirsty child.

He was finding out all about this family. The skeleton find still weighed on his mind. It had brought him frighteningly near to losing his self-control. He realised how important finding out the truth had become to him, it was all tied up with establishing himself as a real man in Chelsea's eyes, and in his own. So he found himself asking questions just like a sleuth. Desmond has informed the police of his new whereabouts and he has been across the road to fetch his belongings from Cope.

'You must move in. For as long as you need to stay here,' said Chelsea. 'Good God, in the circumstances it's the least we can do. Get yourself out of that squalid pub, sweetie. They put all their leftovers into their pasties, and it's been rumoured they pad them out with chicken mash. I wouldn't put anything past that sly bastard Cope.'

The pub was full of lunch-time visitors when Desmond tackled Cope and paid for his one night's stay. 'Well I might as well accept the invitation,' he told him, as Cope closed one eye and regarded Desmond suspiciously. 'It's free. I can always move back if they throw me out.'

'Don't be too sure about that, Hartley my lover,' said Cope, briskly polishing a gleaming glass. His wife peered out at them from her place through the hatch, sensing a contretemps, but there was none. 'You were lucky we found you a room in the first place. I can't guarantee we can do that again.'

So Desmond, feeling traitorous, knowing that Cope considered that by crossing to the other side he was abandoning the ship, felt Cope's eyes on him as he departed clutching his Adidas bag. He knew that Cope would be thinking the nobs had cheated him of custom – as is the way, Cope would add, of folks with too much money to know what to do with. 'Some of us have got a living to earn,' was one of Cope's favourite expressions.

Desmond had dumped his bag in the African room ... always cool ... it faced the north. In spite of the statues and masks, the wooden wildebeests and the fierce assegais, under all this the room still managed to give off the air of a damp youth hostel. It was, as he agreed with Chelsea later, a most strange house. And Enid his mother, like Muriel Dodds, would have sniffed at the standards ... would have gone to complain ... might even have refused to have slept here, had they found themselves booked into such a basic holiday home. They would both have been far happier in a small chalet, neatly equipped, with everything matching.

They would also insist on Rodney Caruthers' paintings being moved from the walls.

But Desmond is happily settled in, and extremely content to be spending a lazy afternoon lying here beside Chelsea.

'Hugo was a gusty man,' says Chelsea, answering Desmond's question easily, her languid fingers touching the grass and toying with the fuzz of it. She sips the lime juice Ruth has brought her and turns over carefully, one hand manoeuvring her bikini top. 'He had more life in him than the rest of them put together. He breathed it into them all, you know? Whenever he was around.'

Chelsea's voice is all admiration, but Desmond thinks he might well have disliked Hugo. Hugo would probably have frightened Desmond and brought out the worst in him. 'We got on terribly well together, right from day one. Right from the day Rufus took me home to meet them! God ... you should have seen Harriet's face. I did ask Rufus, I asked if I should wear something demure and modest, but Rufus told me not to bother, that they would have to take me just as I was. And so I went in pink high heels and hot pants, and I wore a sable wrap.'

Desmond winces. He imagines what he would feel

161

like if he took a girlfriend home like that. And what his mother would say. She'd probably eye him afterwards with that stony look and ask him what he was playing at. He'd heard her commenting over the fence to Freda Jones about the 'nice types' of girls Desmond brought home. 'They've got all the charisma of the back of my electric fire,' said Enid. He couldn't make out whether or not those comments were made tongue in cheek. But Desmond cannot stand nice girls. No wonder he can't keep his relationships going.

'Harriet misses Hugo terribly, in a silent, stalwart sort of way,' says Chelsea. 'If I am in pain I make sure that everyone knows about it.'

'And suffers with you?' asks Desmond.

'If necessary, yes,' says Chelsea, still revealing nothing. 'Harriet expresses herself in solitary ways, like swimming briskly, or batting her golf balls out over the water.'

'And does she approve of you now?'

'No. She never came round. But she's all right. She's got Ruth and Wendy, they are both her types. And of course she adores Gregor. I keep out of her way. Oh we're quite polite and chatty when we meet but we've known each other for fifteen years and never really spoken. Well, she had to accept me, didn't she? She had no alternative.' Chelsea muses and reaches down on the grass for her packet of cigarettes. When she looks at Desmond her gaze is clear and unflustered as the day. Desmond imagines his own eyes are bloodshot. 'I think Harriet is quite a cold person, as is the way of hearty women. Rufus always says she was. When they were children they hardly saw her apart from when she came in to kiss them good night, got up all elegantly for some ball or other. And according to Rufus, Harriet could hardly bear to do that . . . all those needy arms and clutching fingers! Almost in bad taste. She was always cold and aloof. She preferred her children when they grew up. Lots of mothers do, you know. No, the

162

kids got all the attention they needed from Westy the nanny.'

'I would never do that,' says Desmond. 'I would never leave my children to be brought up by anyone else.' And he had to control an embarrassing, dreadful urge to talk to her . . . to confide in her every last detail of his life, throwing himself and all that he was at her feet . . . how appalled she would be.

'Oh I would,' said Chelsea easily. 'I wanted a nanny for Gregor but Rufus wouldn't have it.'

'So he wasn't happy with his own experience, then.' Desmond is pleased he has made his point. He wants to appear intelligent in front of Chelsea. He is scanning his brain to try and imagine what sort of image he ought to present in order to impress Chelsea. But incredibly, he appears to be doing quite well as he is.

'It wasn't like that.' Chelsea's laugh is throaty and deep. 'He didn't think there'd be anyone good enough. There could never be anyone living who could compare with Westy.'

'Did she bring them all up?'

'She was with Hugo from the time he was six . . . then, when Harriet had Rufus, Hugo insisted they find the woman and offer her enough to entice her back to the family. So Rufus had her from a baby . . . Simon and Joel also. And then she died just a couple of years ago. Rufus, of course, was devastated. You should have seen him! He was far more upset than he was when poor old Hugo died. People get very attached to their nannies. Well, I suppose they would. I couldn't see anything in her myself, daft old bat.'

'She must have been ancient,' Desmond considers, 'if Hugo had the same nanny when he was a child.'

Chelsea gives him an accusing look. It comes across as provocative. 'Do you consider me to be ancient?'

Desmond flushes. 'Of course not.'

163

'Well, Westy was my age when she came to Rufus. She wasn't twenty when Hugo was a child. Some buxom, fresh-faced country girl . . . quite untrained . . . No doubt Hugo's parents considered she'd be a natural with children. And when his own children were born, Hugo insisted they find Westy and take her on. Well,' and Chelsea inspects her nails, 'Harriet wasn't on for the job. Harriet had become some big-wig in the fire service during the war. I've always thought her more like a man than a woman. She's so damn hardy.'

'When I met her in the hall she just ignored me completely,' says Desmond, who gets hurt when people dismiss him like that.

'Take no notice of Harriet,' says Chelsea calmly. 'She can be like that. They say she's shy but she's not. She just either likes or dislikes people instantly. She obviously doesn't like you!'

Desmond is hurt. Ridiculously hurt. Why should Harriet dislike him? Is it the colour of his hair? Is it his freckles? Or does she consider him a hanger-on taking advantage of free bed and board? The reasons don't matter. Desmond is still hurt.

Harriet Pilkington's expression is thoughtful as she watches how well Desmond and Chelsea appear to be getting on. Well of course they do – their little scheme is working. Will they approach her and ask for the money? Would Chelsea act in such a barefaced way as that? Or will she retain some sense of decency and send the wretched Desmond?

The police have been round asking questions. She's seen a panda car in the village. They're bound to come here again, what with the skeleton being on Harry's land and Desmond staying here now. What is more, Harriet supposes they will soon date it . . . and sex it . . . and probably find out who she was. Somebody somewhere must have reported the disappearance of

164

that silly woman in the uniform. Inquiries must have been made at the time.

Harriet shudders as she thinks again of that terrible scene.

She supposes that after she left that night, the three of them got drunk, Hugo, the maid and the terrible Rodney Caruthers. It was more than likely they would go for a swim – nude probably – Hugo was always encouraging guests to do that and Rodney Caruthers would need little prompting. Hugo loved to swim in the moonlight. And then, presumably, the accident happened. Unable to save her, the two young men must have dragged her into the cave . . . a very suitable place in those days . . . for the tourists didn't discover Tremity Cove until much later. And Hugo must have considered the cave to be hidden, dry, and unlikely to be disturbed.

Oh Hugo! If you had kept quiet no one would ever have found it! If you hadn't been playing your silly little games with Chelsea . . . fancy trusting a woman like that! And paying all that money for silence over all these years! My dear, the police would have listened to you! They would have understood the whole thing was a ghastly accident! But you were too ashamed, weren't you? I, by my attitudes, had made you ashamed.

And now . . . poor old Harry.

Into the garden of Wild Horses she goes, for Harriet's unease is such she cannot let it rest. Harry is not there. Harry is down at the catamaran. Harriet, knowing she will get nothing out of Harry, has decided to tackle Jessica, Harry's neurotic wife. Harriet should have known better than this. She should have realized that the only effect this could possibly have was to upset poor Jessica further.

Jessica is having tea with Daphne Wainwright. 'Join us,' calls Jessica weakly from an umbrella deep in the shade. Jessica is white from head to toe, with a thick, white liquid that has dried like calamine. 'I've been reading about the effects of the sun . . .' Harriet cannot be bothered to listen. Jessica is always reading about things like this. She changes from week to week, always struggling with some new allergy or neurotic concern. For weeks, now, she has lived on nothing but oily fish, having learned how fit are the Eskimos. Harriet is often tempted to ask: 'Your life is one long misery, Jessica, why do you strive so hard to prolong it?' But of course she doesn't. She just wishes Jessica could find something real to worry about.

Now Harriet descends carefully down in a deckchair and says, chattily: 'That young man, Desmond, seems to have recovered remarkably well.'

'Oh thank God,' groans Jessica. 'You cannot imagine what I've been going through.'

'Chelsea appears to have taken him under her wing.'

'Oh?' Jessica is surprised. They are all surprised.

Harriet frowns before coming firmly to the point. 'Why would Harry do such a foolish thing?'

Jessica leans forward and, with a wobbly hand, pours the tea. 'That's what I kept asking him. But he says he thought it was a man from *The Sun* . . . that he only wanted to shock him.'

'Now Jessica, I want to ask you a personal question.' Harriet's stare is a frank one. 'I want to ask you if you and Harry are having financial problems just now . . .'

Jessica almost drops the teapot and lies back looking startled.

'Are we?' she gasps. And then: 'Harry has not said!'

'Would Harry tell you?' asks Daphne Wainwright in a low voice full of foreboding. 'Or would he battle on, trying to keep it to himself?'

Jessica's voice is nearly a shriek. 'Harriet, what on earth makes you ask?'

Harriet shakes her head. 'I need to know' is all she's prepared to say. 'And Harry wouldn't like it if I asked him.'

Jessica, pale even under the calamine, wets her lips with her tongue. 'Oh my God, don't tell me this!' She thinks about it . . . Harriet can almost see her musings scuttling, cracked, across her dry forehead. 'It doesn't make sense! Only last month he ordered a new car! We are having the tennis court renovated. He's on the council at the zoo and he's just sent them a fortune towards the new tropical house! If we are in trouble, Harriet, then why is Harry behaving like this? Oh God, is it some sort of ghastly mental denial?'

'Surely Harry's not that type,' puts in Daphne Wainwright sensibly.

'Jessica, is there any way you could find out? I have to know.'

Jessica sits up in a vain attempt to come to grips with her situation. 'We all have to know . . .' and then she flops back. 'But Martin James has gone on safari, he won't be back for a month!'

'And even if he was in London, Harry's accountant might not tell you.'

'I'm going to ask Harry right now.' And Jessica rises abruptly from her sunbed, all weariness gone. 'I'm going to ask him, I have to know! It is my right to know!'

Harriet's voice is stern as all the short height of her, up from the deckchair, confronts the striding Jessica, blocking the way. 'No! Jessica, I don't want him to know I am asking. Sit down and compose yourself! You have to try and behave like an adult over this! Harry will only deny it. We have to find out some other way.'

Now Jessica, awkward, does not know which way to go. 'I can't go an hour not knowing,' she says, staring about her with hope of rescue.

'You have to, Jessica, I'm afraid.'

'What has Harry been spending all his money on?' Jessica sinks down again in bewilderment. 'We never had problems before! His investments are sound. He had all that money when Pongo died. At the time, I remember, he said he didn't need it! And that was only five years ago.' Jessica turns to Harriet, accusing. 'I think you are wrong. I don't know where you've got this from but I don't believe it. It is just not possible.'

Harriet is unconvinced. She has wasted her time asking Jessica. There is only one way to find out and that is to confront Harry. She'll have to pick her time, but she sees that there is no option. And after that she's going to the police, something she should have done years ago. 'Will you leave it to me? Will you promise to say nothing to Harry until I have had a chance to find out?'

'I would rather ask him outright.'

'And I would rather you left it.'

'If you're so determined ... but I do resent this, Harriet. You have upset me terribly and yet you refuse to say why.' Jessica almost weeps. 'I can feel one of my heads coming on. The rest of my holiday has been ruined. Penury stares me in the face and I am unable even to ask about it!'

'Just give me some time,' says Harriet, pulling down her straw and shading the determination on her face, the fiery glint in her eye. 'I will just tell you this. There is one person behind all this, I'm afraid, and that is Chelsea! Be careful what you say. Be careful what you do. She is not one of us ... she has never been one of us ... she is a snake in the grass and quite without shame.'

'She's gone mad!'

The two seated women follow Harriet with their eyes as she leaves the garden.

'How absolutely extraordinary,' says Daphne Wainwright. 'What are you going to do, darling?'

'Ask him of course,' says Jessica, swallowing two of her Quiet Life tablets in quick, practised succession. 'I'm hardly going to pretend that nothing's been said. If I'm going to go down the drain I'm damn sure I'm going to have warning. After all,' and she shades her eyes and stares after the departing Harriet, 'there must be time. There are things we can do to protect ourselves . . . we're hardly going to go without a struggle. I shall confront Harry, have it out, and then we'll start getting all his investments and property put into my name . . . or whatever one does, Daphne, faced with these dire circumstances.'

'I think you're being very wise,' says Daphne. 'After all, it's probably nonsense. Harriet, at her age, might well be losing her grip.'

18

After the elation of that first, heady election when Harry Featherstonehough had swept to an overwhelming victory, he had been astonished to receive the first note. A young man, zealous, with the whole of his political career before him and everyone saying what a staggering career it was bound to be, that note had nearly destroyed him.

He was married to Jessica, never the most stable of women. He was the proud father of two wonderful boys, Archie and Jasper. His own father, Pongo, had useful connections; a frustrated politician himself, he had always harboured ambitions for his only son.

The note read: *For the rape of the little maid . . . one thousand pounds . . . to be left in cash at a locker at Heathrow. The locker . . . number 159, will be open. Leave the money and go.*

Rape! That word tore Harry in half. For it had not seemed like rape then. They had been merely children, hadn't they? Boys with the world at their feet and everything to explore. Nellie hadn't really minded. Had she? Oh God oh God oh God.

And if he paid it, where would it end? Harry, although comfortably off, was not, at that time, a rich man. And if he refused . . . the consequences of that were enormous. Jessica, he was certain, would leave him. His career would be ruined. Not only his career, but the careers of all of them . . . although the others, he supposed, might recover on the strengths of their talents alone. He, most certainly, never would.

He could refuse to pay and challenge the blackmailer to bring the whole shocking business out into the open. He could go to the others and together they could fight it, deny it . . . it would be their word against Nellie's.

Ah but Harry knew the great British public . . . no smoke without fire. Even if found not guilty, after all the dirt splashed over the tabloids, he knew the result. They would not vote him in again, guilty or not. They would not want to be represented by someone with that sort of filth on his hands.

Where did he stand? He lay in his chair to think it out. He could go to the others for help, couldn't he? They had committed the crime, if crime there be, together. No one person had been responsible and no one person should be forced to take the blame. But Harry saw that as a coward's way out, sharing the burden was never his way. An independent man, Harry had been brought up not to whine, to grit his teeth and bear it, however horrible, however hard. No, he ought to try and clear up this mess on his own.

He had gone, like a criminal, with the money he could scarcely afford in his briefcase, looking this way and that through sneaky eyes, just like a man in a trilby hat in a film. But he had not worn a trilby. He had worn his favourite deerstalker. The green duck feather in the side always made Harry feel plucky. But he had not felt plucky that fatal day. He had felt dirty, contaminated, paying his way out of trouble, and it felt, as he slunk the long walk across the tiled floor, it felt as if everyone knew what he'd done. What they'd done.

Even his shoes started squeaking.

It wasn't until after he reached home, and was sitting with a drink in his shaking hand, that he realized that now there was no way out. By paying the money he could never cry innocent. His impulsive action, born out of panic, had sealed his guilt.

For ever?

As each month went by and there was no further demand he breathed a little more freely. Perhaps the demand was a one off. Perhaps the blackmailer was human after all, and had only wanted Harry to pay for his crime.

'You're nervous, Harry,' said Jessica. 'You've started grinding your teeth at night and I'm sure you never used to. And you never actually watch the television, do you? I've seen you. You're miles away, thinking of something else.'

'There's never anything on worth watching,' said Harry irritably. 'And I have a great deal on my mind. Mine is a large, highly populated constituency.'

'Well I realize that,' said Jessica. 'But it never bothered you before.'

'Leave me alone, old horse,' said Harry. 'While I'm grinding my teeth at least I know I am sleeping.'

But after the arrival of the second note, Harry had stopped sleeping. It was hard to get the money together and he paid it late. Then, to his horror, came the third. He spent hours roaming round the house in the early hours of the morning, smoking until his fingers turned yellow, drinking coffee after coffee, wondering whether to ask for help. Could he carry this alone? Wasn't his burden growing too heavy? If only he knew who the blackmailer was, perhaps he could find him. Reason with him. Explain how he wasn't a rich man . . . how Nellie hadn't seemed to mind!

'You must make an appointment to see Robin,' said Jessica, fixing her earrings. 'Well just look at yourself, Harry! Look at the bags round your eyes . . . look at the colour of your skin! And you've started to drink too much! Just go and see him! Please, darling! For me! It might be that there's something quite simple gone wrong. Robin will give you some tablets, calm you down.'

'Damn you Jessica! I don't need calming down!'

And this was so unlike Harry – he never shouted at Jessica, he knew she just couldn't take it – that he'd gone to put his hands on her shoulders and gazed at his reflection as it appeared in the pinkened mirror above

her own. And my God! What a ruin he had become! The
eyes that stared back at him could have been the eyes of
a madman! And his face was so tense it looked as if a
scream was readying itself to spout from his mouth. So
Harry had not gone to the doctor. Instead he arranged
an appointment at Brocks Club to meet Hugo.

They settled in leather armchairs with pictures of
horses behind them and gin and bitter lemons between.
Hugo, who of course would never have submitted to
blackmail of any kind no matter what he had done,
carefully read the note, his great black eyebrows knitted
benignly across the bridge of his nose, dragging the skin
to a dagger shape. He looked at Harry and said, in a
voice so level it could hardly be heard: 'Where is the
wench now?'

Harry shook his head dolefully. 'She doesn't live at
Tremity. She married and moved away.'

'What about the husband?'

'A local cowman, I believe.'

'Let's have another look at this note.' Hugo was so
comforting. It wasn't just his bulk and his essence of
power. It was the fact that, of everyone Harry knew,
Hugo was so damn unshockable. There was never an
air of criticism about him . . . Harry didn't feel small
or dirty or disgusting sitting there confessing the worst
sin of his life.

'And you say you have paid up, old man?'

Harry knew Hugo thought him a fool. 'I have paid
twice. As you can see, I am late making this third payment. And I am late because I cannot find the money.
I am not asking you for money, Hugo. I would never do
that. I am asking for your advice. I always imagined I
was a man of the world. Now I find that I am not. And
I have behaved like a bloody fool. Haven't I?'

'Why did you not go to Rufus or Joel or Simon . . .
why did you not ask any of the others for help?'

This was hard for Harry to explain. All he could say

173

was: 'Not on. Not really. The note came to me. Even Nanny Weston, Hugo, you remember Westy . . . Westy would have said: "Square your shoulders . . . lift up your head . . . and take it on the chin like a man."'

Hugo sat back, his rich man's hands smooth on the leather, his wedding ring tight on his finger, the heavy gold chain of his watch strap just showing under his very white cuff. He regarded Harry through heavy-lidded eyes. 'Yes,' said Hugo. 'By Jove, Westy had the right ideas. You don't go whingeing to your friends.'

'Precisely,' said Harry, sweating, for they kept the fires very high in here. Someone was always bending down creakily to add another lump of coal. He counted the panes in the windows and listened to the clock ticking on. The crackling of fires and newspapers made the loudest sounds in the room. A very dead salmon regarded Harry balefully from its lonely haunt under glass, and even its skin looked cracked from the heat and its reeds seemed shrivelled and dry.

'Leave it with me,' said Hugo. And those seemed to be the most welcome words Harry had ever heard in his life. Even Jessica's 'I do' had never had quite that ring to it.

'What are you going to do?' Harry had to ask. For whatever Hugo was intending, shouldn't Harry have been able to see it?

'I'm going to show it to some people I know,' said Hugo, folding the sporting page and taking a gold pencil from his pocket. 'I think the blighter has to be found.'

Harry paled. He didn't really know Hugo. Who were his friends? This could lead to something very dark indeed.

But Hugo smiled shrewdly. 'Don't worry, Harry. Every man has his price. And this, even for a blackguard, is not the most efficient of ways to extract it.'

It was just terribly unfortunate that, in the brief time that note was in Hugo's possession, Harriet had stumbled upon it, drawn her ludicrous conclusions and taken it into her head to overreact. As his wife, she should have known Hugo much better than that. Hugo had dealt with her firmly. He had dealt with the black-mailer, too. For the sake of his children . . . not for himself.

'That's all right, old boy,' said Hugo, a few days later, with a little spiv-like wink and a nod. 'Think no more about it.' So Harry had left it at that. Hugo had never told him the follow-up, and Harry had not asked. Perhaps he hadn't wanted to know . . . fearing to delve into such deep and unsavoury waters. But the months passed and the years passed and no more notes came. Harry began to relax. Harry began to forget. He never mentioned the note to Rufus or Simon or Joel. As far as he was concerned it was over and done with. For ever.

Until Hugo died five years ago.

And then another note had arrived. Not a year after Hugo's death. Saying the same thing . . . only the dropping place had changed. Now it was a deposit box outside a Mayfair jeweller's. Everything else was the same . . . even the amounts. Harry could pay them now . . . well, a thousand pounds every six months wasn't so daunting. But there was always the fear the amount would go up, always the horror that it might come out.

Harry had started drinking again. Sleep was hard to find. He was jumpy . . . well look what he'd done to the man he'd believed was a journalist. And Jessica's neuro-sis on top of it all didn't help. His own foolish actions had shaken him to the core. A sleepy afternoon pretending to work on the boat, rocked by the safety of his friends and listening to Elgar, had calmed him down.

But even so, Harry, these days, is not a happy man.

And it does not help to come home, floppy and sweat-ing with heat, and withstand attack from a whey-faced wife with a cracked skin like an old corpse risen up from a mouldy grave.

'Why Harry, why?' she ranted. 'Why didn't you tell me? I am your wife! We are meant to share things like this . . . things that threaten our whole lives . . . the lives of the children!'

Harry wants to shake her. Has she finally become seriously unhinged?

'Calm yourself, for God's sake, Jessica. And tell me what all this is about.'

Jessica, from behind the drawn curtains of her cool darkened bedroom, rants and raves: 'Harriet has been over. Harriet was insinuating that you were in trouble! Financial trouble! That we were in difficulties . . .'

'Harriet?' Harry is totally confused.

'Yes. And she asked me in front of Daphne! Honestly, Harry, I didn't know what to say! She suggested that Chelsea had something to do with it! I didn't understand what she could have been talking about.'

Harry shakes his head. He sighs. 'Jessica. I assure you we are as comfortably off as we ever were. There is no dire trough waiting for us to drop into. How can we possibly? And how could Chelsea affect anything? It's all quite preposterous!'

'But you haven't been sleeping . . . I know that! I've heard you prowling about downstairs, night after night . . .'

'I have other problems, yes, doesn't everyone? But I can assure you, they are not monetary ones. If I had those sorts of problems, darling, I would have told you. What can I say to make you believe me? You have absolute access to all my papers. There has never been anything stopping you. Even now, if you care to go home, you will find the documents you want in my desk. You know where I keep the key. If you get yourself into a state over this, quite frankly, Jessica, I will be annoyed. Because there is not one grain of truth in what Harriet

176

is saying.' Harry flops down on the bed and shakes his head wearily. He is going to have to have a good talk with Harriet. And where does Chelsea fit in? He asks Jessica again, but she says she is too confused and does not understand.

Harry is a convincing man. Just having him solidly there in front of her is relief enough for Jessica. She can breathe, once more, with relief. She can happily return to her old worries like sunburn and the fact that organic cabbages might well be more dangerous than the non-organic kind. Harry is obviously telling the truth. And now she hears his reassuring voice, she knows, as she has always really known, that what Harriet suggested could not be even remotely possible. Harry is far too responsible a man to get into a mess with his financial affairs. She is light-headed with relief. She almost wants to make love. Almost. But not quite. She turns to him lovingly, and smiles.

'Darling, pop your ball back. I do wish you'd buy some longer shorts . . . they are, after all, the fashion nowadays.'

'These are my old scout shorts and I am fond of them,' says Harry belligerently.

'But you can't keep having the waist loosened and larger and larger panels inserted. They're just not worth it. Scruffy old things. They're worse than Harriet's. They don't even look nice.'

'Well I think they do,' says Harry.

Harriet must be going mad. For everything is quite all right and just as it should be.

But Harry is thinking along other lines. He is making a connection he has, understandably, never made before. Money – Chelsea? Oh good lord, Harriet, what on earth is this all about?

19

'I do wish the children wouldn't light the fire on the beach so early. The tourists think it's something put on by the council and gather round. Sometimes you have to be quite rude to get them to go.'

'They don't understand,' says Harriet, shielding her eyes and watching from the porch as Ruth struggles in the back of the Range-Rover with boxes of food. In the normal way of things Harriet would be bending to pluck out a few of those straggly weeds on the step. She'd get involved with it, go for her trowel, pull on a gardening glove perhaps. But now she just stands there and says: 'It's the way people are brought up today. They think they've a right to be invited to everything. And sometimes get quite obnoxious when they're not.'

Ruth, in her gentle, resigned way, does not contradict. She blows her corn-coloured hair from her face and puffs, vaguely smiling. Where is Joel? He should be helping her with this.

Across the road, through the opened gate, Cope spits a yellow blob on to the stone doorstep of his pub as he watches their preparations. He rubs it in with his foot. These people, they think they control the world. They do not. They tried to buy him off once, and, to his shame, that had worked for a while. But now he sees what a fool he was. He could have milked that old fart, Hugo, for much more than the money it took for a publican's training. Cope smiles. It was a cunning ruse, he thinks to himself, to lull that apology for a man, that loud-voiced Featherstonehough, into thinking the payments would be low and remain low as they had been all those years ago, right back at the beginning. In that way Cope had enticed him to take the bait. But Cope intends to take his time, to make the increases gentle.

But Harry had taken the note to Hugo. At the time, when he'd accepted Hugo's offer, Cope had even been stupid enough to feel grateful. And there was the added concern that Hugo had managed to track him down and was threatening some pretty dire alternatives. 'You and Nellie ... go on the course ... I'll pay for that, but no more. I warn you, young fellow, no more!' There had been something in Hugo's tone that had convinced Cope he meant it. The threat of Hugo's anger had been like being pinned down on an airstrip with a Lancaster coming in to land. And Cope feels that Hugo's children are probably just as prickly. Not so the fat man with the weak mouth and the asinine bray.

Cope watches Harry on television, too. Cope watches from his chair with a cheroot in his mouth, a beer on the floor and his shoes off, and rejoices in feeling as powerful as any prime minister.

After Hugo made his offer Cope had not asked for more. Well, Nellie and he had gone on the course and then been offered a tenancy – that was thanks to Hugo, too. They had been busy, their lives had been full. It was, after all, what Cope had always dreamed of. It got him away from the muck and manure and the tied cottage that was always damp. But, he muses, he still has to work on Christmas day. And then they'd seen the Merry Fiddler in *The Licensed Victuallers' Gazette*. Surprisingly, it was Nellie who had been keen to go back.

'I thought you never liked Tremity. You always told me you couldn't wait to get out.'

'I've changed,' said Nellie, painting her toenails from a bottle of Tangerine Tango. And the smell of it, too, was of tangerines. As she bent down, struggling, white fat like undivided pasta rolled liberally above and below her bra. 'We've travelled so much,' she puffed, laying her fag to balance on the edge of the bedside table in an old

179

groove she had burnt there, 'and now I feel homesick, Kitch. And think of those long, peaceful winters. We work much too hard where we are. I've had enough of all year round trade. The summers will keep us going and in winter we can rest. And with my hip, sometimes, I feel I could do with more rest.'

Not until he knew that Hugo was dead, when Cope returned to Tremity, had he had the nerve or the idea to try it on again. Well, as he told himself, Harry had more to lose, now, than ever he had when, wet behind the ears, he had been member for Carshalton West. Cope has to admit to himself that he doesn't only do it for the money. The knowledge that he has power over people like Harry gives him a special kind of pleasure. It makes him feel secret and big but ordinary, like his hero, The Jackal. *Nobody knows who he really is.* They can look at him and think: Oh look, that's old Cope the landlord, what a dreary life he must lead. Bit of a brigand, isn't he? Bit of a pirate.

And there is excitement in it too, Cope can't deny he is attracted to that. The thrill of sending the note . . . the thrill of treading across the jeweller's carpet, the chink of the doorbell, the cultivated voice he uses to ask for his package, the flourishing signature with which he signs for it. And the jeweller's servile reaction: 'Nice to see you again, Mr Cope, sign here, if you would, Sir.' Hah . . . a little respect! No, Cope doesn't really need the money, although, of course, he'd never sneeze at it. Well nobody can quite afford to do that these days what with inflation . . .

Nellie, of course, knows nothing about it. No, Cope had acted off his own bat. She'd sobbed when she'd made her confession, afraid he might strike her, or leave her, or at any rate blame her for her part in the rape.

'But you had no part in it, did you, Nellie?' said Cope.

'I've always felt there was something I could have

done to prevent it.' Nellie decided that honesty was her best policy.

'Bastards,' said Cope, who preferred to imagine his wife had been ravaged by beasts. 'I always hated that lot! Even as kids they came down and thought they ruled the roost with their la-di-da accents and all their damn money.'

'Yes,' said Nellie tearfully. 'Yes, it was just like that.'

But Nellie would never have gone along with blackmail. She'd be far too frightened to tackle anything like that.

Twice a year Cope goes to London 'to deal with brewery business' he tells Nellie importantly. Nellie suspects he has some woman waiting for him up there because the rep never mentions Cope's mysterious visits when he comes. But Nellie doesn't really mind. Cope is only gone for a day or two and he always tries to pick a quiet time.

Yes, Cope has been a good husband to Nellie. With her hip she could have done much worse. She got smacked anyway when she came home on the night of the rape, limping and sopping wet.

'Swimming!' shrieked her mother, Joan, all hair and teeth. 'At this time of night? And who with I would like to know!'

'Nobody, Mum! Honest! But I've hurt my leg!'

'I'll leg you, my girl, if you don't get up those stairs right now and get yourself cleaned up! Out of my sight! Go on . . . out of it . . . out of it . . .' And her hard, slapping hands and her screeches followed poor Nellie up the stairs.

It was five days later when she was still moaning and limping that Joan finally, accusingly, took her daughter to the doctor. By then the damage was done. She was in hospital for two months with her leg in the air while they tried to repair it. Nellie had suffered a great deal of pain. But after all that it hadn't worked.

181

Things rarely work, in life, for people like Nellie.

She'd been forced to tell Cope on their wedding night for he would assume her a virgin. Cope was that sort of man. A bit old-fashioned in a funny sort of way . . . well . . . when it came to women. So she told him before they went to bed, sobbed out her story over the guest house table, between the plastic tomatoes with their gungey spouts and the green-sprigged squirters of mint.

'Bastards!' said Cope again and again. 'Bastards!'

'Shush!' said Nellie shyly, looking round. For she didn't want the landlady to think them that sort of people.

And Nellie felt better for the telling of it after all those years, and loved Cope the more for his violent reaction. It reassured her. Yes, he really must love her to care as violently as that.

'You might be recognized,' said Cope, when Nellie asked to come back. 'Won't you feel bad to be round them?'

'They won't know me now,' said Nellie with confidence, splaying her toes and inspecting the vivid result. She would have blown on them had she been able to reach. 'They hardly knew me then . . . why would they know me now? I look quite different, don't I? And I am thirty years older.'

And Cope looked at his wife's face flushed with her favourite, Damsel's Blush, at her hair which was wiry, nicotine yellow, at the mouth with its flaky purple smile, and he loved her. But agreed that, no, it was probable she would not be recognized. And even he was ashamed of his next thought . . . for he knew they would not want to rape her now. Nobody would, thought Cope morosely.

But now he cheers a little as he watches them load the Range-Rover over the road. His last demand was made in March, it will soon be time for another. And this time he is thinking of raising the thousand just a smidgeon . . . one thousand five hundred . . . or should he be daring and make it two? The options keep him

182

awake at night, in the same way the fear of them keeps Harry. But Cope's is an eager wakefulness, his pacings are energetic. While Harry's are dragging and slow, full of foreboding and heavy with fear.

Yes, the children have lit the bonfire too early and now they are likely to run out of wood. They co-opt a willing little band of visiting children to run and fetch driftwood while they sit about, avoiding the smoke, and giving their orders. For they own Tremity, don't they? It was they who were here first.

After a day apart, now they have naturally come together, just as the adults do, almost as though they can't help it. Is it fire that calls them, or the outgoing river, or the sense of approaching night?

The beach barbecue is an annual event to which every member goes. They have always done it. Their grandparents did it, but back in those days the beach was not crowded, there was not the permanent group of spectators that there is today.

'Something going on then?' asks a man in shorts and owl spectacles, shuffling forward through the sand.

'Nope,' answers Gregor, staring.

'There must be,' argues the man, spinning his sandals round his fingers. He will put them on when he reaches the car park. He does not want to get sand in his car. 'There must be, for a fire like this one.'

'Nope,' repeats Gregor.

'Have you got permission?' asks the man, sensing exclusion and not liking it.

'We don't need permission,' says sandy-haired Laurence, scowling at the forming crowd which consists of a trail of leaving people, sagging with their beach-going burdens. He gets stared at because he is so like his twin.

The owl-eyed man looks around him, dissatisfied. 'Well . . .' he says to them all.

The visitors raise their eyebrows and shake their heads and mention the dryness of the dunes. They are not used to such primitive fires, such large, uncontrollable fires in such vast, empty places. There is something unnerving about a fire like this tended by mere children. And the deep-throated way it growls and spits is threatening to the nervous. But the Tremity children are not mere children. They are in total control of the fire although they have never been scouts.

The visiting children start to be silly, start to throw seaweed around. The little ones start to cry as a wind gets up from the sea and blows sand in their eyes. The tourists trail away looking up from under the brims of their massive hats and saying: 'Well, we've had the best of the day.'

The Tremity children listen, look at each other and smile. They think they are natives. And from their exalted position they feel sorry for everyone else. 'They have such little lives,' says Gregor, quoting Rufus.

Amelia, angelic as her golf-playing father, frowns. 'Sometimes, Gregor, you can be such a snob.'

'What's wrong with that?' he replies. Gregor is feeling oddly bad-tempered and restless. 'You're as bad. Just because today you've decided to go moral on us.'

You can tell who the Tremity children are because all their jerseys are threadbare, not patched, and their gymshoes are cut at the toes. Some passing mothers, seeing this, feel proud as they watch their own neatly clothed offspring in cosy red towelling, wielding their neat plastic spades and swinging their buckets. Some mothers just don't care, they say to themselves, feeling pleased. The grannies among them say it out loud, casting it over their rounded shoulders. They don't know that there's style and style.

'Have you brought the vodka?' Amelia, not liking to be at odds with Gregor, changes the subject to a more popular one.

Archie and Jasper Featherstonehough, whose dare it is, look at each other out of smoke-blackened faces and grin. 'So you're going to do it?'

'Make the nun kiss Rufus?' Kate and Holly have been out all day, have missed all this. They are avid to hear the answer. They lick their pretty pink lips.

'It's a silly dare anyway,' says Amelia, burying her toes in the sand. 'Because obviously we can't actually make this happen. But getting the nun drunk is the best we can do.'

'It'll be easy, actually,' says Ferdi. 'Her tolerance level will be so low.'

'She never touches the stuff,' says Laurence. 'I've only ever seen her have a glass of white wine . . . and then only sometimes . . . on special occasions.'

'Are you worried about Chelsea, Gregor?' asks Amelia out of shaded eyes, and slightly smiling.

'Why would I be?' But Gregor has never been able to take his mother for granted. The sand Gregor throws is almost reaching Amelia's arm.

'She might be jealous.'

'I should think she'll just laugh,' says Jasper, a rotund image of his powerful father but steadier, and dull, and with a soft mouth, just the same. Jasper can always be relied upon to stick up for Gregor, just as Harry backed up Rufus in the old days.

'When are you going to start?'

'We'll do it when it begins to get dark,' says Gregor airily. 'We'll do it when everyone starts getting silly. And I want Ferdi to play his violin.'

'No,' says Ferdi, flushing so that all his freckles turn brown. 'That wasn't in it. I'm not doing that.'

'Atmosphere,' says Gregor. 'If you're on our side you must see that atmosphere is going to count.'

'Love songs, do you know any?' asks Kate Wainwright, thrilled.

Ferdi hates this. Ferdi hates playing his violin in front

185

of anyone, most of all his peers. The minute he picks his
instrument up his father, Joel, is on edge. And it always
feels as if Ferdi is playing for him . . . and he's not . . .
although it is always Joel's eye he catches. And Ferdi
knows Joel to be scornful of love songs.

'We won't laugh at you, you know,' says Kate sarcas-
tically. 'After all, this is all for a common goal.'

'You have to do it, Ferdi,' says Gregor. And that seems
to be that. He takes the bottle of vodka from underneath
his towel and reads the label. 'Almost pure alcohol, well
that should do the trick.'

'Excellent,' says Amelia Pilkington, giving Gregor a
steady smile. Which he carefully ignores.

Gregor does not need Amelia. Gregor does not need
anybody.

20

Well, who would you want to sit by? Not a very enticing lot, are they? Would you try and talk to Rufus as he sits apart, spread on the side of a dune and drinking? Or would you assume that Rufus might feel himself intruded upon? Maybe it would be safer to tackle the faded, always smiling Ruth, but she's too busy to bother. She's not doing the interesting things, like the cooking, no, she's leaning over a hot brick with pink fingers gutting a trout.

How about Wendy with the thick brown bob and the royal accent and the *Country Life* features? Wendy is gossiping with Daphne Wainwright and Alice Harvey-Lees about someone they know who has just bought a castle in Spain. They are so absorbed by smoke and conversation that it is hard to know which they keep closing their eyes against. 'It's even got a moat which is clean enough to swim in. And they heat it . . . just like a swimming pool. I could never abide warm swimming pools . . . it's like finding yourself on a warm lavatory seat. Not pleasant. I didn't know you could buy castles in Spain,' says Wendy, measuring the gin out fairly.

'You can do anything now, darling, now we're all one as it were.'

'But I haven't met anyone yet who says they would actually use the damn tunnel. I mean . . . if you were a terrorist what else would you bother with? One bomb lobbed from that high-speed train and that's it.'

'They say it's quite pleasant to drown,' muses Wendy.

'And how do they know? They say you can get a high from masturbating and half-hanging yourself at the same time, people are being found dead all the time all over the place from trying it. I'd never forgive Felix if he did that to me. There'd be absolutely no sense of dignity at the funeral. No. Personally, darling, I'll give that a miss and stick to my gin.'

You wouldn't be wanted in Harriet's little huddle. She tries to talk to Harry, but Harry is so angry he can hardly hear her. 'You upset Jessica, darling! You really did! You know what she's like, you know what I have to contend with. It's quite beyond me, Harriet. I just don't understand what made you go and approach her like that. Why didn't you come to me if you'd got those extraordinary ideas into your head?'

'Don't bother to defend yourself to me, Harry,' says Harriet, with a folded, decided look on her ancient face. She digs her golf club into the sand, hard, to make her point. She likes to have it with her in case she feels like a quick knock. She has tied her straw on with a scarf and resembles a pioneering woman aviator. The straw is firm as her resolve is firm. She doesn't really care if Harry has failed in the payments or not. She is convinced it is her turn now, and that Chelsea is merely biding her time. Harriet is going to speak to the police tomorrow. She is going to tell them about Hugo, about the blackmail note she found, about the maid and the skeleton. And Hugo's little habits? Well, Hugo is dead, and the press can make of it what they damn well like! It might be unpleasant for the children for a while – after all, he was their father. But, and Harriet is stern with herself, even that could not be worse than having this awful blackmail threat hovering above your head for ever. Well look – Harry could have killed a man!

'I have worked it out, but now is not the time or place to discuss it, Harry. I will just warn you now, and tell you that I know who is sending the notes. It is Chelsea ... aided by that poor little man she

188

is falling all over this evening. We must talk, Harry.
But tomorrow will do. Because I have decided to do
something about it!'

For once in his life Harry goes silent. Astonished.
How does Harriet know about the notes? Could it be
that, all those years ago, Hugo confided in her and
explained about the rape? How extraordinary! And
how shaming. Harry can hardly bring his eyes up to
meet hers. Harry had always supposed Hugo kept the
darker side of his life well separated from that of his
family. But it is also peculiar how Harriet has come
to the extraordinary conclusion that Chelsea is at the
root of it all. Harriet is right. They must talk. Because
if it is Chelsea then Harry needs to know how and
why, and how are they going to stop her from taking
this any further. Yes, Harry and Harriet's conversation,
taken in quiet, frenzied bursts, is private. And extremely
confused.

Harry is under a double pressure tonight because
Jessica has told him to keep an eye on the children.
'Don't expect me to be on the alert, not after this
afternoon's shock. I want a quiet, peaceful evening.'

Harry cannot remember a time when Jessica was last
on the alert. But he is trying, half-heartedly, amidst all
the confusion, to locate Archie and Jasper.

'Why are you so worried?' he asked her. 'They'll be
with the others. They're perfectly safe.'

'There's evil abroad,' said Jessica with one of her
knowing looks, Jessica, who never misses the news or
the local section that follows. She was readying herself
to come out when she gave out her warning, rolling
up little balls of cotton wool to put in her ears in
case of strong winds. 'They've found the body of that
waitress . . . horrid. Strangled. At the bottom of a cliff,
all mangled by the sea. Can you believe it? And it's not
far from here, Harry, so really we ought to be keeping
an eye.'

189

And Jessica had coated her lips with the white grease she uses for skiing. And then she'd come forward and kissed him.

Chelsea doesn't want company either. She is lovely tonight, toned down. For once she is untarty, in faded shorts and a sweater. She has not bothered with make-up and this makes her look twenty years younger. Her black hair is windblown and natural. Her violet eyes sparkle. She has Desmond Hartley in the palm of her hand and she knows that Rufus is staring. Bewildered?

Desmond, of course, is quite overwhelmed. Perhaps he would be grateful for a brief interruption. Now, every remark Chelsea makes is heavy with innuendo. But there's no need for Chelsea to take it that far. Desmond is almost hysterical with desire already. Has been for some hours. All he wants to do now is to put it into practice. He's not even afraid of feeling ridiculous any more. He's way past that stage. The air around them is dense with sex. He boils like a living lobster. If Desmond's hands shake now, it is not because of the skeleton. Sod the skeleton.

But what about Rufus?

Sod Rufus.

Only Chelsea keeps an eye on Rufus, sees how Rufus watches her, sees how Rufus frowns when she laughs, or when she strokes Desmond's hair. Rufus looks dark there, deep in the shadows. But his eyes are watchful and glint from the light of the fire.

See, Rufus! Chelsea's actions speak louder than words. Watch, you bastard . . . two can play at your mucky little games!

'I cannot stand much more of this,' says Desmond, his voice hoarse and thick.

'Wait. Wait.' And Chelsea raises a manicured finger to Desmond's lips. 'In a moment we'll go back to the house . . . it's empty . . . but we must take care. You go your way and I'll go mine.'

And Desmond's heart thumps so hard in his chest he feels he might die before he can actually make it. And Christ, will he make it?

Perhaps one might imagine one could drift away and make friends with the children? In this, one would be badly mistaken. For the children do not want adults around . . . that is not the custom at Tremity. At home they might be welcomed into adults' conversations and might include the adults in theirs. Not here. And they have their own preoccupations to deal with this evening. They are as one. They run as a band. As their fathers before them ran as a band. Resenting intruders.

Simon has a chef's hat over his curls but his sweater is, as always, neat, golfing, and emblemed. He is slightly concerned about his mother. She was a little odd on the golf course. Joel, Toby and Felix help him, all with drinks in their other hands. The cold food is laid on a brick-propped door, as it has been laid over the ages. Same door. Same bricks. Even in this such small detail they do not deviate. They cook the fish over the embers, the steaks can survive the fire. The spare ribs are for the children, the vegetarian sausages for Wendy. All the vegetables happen to be stuffed, tomatoes, aubergines, celery. The stoic Ruth has done that. And the salads are quite exotic . . . the dips smell richly of garlic and herbs.

Something would stop you approaching Helen, even though she sits alone, even though, of all of them, she appears the most lonely. But she is lonely as the sea is lonely. It would seem that there can be self-sufficiency in loneliness, for there is a look of sad satisfaction on Helen's face, as there is in the way the waves reach out

191

to the shore and retreat, leaving only impressions there. She, too, stares with interest at Chelsea's performance, knowing it to be a performance, and wonders. She, too, stares at Rufus, as Chelsea does, but Helen's is a different look. Not a questioning look. But a knowing one.

Tonight it is essential that Helen keep alert. Helen is determined not to let Rufus or Chelsea out of her sight. She has watched them carefully since three nights ago when she found the change of clothes in the cave. Helen has been quite aware of the danger since she made her discovery. Fascinated by Rufus, repelled by Rufus, she had taken to following him last year. All those night-time walks . . . and where did he disappear? Helen had crouched. Helen had made quiet her breathing. Helen had waited, and at last Helen had found the place . . .

She remembers her sandalled steps on the sand and the horror with which the 'thing' had dawned on her senses. She had swallowed, and swallowed again but Helen had been unable to prevent the vomit that rose from her throat. More terrible than the thing itself had been the clothes it was dressed in. Absurd clothes, the black uniform of a policewoman, starchy and neat, the buttons so brightly polished, and so much more dreadful for that. Worse than any demon one might meet with in a nightmare. And before they left for London the last thing he'd done had been to change the clothes so that now the spectre resembled a nurse, neat in a cap and apron with a cloak tied carefully at the neck. Obscene. Terrifying. And the cave was rank with the atmosphere of pure evil. It was not the evil of the girls she taught in her school. It was not the evil taught her over the years in the convent. It was a very different evil . . . not deliberate . . . not even satanic, but sick, sick, sick, ancient as the rocks themselves and rotten to the very core!

And then, of course, the news. She had seen and heard the reports of the killings on the news. And then she had known . . . but wanted not to know, certainly wanted it not to be true. For how could she possibly believe it? She sat in her chair with her feet on the faded patch of carpet and the angle-lamp shining down. The scrapbook told the story. She turned the pages slowly over and over.

Helen had sent for the local papers . . . Bolton, Liverpool, York . . . and there were the murders on all the front pages while Rufus stayed hidden among the art and the thin bits of supplement.

And now it is Chelsea's turn.

But why, Rufus? Why?

Helen had smiled two weeks ago when she'd found the robes of the nun. She had smiled because she had realised long before then that one day soon it would have to be her turn. And she'd smiled at the fact that Rufus could go so wrong . . . he . . . the great lover of perfection. You thought I lusted after you, Rufus, you thought you saw love in my eyes. And love does not fit in a nun's eyes, does it, my dear . . . if there is a place for that under a veil then is a cold, rigid love, not passionate, not vulgar, not lit with such dark desire.

Chelsea is right . . . everything here is wrongly perceived by people who know no better . . .

Every now and then the nun reaches down and sips at her drink. Not because she is thirsty, or because she particularly likes pineapple juice, but because it gives her something to do with her hands. It is a habit, as drinking is, in company, alcoholic or not. And when her glass is empty one of the children is always at hand to fill it again. She ignores them. She just nods if they ask her whether or not she wants any more. She has more on her mind than whether her glass is full or not.

Helen does not like Chelsea. But she is not prepared to let Chelsea die. Helen has her own plans. So she watches. Fiercely.

It is warmer, here on the beach, than Helen imagined it would be. It must be the heat from the fire. It must be the warm, dry sand. She is thirsty. Getting thirstier. She sips. And she sips again.

Helen cannot approach Rufus. That's not the way it works. But Rufus can approach her. And he does, coming to sit beside her and stretching his long legs before him. He is very animal, Helen can feel that. 'Are you enjoying yourself?'

Helen smiles wistfully. 'Oh yes. I am.'

'We always do this.'

'I know,' says Helen. 'It was nice last year, too.'

'There's a security in ritual, don't you think?'

And Helen, who knows all about that, nods and smiles again.

'Perhaps we'll go out in the boat tomorrow. Perhaps we'll take a picnic. It's time we went off on our own again.' Rufus expects the nun's eyes to light up, and they do.

'As long as it's not too rough,' she says. 'I was seasick last time.' Yes, she was, and that was most embarrassing.

'Look at the sky,' says Rufus, staring out. 'That's a sign it's going to be another hot day. The sea will be calm. We will only go if it's calm.'

'What about Chelsea?'

Rufus looks across at his wife. His tone doesn't change. He is placid and easy. 'Chelsea can come if she wants to, but Chelsea won't want to. Chelsea would rather sit in the sun in the garden.'

'Yes.'

'You could take your sketchpad.'

'And paint on the water?' Helen laughs.

'Try it,' says Rufus. 'As another experience.'

'Nothing good would come out of it,' says Helen. 'It would be a waste of paint and canvas.'

'So is nothing worthwhile, without there being good at the end of it? Is good so important to you, Helen?'

Helen feels dizzy. She shakes her head to clear it. What

194

answer does Rufus want? She's finding it hard to find her words, and harder still to say them. What is the matter with her? Why is she feeling like this? When Ruth and Wendy, Daphne and Alice, strip and go wandering off towards the sea, Helen fights the strangest urge to go with them. Their bodies are white against the night and when they disappear into the darkness they look like ghosts, never there. When Ferdi takes up his fiddle and plays, Helen wants to cry. For the tunes he chooses are eerily sad, they match the mood inside her. When the wind gets up and blows the little tops off the dunes, Helen wants to fly with them . . . fly off into the air, to a safer place.

But she can't. She is here. Passive, submissive and plain. There is only now and she is who she is and nothing can change her. She is not surprised to hear about the picnic and she knows that the time is right. She would have liked a little longer, but life's not like that. You cannot always choose the time or the place, you can never be really ready. Not totally.

Not for death. No, Helen's not ready. And Helen does not intend to die.

If you were a stranger it would be more comforting to leave the dunes behind, the fire and the people around it and go up the road, as fast as you decently could, towards the lights of the pub. For here there is much conversation, albeit rambling and drunken. And here there is Cope, lording it over the bar and putting forth his opinions. You could laugh at Cope, or agree with him, but you could not shout Cope down. He, after all, is the host, and he will not have that.

You could sit on a stool at the bar, next to the friendly policeman. Off duty now, PC Arthur Buckpitt is not concerned about the calling of 'Time'.

He is Devonian and he doesn't slip in or out of his accent. He can't. For Arthur is an honest man and he drinks an honest pint. None of that real ale nonsense. 'That skeleton they found . . . 'Twas that old bugger Widgeon who disappeared alluv thirty years back . . . That mazed moron must have crawled into the cave an' died there. TB they say, most probably. 'E had it bad. They tried ter keep 'e in hospital but the bleeder were allus dischargin' 'isself. Couldn't bear ter be indoors, see.'

Cope lifts a glass to the light and inspects it. He says: ''E ran off after being caught whipping some tools. I remember . . . so stupid he thought he could auction them off an' get away with it.'

'Aye, well . . .' And Arthur Buckpitt stares morosely into his glass. 'It do come ter uz all in the end.'

'It do that,' says Cope. 'No matter how much money we've got. No matter who we are. We all make old bones in the end.'

'Unless we're cremated, of course.' Arthur perks up briefly only to sink again.

'Well . . . yes . . .' says Cope, his mind on a large order. 'Then we only make ashes.'

There is a short silence. Cope serves a boy who might well be under eighteen. Arthur sees this and ignores it.

'Nasty business with that waitress.' Arthur wipes the foam from his lips.

'Oh?' says Cope, and Nellie peers out from under the hatch.

'Yep.' Arthur is making a swirling pattern with his finger in the beer dregs left on the bar. Cope moves forward and wipes up the wet, leaving Arthur's finger just pushing.

'All decked out wi' 'er uniform on. One of 'er friends thought she accepted a lift, but it were too dark ter see who it were.'

'These girls will do that,' says Cope. 'It doan seem to matter how much they get warning.'

196

'They never found that nurse,' says Arthur. 'We're looking up country fer 'e.'

'Mebbe 'tis the same man. Maniacs . . . some of they.'

'Different methods,' mutters Arthur. 'These murderers tend to stick to the same ways.'

'But the uniforms,' says Cope casually, measuring out a careful double.

'Aye, they're beginning to see somethin' strange in all that.'

'I better take my pinny off,' screams Nellie. 'Or I'll be the next one.'

Arthur nods and raises his eyebrows. 'No one's safe these days,' he says. 'Go on then, I'll 'ave a pasty.'

Nellie retreats. 'One pasty coming up,' she says. 'On the house.'

Arthur looks round in his policeman's way. He has been in the force for years. He can't help it. 'Busy tonight,' he says. 'None of them that I recognize.'

'The locals come in in the winter,' says Cope conversationally, for Arthur knows that. 'And then of course, those lot over the road are holding their beach party tonight. Not that they'd be in anyway. They don't patronize the likes of us.'

Arthur nods. 'Nothing changes, do it?'

'Not here. No it don't.'

'Poor old bastard,' says Arthur.

'Who?'

'The old tramp, of course. Who else? Why, did you think I were meanin' yourself?'

And they both laugh, as men do in pubs, over-loudly.

21

How far is Chelsea prepared to go? She has promised Desmond everything. He is her slave, worshipping, adoring, but he is a man and absolutely desperate for her. Well, in for a penny in for a pound. Chelsea expects Rufus to appear on the scene before this performance reaches its climax, but if he does not, then Chelsea is quite prepared to play her part fully, up to the bitter end.

She does not dislike Desmond. But she feels nothing more powerful for Desmond than a slight fondness. And making love with Desmond might do him the world of good . . . she can see that he lacks confidence . . . well, Chelsea's expert ministrations have done wonders for men more wimpy than Desmond before now. She will see how it goes and respond accordingly.

Chelsea has never experienced the slightest twinge of desire in her life . . . well not for a real live man anyway. What she gets up to under her covers is entirely her own affair. Mechanical, that's what sex has been for Chelsea. Not that she isn't expert at it . . . not that she doesn't give enormous pleasure . . . and she's always pretended to love it. She's very good at that.

Nor is she passive, she does not lie dormantly thinking of England, oh no. Chelsea's sexual experiences are tremendously energetic and there is nothing she baulks at, nothing she will not do. It's just that she's never felt anything, as if her body is extraneous to herself, something to barter, or bribe with, like money or services. It's always been as basic as that. Sometimes Rufus had even called her his rubber doll. And he'd treated her a bit like a rubber doll, too.

Desmond is going to have an absolutely wonderful time.

Chelsea cannot get rid of the terrible suspicion that she could merely be one more to add to Rufus' disgusting collections . . . the perfect whore – indifferent to sex and unfeeling. Immune to the heat of it. Shielded from the blast of it. So indifferent, in fact, that she is willing to perform in order to satisfy someone else's desire.

But, considering the nun, while sitting by Desmond's bed at lunch time, watching him flop that quiche into his mouth, she realised that Rufus intended to possess Helen . . . just as he would take any specimen he desired, as cold-bloodedly as that! The realisation of this shocked Chelsea, as she followed, for the first time, Rufus' twisted perceptions and saw that yes, she could be perceived as the perfect whore. She had dismissed the thought as unbelievable, but a little of Chelsea had been left to wonder . . . if that were true . . . if that were true then what would happen if I, like that ass's jawbone all those years ago, was flawed?

Wanker.

The conscious, sensible side of Chelsea said: Well, if he can cheat me, then I can certainly cheat him, teach him a lesson that will bring him back to his senses. Chelsea is disgusted. How can her husband possibly want to go to bed with a nun? And everything points to that.

She ponders on all this as she goes, as she keeps to the bank, following a channel of inflooding water. Desmond will go the road way . . . she will climb up the cliff path when she reaches the house because she knows the landmarks better. Or thought that she did.

But Chelsea has never been the bravest of souls. She is not a night walker, not now. And, long ago, in the days that she had walked the streets, well, then there had been the comfort of street lights, and car lights, and porch lights from terraced houses. There had been the hard security of a pavement under her feet. This total darkness unnerves her. It goes with the sounds of the moving river, the gaunt, black outlines of the cliffs, the occasional splash in the distance as if something unknown and not friendly is swimming under the surface of the creeping water. Her feet disappear in the black, oily water as if her legs have been severed at the ankles. Chelsea carries her sling-backs close to her chest like a city child clutching new ballet shoes. As if they are something precious.

She has never cheated on Rufus before, not since their marriage. She has enjoyed being married to Rufus, strange though his family undoubtedly is and hard as it was to fit in. After the first, initial attempts she had given up trying. Well, Rufus told her not to bother so she didn't. The wedding, she supposes, could be called frightful, and probably had been by most people there. A society wedding . . . the papers were there, the cameras flashed as she came out of the little village church bordering the grounds of the house that was Harriet's and Hugo's country home. That was Rufus' home.

Top hats and tails, and all the women in hats and gloves, even the children looking like models out of a wartime magazine . . . those awful tailored coats and shoes with straps on and the little boys wore boaters.

'We can't have my side of the church and your side because you haven't got enough family to fill the pews,' said Rufus, making the guest list. 'We'll just have to mix them all up.'

Mix them all up! Hah, that was a laugh. Because Muriel and Wilf, posturing like that and on their best behaviour, were a ghastly sight to behold. And with them, in the bus that they hired, came those reckless drinkers Aunty Madge and Uncle Reg, Cath and Aida, Joyce and Dennis . . . oh, and many, many more of their ilk.

And on the other side – they might be undivided in church but the divisions were surely there – was

Rufus' stiff-necked lot, poker faced, looking askance at Chelsea's family but having to mingle for decency's sake . . . for poor Harriet's sake. The noses they looked down were very long. And they seemed to snort, like horses.

The chord that announced Chelsea's entrance to the church could never have been strong enough . . . ought to have been a minor one . . . ought to have been held longer. Wilf, overcome by the whole situation, stubbed out his cigarette in the porch, fingered his neck under his Moss Bros collar and muttered: 'If I don't do this right my life will be on the line. This is the most important day in your mother's life and she's convinced I am going to spoil it.'

But Chelsea told him: 'It doesn't matter what you do. We're here now, aren't we. I'm where you have always wanted to be!'

'I haven't. I never wanted to be involved with people like this. It's Muriel. Look at her face! She thinks she's arrived in Heaven. She thinks that now she's related, all these people are going to call her up and be her friends. She thinks her life is suddenly going to change. She's having the front room done up . . .'

After years of estrangement – Chelsea's mother had informed all her friends that she had disowned her daughter – Muriel had succumbed. She had been lured by the posh invitation, excited by Chelsea's telephone call, tempted by the possibilities of telling a different tale: 'My daughter lives behind Harrods, my daughter is a lady . . . one of the Pilkingtons, you know . . . a very old family.'

Yes, Muriel, Chelsea's mother, had even, conveniently, forgotten the sordid details of Chelsea's diary, the nasty photographs she'd found in her drawer, the packets of Durex under her bed. She had even managed to put to one side the label she herself had tagged her with – the name, June – so surely designed for conflict, a branding iron unlike any other, the chain attached to the kitchen sink, to one man's bed and the factory bench. Yes, she had even managed to get her tongue round the new, rather terrifying name of Chelsea.

Muriel had not gone to Moss Bros, it might have been better if she had. Instead, she had pored over the catalogue, night after night with Aunty Madge and between them they had eventually chosen the most expensive item in it, with Muriel saying thoughtfully: 'Well, that ought to be all right.' But not considering whether those cruelly black and white slashes would suit her, would match her yellowy smoker's complexion, would really do anything for her flour-bag figure. And the pillbox hat with the bird's wing on it had turned out to be, to Muriel's horror, the fanciest hat in the church.

Chelsea, not giving a damn whether her mother decided to come or not, might have lost courage at that moment, when she paused there for the eight bridesmaids (strangers all) to form a parade behind her. Even they did not look sweet as bridesmaids should, for they were pale, like sacrifices in their simple, white, almost communion dresses, but the bouquets they carried and the bands round their waists were scarlet.

Chelsea might have lost courage then, had she not peered forward through the cloud of white and caught sight of Rufus' face as he waited, looking oh so gorgeous, oh so handsome, down at the front of the church. So she kept on walking, dragging her father beside her, and she kept her eyes upon Rufus and he kept his upon her. And those eyes, they were full of self-congratulation . . . full of admiration and satisfaction . . . Chelsea knew, then, that she was just right. And that everyone else in the church would just have to lump it.

There was no expression at all on the vicar's benign old whiskery face. Indeed, so whiskery was he that Chelsea suspected he could not see out between them, for he had that way of lifting his head very high in order to peer, as if there were half glasses there, about to slip down his nose, but there weren't.

And afterwards in the marquee . . . my God! Muriel's prim face went primmer, her mouth became more of a permanent O as she squeezed out the words she had practised at home before coming, as she squeezed in and out of the groups, trying to deny her black and white image (she should have stuck to the well-tried beige), trying to squeeze into a mould of some kind, preferably flat, preferably transparent. For Chelsea was not one of them. Chelsea stuck out like a sore thumb as did every member of Muriel's family.

Wilf stayed at the side of 'this bloody tent', pretending not to be there, knowing that he would take the flak, knowing his wife loathed him, while his relatives took over for him, stamping all over the wooden, oyster-carpeted floor. Everything was oyster, the awnings were oyster, the table cloths oyster, the lamp shades were oyster, the napkins were oyster. It was a very good thing that they had planned a sit-down meal because there were certainly those on the bride's side, by then, who could not stand.

Hugo appeared to enjoy himself. Hugo had a permanent sparkle in his eye. And it was Hugo who introduced Chelsea to 'Westy . . . my dearest friend. My old nanny.'

And old was the only word you could honestly use. For Westy doddered about in her electrified wheelchair, careering about uncaring of obstacles like flower displays and catwalks. 'She had a stroke last year and unfortunately it has left her half paralysed,' Hugo whispered. 'But there's life in her yet, she's only seventy-five.'

But out of Nanny's throat came the distinctive crackle: 'Come here, let me look at you, child.'

So Chelsea obeyed, bending slightly to bring herself into line with the old woman's face.

And then it was Rufus who came to stand by her and say: 'Well, Westy, what do you think of my bride?'

And a secretive smile crossed the haggard old face, the lips folded in, the chin became pointed, and Nanny merely looked up at Rufus and nodded benignly.

'This was my favourite child,' strained Nanny to Chelsea who wanted to back away but could not for she was being gripped by a dry, clawlike hand, and her arm was being stroked in a most intimate fashion. Repelled, Chelsea shivered. Nanny smacked her lips together as if savouring a new and particularly interesting flavour. 'There was nobody else ever quite like him, my dear.'

'Yes, yes I know,' agreed Chelsea weakly. 'Rufus is very special. Have you got champagne? Can you see from where you are? Would you like moving nearer?'

Nanny's head wobbled dangerously. Skin stretched tight across bone as she answered: 'Nearer to what, my dear? I wasn't aware there was anything going on that I particularly wanted to see. And I have everything I want.'

'Isn't she wonderful,' exclaimed Hugo, proud, in a strange kind of way, as if this old woman was some creation of his that he had brought here today to put on display. But then, uneasily, Chelsea realised it was she they were speaking of . . . not Nanny . . . this was not the way the young speak of the old who have managed to cling on to life. No, it wasn't like that. 'Isn't she wonderful?'

'Indeed she is,' agreed Nanny toothlessly. Nodding. 'Gorgeous. Oh yes, dear boy, indeed. I would go so far as to say she is perfect.'

And Hugo and Rufus stood, like guards at Nanny's side, stiff in their formal attire with contented looks on their well-scrubbed faces. Looking very pleased with themselves.

And that was the first time, Chelsea thinks to herself now as she reaches the rocks that lead to the cliff path, that was the first time that she felt she was being presented . . . like hands might be presented after washing, like a model aeroplane might be presented after sticking. She had dismissed the strange feeling, of course. Because how could it possibly be like that?

There had been other children, other houses.

After that Nanny lived on in luxury, pampered and paid for by Hugo. The home she was sent to after her eventual retirement was not like a home. There the residents were cosseted . . . they dined on smoked salmon and duck, wine was served with their meals. They sat on verandahs under rugs and had fridges built into panels in their walls. Chelsea rarely went to visit and Rufus didn't encourage her. He preferred to visit his Nanny alone. His visits were oddly regular . . . as though he went to report on his progress . . . but Chelsea, knowing nothing of nannies, assumed this was probably perfectly natural.

When the telegram came that told them Nanny was dead, Rufus went white. He sat at the kitchen table with the paper in his hand and drooped.

'It had to happen,' Chelsea tried to comfort him. 'She wasn't well. And she was old . . .'

'Shut up . . . cunt . . . you don't know what you're talking about.'

Chelsea flinched, her hand flew to her mouth. She backed against the sink. Never had Rufus spoken to her in that way. And for a second she felt she had not known him . . . had never known this man who wore that haunted expression, who bared his teeth like that. A mask had slipped. And underneath that mask was someone she could not recognise. For there was something rotten there ... and evil ... she had not gone to Nanny's funeral. Rufus had not asked her to go with him.

Chelsea wishes she had not had that thought just now. She is nervous enough without that. It hadn't lasted, of course. Rufus had risen from the table, all apologetic, had taken her into his arms, had said: 'Forgive me ... I was not myself.' But it had taken a while for Chelsea to forgive him, and she'd thought she had forgotten, but she hadn't. That look on Rufus' face she sees before her now, quite clearly.

Where is the place? Where is that familiar lion-shaped rock at which point she can turn and start climbing ... up over the rock to reach, after just a few yards, the wicket gate? She will pass through that and come to the winding track that meanders sideways and on, right to left, until you are puffing and out of breath, until you reach the first of the privet and you see the first iron chair, you scent the pines. Where is that rock? In her haste, deep in her dark musings, surely she cannot have passed it?

Chelsea's breath is coming fast now, and it isn't exertion that causes it. It is fear. Fear of being lost, fear of the rising water level, fear of the dark, fear of her memories and of her realisations. For has Rufus ever honestly loved her, other than in the way he loves his prize armadillo armour-plate or the bony tail of the ray? Somewhere, in a cave above her, a human skeleton was found. Who was the woman dressed first as a nun and then as a whore? For Chelsea has no reason to disbelieve Desmond. He is a most simple, honest man.

And why should these clothes be draped on a skeleton? Who would do a thing like that? They would have to be mad, wouldn't they?

Madness . . . Chelsea shivers with sudden chill. Chelsea can smell her own terror now. She thinks she hears sounds . . . feet paddling in water not far behind her . . . feet which, no matter how fast she moves . . . keep coming nearer. Sounding louder. She turns but can see nothing but shadows and flowing water. But behind the last rock . . . what is there . . . or the one before that . . . such shadowy, bulky hiding places along these estuary sides!

She wants to stop where she is and scramble on to something high, never mind that it is the wrong place. She wants to lie down and press herself on to the rock . . . press herself down until she disappears, or pull herself high by branches, hide herself in creeper. But if she does anything untoward, might she precipitate the crisis . . . if crisis there be? There is nothing but fear.

She must keep her eyes fixed ahead of her. She must keep her breathing steady. She must not falter nor turn round any more. That would be foolish. If she turns round she will see eyes, and what expression would she see in them? Would she recognise it? Would it be human?

She has to pretend there is nobody there . . . if she pretends then there won't be. This was a game she played as a child, hiding under the covers with one eye peeping out suspiciously at the corners in the room and at her half open toy-cupboard. There was never anything there then. So why should there be now?

But she isn't a child any longer and there is someone there. His breathing is louder, now, than her own. The water swirls warm round her ankles . . . feels as if she has peed. She stops her own breathing and immediately she hears his. Hoarse and half strangled, urgent breathing. Breathing for her? It's no good. It's no good. She stands still, listening, aware as the wildest animal. But she knows, with dawning horror, that she is not the wildest animal in this place. Compared to the one behind her there is no wildness in her.

'Please God, please,' she sobs, 'for the sake of Gregor, make this all be a dream and let me wake up, please please God, please . . .'

Scream? She has no strength to scream with. Her strength must be preserved now, preserved for defence.

There is no defence for Chelsea. She sees nothing. The blow, when it comes, comes from behind. It bursts in her head like scarlet flowers, like all the bouquets of her bridesmaids. It puts out the fear for ever and leaves the cold white lily of death in its place.

22

'Leave her just where she is. Don't move her!'

'But she's going to slide off in a minute!'

The beautiful Chelsea slops in the water, half off
the rock and half on it. Displayed for the last of the
photographs.

All the lights in the house are on and the drive is
packed with cars. The mounted searchlights mottle the
cliffs and men move in and out of the beams like cartoons
on a fuzzy screen in a musty old cinema.

Desmond is crying. The tears just fall down his face,
one after another in relentless, wet desolation. This has
broken Desmond's heart. Because it was not just sex for
Desmond . . . it rarely is just sex. No, Desmond imagined
himself in love . . . not only that . . . this is almost too
painful to relate but he dreamed that Chelsea cared for
him, too. He sobs, quite out of control. Don't laugh at
him, it's not funny, it happens, and sometimes it takes
even less than twenty-four hours.

He had even, in the secretive, hopeful dark of his
soul, made plans. Pathetic plans. Manly plans involving
Renfrew. And in his fantasies he and Chelsea would go
away from here together and . . . but this is too much
to bear. It would be unfair to Desmond to tell it.

Now he just wants to go home.

He found her, of course. He was waiting, heart pound-
ing, breathless, in the darkened house, for half an hour
before he decided he'd better go and meet her. She'd said
ten minutes. Had she changed her mind? He'd found a
torch among the chaos in the kitchen and made his way
down the path, still tortured by his needs and eager to
get on. He'd imagined what was going to happen most
vividly. Many times. He'd had all afternoon to imagine

it. And all evening. And his fantasies were too powerful to deal with. Perhaps it is better that Chelsea is dead for she certainly could not have lived up to them. She would have fulfilled his sexual dreams, but how she would have laughed at the other ones.

Desmond, quite quickly, became afraid. But his fear was concerned with Rufus, and what he would do if he found them together. So he stopped and listened and looked back over his shoulder now and again as he descended. He was not looking in front of him when he opened the wicket gate, when he closed it behind him and pressed on, careful now, after his first distressing experience on slippery rocks.

He had almost stepped on her hair.

And Desmond had nearly passed out for the third time. She was limp, and – awful to say this – but she was almost more appealing as she lay there, her head to one side, her arms outstretched as if calling to some great, eternal mother. That she was dead was beyond any doubt, even to the trembling Desmond. For no one could survive such a gash to the head. No fall, no foolish, misplaced footstep could have brought her this most violent of wounds. And beside her on the rock lay the golf club, its silver head lethal and wicked in such a black, starless night.

Desmond had knelt down beside her and wept. Just like a child. Stroking her. Dreaming her. Loving her.

It then took enormous effort to retrace his path, up and up and up and up into the darkened house. He could hardly see through his tears. He turned on the lights and was struck, once again, by the stark neglect of the place. He dialled. He waited. He told them. They came. He wept again and again.

The children have been packed off to Water's Edge in the care of Felix and Alice. Who is is going to tell Gregor? And when? They think it has to be Harriet, but Harriet is

210

with the police. She has been with the police, in Hugo's old study that is used as a laundry room now, for ages.

On arrival, Detective Inspector Ainsworth, Desmond's Pluto, had eyed Desmond with a certain amount of distaste, as if to say: Not you again, are you always drawn to the morbid like this? But this time Desmond was not prepared to be so craven. He was at the end of his tether. He refused to be treated like a particularly irritating fool. None of this was his fault and he never wanted any part of it. He did not give a toss about Inspector Ainsworth or about what he thought of him. He didn't give a toss about anything. All he could think was that Chelsea was dead . . . all he could feel were the new depths to which he was plummeting.

In the drawing room Rufus was being plied with brandy. A man in torment: 'I cannot believe it. It has to be wrong' is what he repeated again and again. 'Chelsea never went off on her own. Never. Not anywhere. She wasn't like that.' He cried like a child. He stamped his feet and he cried, sobbing loudly, clutching a cushion, so they had to close the door because the sound was too distressing. Wendy stayed with him.

'I did it,' said Harriet aggressively, for the third time, pushing her family away when they shushed her. 'I hit her on the head with my niblick.'

'That's a nine iron,' said Simon wearily, explaining to the young, bemused policeman who sat with them in the kitchen. 'As if the type of club it was mattered. Take no notice of her. She doesn't know what she is saying.' And Simon returned his head to his hands.

They sat round the kitchen table, frozen in various attitudes of horror while sandy costumes dried above. Unable to say much. Unable to account for any of it. And irritated by Desmond's sobbing.

'You were here, at the house, you found her,' said Joel to Desmond. 'I thought we were all on the beach.'

Desmond was not prepared to lie now, no, not to anyone. Not even to protect himself. He was past caring. 'I had arranged to meet Chelsea here' is what he told them.

'For what?' asked Ruth. 'For what reason?'

Desmond, desolate, shrugged and stared out in front of him.

Even with the door closed the others could still hear Rufus' sobs. All they could do was shake their heads and shiver.

'She was always so vibrantly alive,' said Ruth, trying to conjure Chelsea up in her mind and guilty to find that she couldn't. All she could hear was her chronic cough. All she could see was smoke.

Harriet, too restless to be able to sit down, paced the room and the others, they watched her.

'Where is the nun?' she suddenly asked, stopping her pacing.

'Up in her room. Drunk. The children did it! Some dare! We had to carry her to the car!'

'When are they going to talk to me? When are they going to listen?' said Harriet.

Everyone frowned.

'I'm perfectly serious,' said Harriet, glint-eyed under her hat. 'And I had very good reasons.'

'Oh Mother, be quiet,' said Simon, not gently. 'I know you are suffering from shock, well we all are, but you are making everything worse. You disliked Chelsea, we all know that, but you could not have had reasons as powerful as that. You could never murder anyone! We know you are upset . . . we are all upset . . . but you are just making yourself ridiculous.'

But even as he spoke, Simon's memory took him back to the golf course conversation he'd had with his mother that afternoon. A very peculiar conversation . . . as if she was trying to tell him something. And he hadn't under-stood. He stared at her as she paced and he remembered her tone of voice . . . hard when she mentioned Chelsea . . . iron hard and full of hatred . . . full of suspicions. She had not sounded herself. But, no matter how strongly Harriet felt, it was way beyond the realms of belief that she would stoop to this, this sort of twisted revenge. For what?

No. It was quite absurd. Of course it wasn't possible.

But later, when interviewed by the heavily sweating Inspector Ainsworth, Simon mentioned it. He had to. He'd nothing else to tell them, and they surely would not suspect . . .

Next door at White Horses Harry Featherstonehough struggled on the horns of his own dilemma. He could not confess to the blackmail . . . not after standing against it so staunchly for so many years. If Harriet mentioned it then he would deny it. The police came to fetch them from the beach and after that there was chaos. They had found the nun, drunk, quite comatose behind a dune. Extraordinary. They had bundled her into the back of the Range-Rover and put her to bed. Then they had all been ordered to their own houses. But he had to mention the money because Daphne knew of Harriet's suspicions . . . and Jessica. And someone would be bound to bring them up.

Harry was being interviewed. Mercifully Jessica had time to whisper urgently: 'Slip a pair of trousers over your shorts, darling.' And Harry had quickly done so. He felt grateful to her for that. Harry felt exposed, he felt threatened enough without anything extra to contend with.

He sat in the dining room next to the huge inspector. They might have been about to share a meal. They both rested their arms on the table as if about to grasp a knife and fork.

'I do not know who was on the beach or who was not,' Harry said tiredly, for he had drunk more than his allotted amount that night. 'It was dark. It was

213

impossible to see. And nobody stayed in the same place. Hell, I didn't even know that Chelsea was missing until the police came and told us. Anyone could have gone after her. I am sorry. I would not have known.'

And then, half an hour later, as the interview ground on: 'Harriet talked to me about her suspicions. Yes, only this evening she told me. She'd got the ludicrous notion into her head that Chelsea and what's his name, Desmond, were blackmailing me! I didn't know what to say. Of course I denied it . . . I wish I'd spent longer reassuring her . . .'

'Why do you wish you'd spent longer, Sir?'

Harry gave the inspector a bleary-eyed look. He rubbed at his tired eyes with a red and white spotted handkerchief. 'I don't know. I just wish I had.'

'You think Mrs Pilkington killed her daughter-in-law?'

Harry shook his head wearily. 'No, no, of course I don't. I'd never think that,' he lied.

'But you are not being blackmailed, Sir?'

'Of course I am not being blackmailed! By Chelsea or anyone else. This is all too absurd!'

'Would you say then, that Mrs Pilkington had some fairly bizarre ideas in her head?'

'Well, not bizarre . . . she is getting old, Inspector. She is entitled to get things muddled.'

'Muddled?'

'Yes, muddled! Muddled! Muddled! Hell!' Harry banged his fist on the table. Harry was getting impatient. He was not in the House of Commons now. The inspector gave him a warning look.

'She is old and yet she is fit? She is a strong woman?'

'Fit as a fiddle and strong as an ox! An example to us all!'

Harriet tells the huge man in the shirtsleeves: 'That vixen was blackmailing Harry! She blackmailed Hugo

214

all his life, and then, when Hugo died, she turned her evil intentions upon poor Harry. I am relieved now, actually, that it is all coming out.'

'All?' The man was patient. He regarded Harriet through questioning eyes. There she sat, her hat tied tight on her head by a scarf covered in horses, and her eyes a furious blue. The legs that showed below those knee-length khaki shorts were strong legs . . . the legs of an outworn athlete . . . all sinews and muscles and veins. She was, as everyone said, an extraordinarily powerful woman for her age. And most determined to speak out.

'You will think ill of poor Hugo.' Harriet raises her head like a martyr and stares wide-eyed as a martyr would. 'But I am prepared for that now. We are a close family. We can withstand one tawdry little scandal.'

The inspector has all the time in the world. 'Can you explain?'

'Hugo was a man of passion . . .'

'Ah yes, of course.'

'Of very great passion, Inspector, actually.'

The inspector waits. The young man taking notes edges more comfortably into his high-backed chair. It creaks and Harriet looks at him sternly. She puts him in mind of his old headmistress.

'There was an accident . . . some years ago . . . a young girl dressed as a maid died . . . she was staying here at the time with Hugo and an old RAF friend, Rodney. I came upon them and found them behaving unfortunately.'

'How long ago would this be, Mrs Pilkington?'

'Oh good heavens, let me see now . . . Rufus is forty-five . . . it happened the year before he was born. And they panicked, they hid the body in the cave. That, Inspector, is the answer to your skeleton mystery. They hid the body in the cave and should have said no more about it. But Hugo was a lusty man and attracted, sadly,

215

to girls like Chelsea. She proved too much for him, poor dear. He played his sexy games with her.' At this point Harriet lowers her eyes, picks an invisible thread off her knee. She bites her lip and, finally, in order to speak, she gazes up at the ceiling as if she spies something fascinating there. 'Hugo enjoyed dressing up.'

The silence is hard to define. It is impure. Because the inspector feels like chuckling but can not. And Harriet feels like crying but will not. And the young man taking notes starts to doodle with his Bic.

'He must have persuaded Chelsea to indulge him in his nasty little habits . . . for she knew, you see . . . she knew about the nun and the whore. Hugo must have confided to Chelsea, the silly fool must have told her about the maid and where they had put her.' Harriet sighs very crossly. 'He was never a good judge of people! Hugo could be such a fool! And then of course, he had to pay her. I found a note in his jacket . . .'

'Can you remember what the note said?' The young man looks up. The inspector's tone is too gentle. He considers the woman insane.

Harriet repeats the note she found, word for word: '*The money for the maid is late in the paying. My warnings are not empty threats. You and yourn cannot destroy someone's life and get away with it, no, it dont matter how big you are.* That's what it said, Inspector. That's what it said, to the letter. And it was because I wouldn't do it, you see. I was appalled by Hugo's sexual perversions. But he was a good man, a good husband, and a good father . . .'

'Apart from his nasty habits?'

'Exactly.'

'And why did Chelsea and Desmond decide to expose the skeleton at this particular time?'

Harriet's tone is impatient. 'Because they tried to blackmail poor Harry but Harry could no longer pay! Can't you see it, Inspector? My goodness, I would have thought it as plain as the nose on your face! They decided to turn their attentions to me! The skeleton and the whore – don't you understand – only I could have known about that. Pay up or else . . . that was the underlying threat.'

'But you were not asked for money?'

'No. No. But I would have been. In the next day or two.'

The inspector crosses his legs. 'I have to inform you, Mrs Pilkington, that the skeleton Mr Hartley found in the cave was that of a man aged about sixty-five, who died from tuberculosis. And he has been identified as one William Widgeon, a person of no fixed abode, who roamed these parts in those days.'

'That cannot be. I am not a fool, Inspector, and most unlikely to fall for any of your grubby little tricks.'

'I'm afraid that is how it most certainly is. And Mr Hartley, who discovered the remains, mentioned a nun's outfit but we have not been able to prove or disprove this. I think, Mrs Pilkington, that you have become most confused. You did not like the deceased, your daughter-in-law, I believe.'

'No!' Harriet speaks fiercely. From a stack of faded magazines she takes a copy and fiddles with it angrily. 'No, I certainly did not like her. She was wrong, so terribly wrong for dear Rufus.'

'And did you always feel this way about her?'

'I hated her from the start! If you had seen the pictures . . .'

'Pictures?'

'I found them before I even met the woman, Inspector. Grotesque, frightful, degrading, humiliating pictures . . .'

'How strong was your dislike of your late daughter-in-law, Mrs Pilkington?'

Harriet rises gallantly from her chair, for this is her hour. She has rolled up the copy of *Horse and Hound* and beats the desk with a threatening urgency. She leans over the desk, grips the sides, ignoring the pile of clean towels, the stack of ironed pillow cases, and her face, under the angled light, is tight and white with furious disgust. She is a fearful sight. She will protect Harry no matter how terrible his actions have been! For this is her own crime . . . committed by her against Hugo many years ago!

'I loathed her!' she spits. 'I loathed and detested her and considered her filthier than the dirtiest creatures you find at the bottom of any sewer!' Her great distaste is so vehement, so venomous is the anger in the throttled words, that the inspector has to move back, has to wipe the spittle, discreetly, from his hand. 'And yes, and yes, and yes I killed her! As I have always wanted to kill her . . . to rid the earth of such a creature living upon it!'

Just half an hour later the inspector goes to sit beside Rufus. He is tired. They are all tired. This has been a long night.

'Mr Pilkington,' says the inspector gently, as if to nudge a sleeper awake. 'I hate to tell you this. I hate to have to be the one, but the answer to this is distressingly simple. Over the years your mother has built up her hatred towards your wife, has contained it, has nurtured it, until, in the state of senility she is now in, she has allowed her resentment to get quite out of control. She is nearly eighty years old, I believe. Well, we do not relish the prospect of taking persons of her age into custody but unfortunately we have no choice. Naturally there will need to be psychiatrists' reports and they will confirm her state of mind. That will be quite enough for the courts.'

The inspector shakes his head again and emphasises softly: 'On top of everything else you must be going through tonight, I am so sorry to have to tell you this.'

Rufus lifts his bemused face towards the sorrowful policeman. It is a face quite worn out with tears. 'What are you saying, Inspector? That my mother hit my wife on the head with a golf club? That my mother killed her?'

The inspector is too tired, or too unwilling, to answer. 'I will speak to your brothers.' And he rises to go, touching the shoulder of the suffering man.

And when he looks back from the door, Rufus, who has asked to be quite alone, puts the policeman in mind of a child. It is the way his fists are clenched, he thinks, and it is something to do with his twisted hair and his terrible, hidden anger.

This whole affair has proved most unfortunate. And all rather embarrassing.

23

The morning after the long night, and with Harriet away the place feels empty and echoes, much as it did when Hugo left it. The newspapers lie abandoned on the step, fluttering slightly every time an early morning car goes by. The sunlight blazes through the window and rests on the thick pottery pieces that adorn the kitchen table, drying the loaf that is left there. The residents, allowed to go nowhere, hang around the house listlessly, trying to avoid the police who appear to have got themselves into every room, like window cleaners.

'I feel like a goldfish,' says Joel. 'Stuck in a bowl without any weed.'

'And the cat has just come into the room,' says Ruth, because of that threatening feeling.

It is as if Harriet is dead. They have no respect for her things.

No one can really believe what has happened. Everyone is under the firm impression that there has been a dreadful mistake which will soon be rectified. The family solicitor, Arnold Lambert, is on his way down from London. As soon as he has spoken with the police they are sure that Harriet will be sent home. They took her away in a police car in the early hours of this morning. Simon and Wendy insisted on going with her. They stayed with her through the night, 'In a police cell, darling,' shrieked Wendy, phoning Ruth. Can you believe it? An old woman of eighty? Wouldn't you have thought they'd be a fraction more sensitive? But I suppose they did keep the door open – when Simon demanded it.'

Joel and Ruth set off first thing in order to take their place. 'We won't leave her alone for a minute,' said Joel. 'Heaven knows what else she might say in the state of mind she is in. She seems to have gone quite bonkers.'

Everybody ignores the nun when she comes down the stairs, hung-over. Irritated by her presence at the best of times, now her quiet, whitely worn image is intensely disturbing. She has never been more of an outsider than she is this morning. The family want to close in, draw together, but all the time she sits there. So they can't close ranks. You'd think she'd somehow sense this and drift off, wouldn't you?

Rufus is out, somewhere on the cliffs with Gregor, somehow dealing with the undealable with.

The village, of course, is agog, avid with anticipation. Alerted to the drama by the noise and the lights of last night, faces thinned by scandal, they congregate on every corner and rumours fly like their beady eyes do, and their words caw and squawk like the seabirds.

Across the road, Cope, who would under normal circumstances be loving it, is a nervous man. He considers murder to be quite a few steps up from blackmail. He doesn't really consider what he's doing to be morally wrong . . . to his mind it is more like extracting compensation for his wife's hip, fairer to confront the perpetrators of the crime than to milk the state as some people would. Why shouldn't they pay? It's not as if they can't afford it. But he fears that once the police start sniffing around, and my God they will sniff around murder, they might uncover his little crime and that would be most inconvenient.

Rufus is dealing with Gregor. The other children are told, gently, by their parents.

Sombre, in the White Waves garden afterwards, their

221

energy gone and fear in their eyes, the children contemplate the enormity of the consequences of their actions. 'Because it has to be Helen,' says Amelia. 'She didn't kiss Rufus. She went one step further and murdered Chelsea instead. Before she went down.'

Archie Featherstonehough says, with his eyes well down: 'Gregor will be thinking this, too.'

Angrily, guiltily, Holly Wainwright says: 'Why did the police make such a mistake? Why didn't they arrest the nun? Surely it's not so difficult. I wish we'd been asked. We could have said.'

'What . . . and have everyone blame us?'

'No,' says Holly, cast down. 'No, I suppose not. But we can't allow it to go like this. When will they let Harriet come home? When will they realise their mistake?'

'They might never recognise it.'

'Oh God,' says Thomas Harvey-Lees. 'We ought to tell them. After all, we weren't to know. Perhaps Gregor will say something.'

'It was a stupid dare, Thomas,' says Amelia, not flirting with anyone this morning. There is no longer a leader in the garden. 'Really, really stupid.'

'We didn't think you'd do it,' says Thomas, hurling the blame back furiously.

'Well it's all ruined now.' And, bleakly, Amelia seems to have summed it up.

And will they always be like this, perceiving things wrongly all through their lives? That would be sad for them. They should not play so many wild games. They should not be given such reckless freedom or else they will find themselves carrying their sins for ever, like their fathers.

Harry Featherstonehough, next door and calming hysterical Jessica, blames himself for the arrest. But he still does not see how he could have behaved otherwise. To admit to the blackmail notes would have

222

been tantamount to confessing to rape. By now that word, even in his mind, slaughters him. He'd never liked it – well who does – even when it's applied to a crop, but now, when he hears it, it doubles him up. It brings hot bile to his throat. What would Nanny Weston have advised him to do? To carry the can? To come out into the open and take it like a man? But what about the others? He is not the only person involved in this. To tell and get his friends into trouble would be like snitching at school . . . unforgiveable. But he's landed Harriet in trouble now, hasn't he? Not for a moment did he believe the police would take Harriet's ramblings seriously. Harry had never considered Harriet capable of murder . . . but it does look as if . . . why the hell has the woman taken such a desperate step?

Through it and through it he goes but he finds himself in a circle, hemmed in and unable to find a pathway out of it. And what about Harriet . . . how had she discovered the blackmailer was Chelsea? Had Hugo told her? And even more important . . . what is Desmond going to do now? Desmond, who, if Harriet is to be believed, must be in possession of all the facts, who, even now, is sitting pretty, a guest next door. Not only does he know about the rape, but, even if they get Harriet off, Desmond must know that Harriet did it. Would the man have the pluck to carry on blackmailing by himself now that Chelsea is dead? Or will he go off with the tail between his legs, frightened away for good?

Harry doesn't know. Harry is going through mental torment. How much will Harriet tell the police? Perhaps the rape will come out anyway.

Later that morning when Simon and Wendy return, Harry can't get between the garden hedges fast enough. It is the not knowing that slays him. He has to find out what Harriet is saying.

*

They all gather round the kitchen table, faces expectant and nervous.

Simon shakes his head and Wendy puts on her most sensible face. 'It's looking bad,' says Simon. 'Harriet won't stop talking. She says it's like balm to get this off her chest. She refuses to grasp the fact that the skeleton was old Widgeon. She insists that it belongs to some maid who Hugo, can you believe this, hid there? She's going on about nuns and whores and about how Hugo made her dress up. She's insisting that Chelsea was blackmailing Harry, that Harry failed to pay up, that Chelsea had turned her attentions to her!' And then Simon looks directly at Desmond. 'She is saying that you were in league with Chelsea . . . that you put the costumes in the cave and led the police there deliberately in order to frighten Harriet.'

This is madness. Desmond, after his night without sleep, is exhausted. He is no longer interested in phoning his mother, it isn't his mother he wants. He wants Chelsea. And if he can't have Chelsea . . . and it's taking a while for him to absorb the fact that he cannot . . . then the last thing he wants to do is to go back home. Enid can say what she likes, do what she likes, Desmond is beyond all that now. He has, in spite of the odds, grown up.

This whole place and everyone in it is crazy. He's never heard anything so absurd as their wild conjectures, and he says so. Why is Harry staring at him like that? Why are they all staring? All save for the nun, Helen, and she plays with the crumbs on the table, seemingly not interested, seemingly not listening.

'I'm not even going to bother to talk about this,' says Desmond as he proceeds to do so. 'I don't know what's going on, but I've had enough of it. You are all round the bend and I'm not getting drawn into it. I wish that

I hadn't found the skeleton, it's beginning to feel like the worst thing that's ever happened to me. I certainly would never have concocted a story, and I never met Chelsea before yesterday.'

'You were getting on very well for people who'd never met,' says Harry, lowering his head like a charging bull; his eyes are red also.

'That sometimes happens,' says Desmond. 'There's nothing unnatural in that. And nothing sinister, either!'

'Were you being blackmailed, Harry?' asks Simon suddenly. 'Is Mother completely out of her mind? Is there substance in any of this? Could Hugo possibly have hidden a woman away . . . for all these years . . . as a result of an accident? And could all this have been preying on Mother's mind, with none of us knowing anything about it?'

'I know nothing about it,' says Harry, who by now is totally bemused.

'Then it must have been Mother,' says Simon, his face a picture of total amazement. 'It must have been Mother who killed Chelsea! Because she'd got this story into her mind! It's quite bizarre! She was such a sensible, down to earth sort of person! It's incredible!'

'I'll never be able to believe it,' says Wendy, worn out by the night's vigil. 'Even if they proved it to me . . . even if somebody saw her . . . I'd just not believe it. I'm sorry! But that's that. She's saying she's the one who killed Chelsea. She's perfectly certain on that. She won't be budged. It can't be true because even the police don't really believe it but they say they have no option but to "pull her in". Someone else must have done it and Harriet must be taking the rap.'

And everyone is of the same opinion. Except for Harry Featherstonehough, who believes that Harriet has done it and has made up some fantastic story in order to protect him and her children . . . And Harry contemplates

Desmond most carefully while he considers the sad, mad nobility that is poor Harriet's.

Yes, Helen is quiet. She, as well as Desmond, thinks about Chelsea. Helen has never liked her but when she thinks back to the conversations they had, she remembers Chelsea saying: 'They are not in the real world. They perceive everything wrongly, even the cat! They've had it all too easy, that's their problem.'

And Helen knows that Chelsea was right. Look at them now! Motherless, without Harriet. They know nothing of ordinary people from whom they have distanced themselves without even realising it. They live in a bubble from which they descend, every now and again, to play with the world, to tweak at it and provoke a response, before going back into retreat once again. They cannot see wickedness in their own kind so they have to look for it from without. They look for it there and they find it. They would do anything to protect themselves. Anything. But things have gone wrong and Harriet, in order to protect somebody she loves very much, has made up this absurd story. Helen feels sorry for Desmond, for he is new to all this. And bewildered. And frightened. And the only one among them who is truly broken hearted.

When Desmond gets up and says: 'I'm going for a walk. And when I come back I'm going to pack my things and move back across the road,' Helen waits five minutes and follows him. But she takes a separate path because the nun prefers to walk alone. And she needs to watch Rufus.

But the one thing Helen cannot understand is why Rufus, having decided to kill her first, changed his mind so suddenly, changed the robes on the skeleton, and decided to murder his wife instead.

In Rufus' twisted mind, it must have been something

very important. In what way was poor Chelsea imper-
fect? For that decision was made two days before Chelsea
met Desmond . . . that's when the clothes were changed.
No, Helen knows it was not Chelsea's games with the
innocent Desmond that gave Rufus the need to kill her.

24

Gregor is calm. Gregor is sensible. Gregor is a miniature version of Rufus and therefore perfection. Now that his mother is dead Gregor knows he will grow closer to his father and this thought does not displease him.

As his son leaves him to walk back across the dunes towards the house, towards his friends, Rufus walks on alone, head down, hands deep in his pockets, taking in heady gulps of sea air as he nears the edge of the incoming tide. He likes to walk half in and half out of it, as he did in his childhood, when Nanny would always say: 'Jump back! Jump back! Don't let the waves wet your shoes!'

That was when he was very small and Nanny used to come to Tremity with them. The wave edges look dirtily frothy. Rufus frowns. He wishes that Gregor could have had a nanny to look after him, rather than Chelsea. Having Chelsea as a mother for Gregor was never the best solution but although Rufus had interviewed a whole series of women, women with marvellous references, women with long experience, there had never been anyone good enough, never been a nanny he felt could come near to giving his son what Westy had given to him.

His sunken, hollow eyes stare with the pain of a man in mourning. Or a man locked in madness, doomed to spend the whole of his life marching to the beat of that frenzied drum. Dear Westy. Why did you die?

The nursery at Burford was a warm place, warm like a womb, like a brothel because Westy had a terrible fear of the cold, and fires were kept lit day and night, winter and summer alike. It was a place where things were 'done' to you, sometimes whether you liked them or not. It was brightly lit with high ceilings and big, wide windows that looked out on to the parkland.

It was all painted a cool pale green. Westy loved the colour green. '*All round my hat I will wear the green willow* . . .' she used to sing, her great bulk tripping daintily across the nursery floor . . .

There was hardly ever a moment when Westy was not there, in the nursery or in Rufus' life. Large in blue cotton and starched linen cuffs . . . and a broad, crisp apron with a pocket full of cotton buds, that crossed over at the back and was done up at the sides with little rubber buttons. Westy was firm and shapeless like a punch bag, and her broad-browed, unlined face reminded him of a baby's. Her skin was like a freshly shaved man's and her hair, which was long, was pulled cruelly back, flat, and screwed at the nape of her neck in a bun. It looked as if it was painted hair. Westy smelled of soap and her hair smelled musty like the inside of her coats. She used to fetch the washing from the nursery fire guard and sniff it deeply before she'd take it to the laundry cupboard and put it away. Sometimes she used to let Rufus pull up a chair and help her. And then she would spring at him and sing, as he balanced there: '*And if one green bottle should accidentally fall* . . . whoops a daisy.'

The day nursery was where they spent their days and ate their meals. Seated near the fire on tall, rush-bottomed chairs, they ate off a table that was never entirely free of Plasticine, or of the smell of it. The dishes were brought upstairs by the maid, Shirley, and it was Westy who moved the silver lids off the dishes, stuck in her finger and tasted each one, saying: 'Could be a little sweeter, could have a tickle more almond in this.'

'I'll tell Mrs Abbot, Miss Weston,' stammered Shirley, always, as she backed out.

Westy ruled not only the nursery but the whole household as well. It was not until he grew older and the world evolved and grew larger that Rufus became aware of the fact that many walked in fear of her. Not only the lower servants at Burford but many of the guests as well, and certainly visiting nannies who came with their charges for tea . . . he used to watch and notice how this thing worked, how Westy, with only a look or a glance, could order silence or extract obedience or quell a rebellious heart.

And it wasn't that she was outwardly unpleasant. She was just terribly honest. And absolutely certain of her position, her tread was a sure one. Everyone always wanted to please her, and, for reward, they would be graced by that little smile.

Or a star.

Nanny seemed large at the beginning. As Rufus grew she shrank, but never her dominance over him. That remained, like the giant she had been, like the shadow bending, like the bath water bubbling, like the sheets billowing, like the fire roaring, like the voice singing: *'Here we float in our golden boat . . . far away . . . far away . . .* Oh, where's that naughty soap gone? Move up a little bit and let Nanny find it. Whoops.'

Harriet would come rarely. 'Your mother is a busy, most successful woman, and only needs to know that her little boys are all right. Some children never see their mothers or their fathers. They go away . . . right across the world for years. You are lucky. Your mother comes to see you almost every day.'

The routine was strict and never varied. The weather made no difference to whether or not they would go out for their walk at ten, after their dose of cod liver oil. Come rain come shine they went, and they always took the same route . . . down the drive, turning right by the footpath over the steep beech meadow, up through Shooters Wood, back and round to the path again, up the drive and home. Westy was always dressed in her hard grey coat and black lace-ups. She strode out in front of them with her tough, felt hat straight on her head and

230

she carried her head high. '*I love to go a-wandering along the mountain track, and as I go . . .*' sang Nanny. And they would all rush to catch up so they could join in with the chorus.

'*Picnic time for teddy bears,*' sang Nanny. But it was never merely a walk. It was an experience from which the Pilkington brothers invariably came home exhausted. For Westy liked them to bring her things to look at, and there was much competition between them in trying to find the best. A foxglove, rusty at the ends and drooping, was discarded, dropped on the path: 'Surely you can do better than that.' A leaf that was slightly torn, in spite of the beautiful pattern, was laid in Westy's hand while a critical finger stroked it. 'There's not a lot right with this one.' One day a caterpillar was dirty, the next day it was acceptable. It was hard to find the perfect item . . . it took great cunning and energy. But the reward, when you did, was a green star when you got home and one of Westy's rare, slant-eyed smiles. In through the kitchen door they would go, scraping their boots with care, to collect the tray of cocoa and the digestive biscuits which Westy would carry upstairs for elevenses. Westy would leave the baby of the day in the big, black pram outside the kitchen door. She would go down for the baby at twelve thirty, lunch time, and come with it into the nursery singing an invented verse of 'The Quartermaster Stores'.

'*Lavender's blue dilly dilly, lavender's green . . .*' After lunch you would take off your trousers, fold your shirt over your chair and go to bed for an hour. This was a silent hour and no one would dare to break it. From two until three Westy would play the piano and they would sing songs, or she would tell them a story. If they'd been good they could choose the book, if they had not then Westy would. '*I'm a troll, troldy-role . . .*'

Afternoon tea was a very important meal. There were always crumpets, sandwiches and lots of cakes. It was always a bit like a party. Rufus, Simon and Joel drank orange juice but Westy had a pot of tea to herself. Very often other children came, and after tea they would get the toys out and play while Westy shared her pot with the visiting nanny or nurse, and watched over the children from her rocking chair with the big cushions in it.

The rocking horse had nanny's eyes and the jack in the box was patterned like Westy's Fairisle cardigan.

In spite of the strict routine there were charts on the wall, as if Westy felt that without them things might slip. Checklists, which Nanny was always filling in with ticks or crosses ... whether Joel had drunk his milk ... whether Simon had been to the toilet ... whether Rufus had picked up his toys. But these ticks did not guarantee you a star. Only Westy's mood ever guaranteed one of those. You might think you were going to reach the magical number of ten ... the end of the month would come nearer ... there were eight beside your name. Breathless, you would try to be good. You would smile. You would brush your teeth till they ached. You would brush your hair fifty times. You would rush about on your walks until you had a stitch from running. But rarely did anyone reach the ten ... Simon gave up trying.

Only Rufus reached the ten. And only Rufus knew that he would.

The night nursery formed one arm of a stumpy U, Nanny's bedroom the other. There were cupboards and bathrooms in the space between and the day nursery at the bottom. If a baby would not stop crying it was put in the laundry room from where the sound came, muffled, 'and therefore tolerable'. Westy never allowed the boys in her room, or her visitors, either. 'It's my private place and Lord knows, with my long hours, I need some privacy. *Said Alice.*'

When Westy went out, which was rare, with her hat and her coat and her handbag, they had tried the door but found it, as they had expected it would be, locked. And Westy had taken the key, that must have been why she had patted her pocket. But Rufus knew what it looked like in there. He had always known what it looked like. His earliest memories were all of that room . . . nothing to do with the nursery.

Outside the door there was a little bucket of coal and a plaque on the door with a forget-me-not on. The plaque was at low finger level, so they could touch it. And they did. The plaque was a shiny oval and it fascinated them.

Once Joel drew it, and took it to Westy, so proud. 'That is nothing like my forget-me-not,' said Westy. 'That looks more like a bedraggled piece of seaweed. *Two jelly fish, sitting on a dish, two little jelly fish sitting on a dish.*' Joel had not got his longed-for star.

The first time Rufus went to Westy's room was the night he got up, soaking wet and frightened, not knowing where he was. It was dark in the day nursery except for the small glow from the fire, but that cast frightening shadows. He sucked his thumb and began to cry. It must be late because normally Westy sat up by the fire, darning, mending, reading, until she was sure they were all sound asleep. '*Like a diamond in the sky, Twinkle twinkle* . . .' Only then would she go to her room and shut her door behind her.

But on this one, most terrifying night, Rufus had not dared face the darkened bedroom where the source of the nightmare lay. He had started a terrible wailing . . . and that sound frightened him more . . . he thought that his heart would burst from his chest, there were devils in every corner, devils like gargoyles in the church with silver lights in their eyes. They had him cornered now and they were coming . . .

A crack of light showed under Westy's door. Rufus hurled himself at it. 'Westy, Westy, I'm scared.' And he sobbed and he screamed and he banged at the door which seemed the only safe refuge from his child-ish Hell.

He had shrieked at the sight of Westy in her nightie and with her hair down like a witch. He had shrieked and trembled and dribbled and fought . . . for this was the ultimate horror. Westy had changed into one of them! Westy was a wicked witch.

Finally Westy had slapped his face and drawn him after her into the room where the light was bright and safety beckoned. Inside was a high walnut bed covered with a cream, lace bedspread which was folded carefully down. Rufus was shivering. 'Get in,' said the witch, 'and get warm. And stop that noise before you wake your brothers up. Hush, child . . . even the servants will be able to hear you from where they are!'

And Westy, understanding about the shock, had put her black macintosh round her, had buttoned it up so that none of the nightdress showed any more. 'Look,' she said, 'I am drenched as poor Piglet in the rain.'

She'd got into bed beside him, undoing his wet pyja-mas and pulling them off. She had pulled his wet, trembling body on to her own and, as the tension went out of Rufus, it flopped. 'Get dry,' she said. Gaberdine and urine and the smell of cheap scent. Drowsy now, still wracked by the occasional, silent sob, thumb in his mouth, Rufus had said to big, warm Westy: 'Tell me a story.'

Westy, who had turned the light out, chuckled to herself. 'This puts me in mind of your own father when he was a little boy . . . not much older than yourself.'

'Why, did he used to sleep in your bed?'

'Sometimes he did, oh yes, and if he was frightened we used to play games.'

'Can I play them, too?' Rufus spoke like a baby, wanting to be a baby again.

'They were far too grown up for a little boy like you.'

Rufus sniffed: 'But you said that Daddy was the same age.'

He could feel Westy looking at him through the darkness. 'He seemed so much older than you. But then all my little boys seemed older then. Maybe because I was so much younger.'

'What were the games?' Rufus sucked his thumb, untroubled now, and important, and safe, in Westy's great bed. Such a special place, and so secret.

'Well, your father would touch me and guess what I was pretending to be. He was never allowed to look. He had to feel in the dark.'

'But I know what you're wearing because I saw so it wouldn't work.'

Rufus was suddenly untired. The game sounded so exciting. Playing it with children would not be the same. It could only be played with Westy and he had to persuade her or die.

He sat up in bed, all alert. 'Put something on . . . put something on and let me guess.'

'Oh I don't think . . .' said Westy in her needing to be persuaded voice. Rufus knew he would get his way.

'Please, Westy.' He pulled at the hard macintosh sleeve. 'Please, please let me guess. I think I'd be better at it than Father!'

'Cheeky devil,' said Westy, teasing now. 'Your father was always very good at it.'

'He never told me you played it.'

Then Westy got cross. 'With grown-up games we don't go round telling people what we do,' she said stiffly. 'I can see you're too little to understand.'

The desperation inside him was growing, his voice was tight and urgent. 'I'd never say.' He shook his head and crossed his chest. 'I'd never, ever say.'

'I don't know . . .'

'Please, Westy, please! I am not even slightly tired.'

235

'But you are a baby boy, with nightmares. Your father never had nightmares. Your father never cried.'

'And I won't again, if you'll play the game with me!'

Westy lay and thought in the dark while Rufus willed the outcome. I will go without cake tomorrow, I will learn my seven times table, I will never pull Joel's hair again, God, if only you will make her!

And then Westy rose from the bed and the macintosh crackled. Rufus turned over on his side, determined not to look. It was warm and soft in Westy's bed and it smelled very strongly of her. But he listened, as he had never listened to anything in his life before. He thought he heard bats in the air outside and far away a vixen calling. He could hear the fire, very loud, in Westy's grate, although he knew it was dying. He could hear the creak of Westy's wardrobe door, and the metallic sound of a spindly key turning.

And then she was getting undressed. He knew this as surely as he knew his own name, as he knew the creases on his own small hands. There was a moment when he knew she was naked and still he did not turn over. He dared not cheat and be forbidden from playing the game. His father's game. Hugo's game . . . Hugo who was so good at everything . . . who was so confident of everything. Hugo, who was loved by Rufus' beautiful, cool-kissing mother.

And then Westy got back into bed and said: 'Well, my charmer. Now you must guess who I am.'

'You're not Westy any more,' Rufus whispered. 'You've stopped smelling like Westy.'

'*What are little girls made of,*' sang Nanny, softly from a distance.

And then Rufus whispered no more, because his hand went out to Westy's face and came down it, coolly, with tentative fingers. Down to her neck his childish hands went, and there was a velvet collar there, with a sharp buckle like a big brooch at her throat.

There were silk straps on Westy's shoulders, and at the place where her bosoms were he could feel the hard bone of a corset, but covered in silky material, with little, sharp metal things that he could slip under his nail and he knew there were sequins there.

Down to Westy's waist and the bones clutched her cruelly. The flesh was very hot there as if it contained a long-burning fire that was smothered with old leaves. He felt the shape of the waist, the waist that was normally concealed underneath that neat white apron band.

Then, to Rufus' astonishment, came the layers of netting, and although he could not see them for it was pitch dark under the covers of Westy's bed, in his imagination he could picture the colours, reds, and oranges, and purples ... and he fingered the tight suspenders that dug into Westy's thighs, and the soft, giving flesh around them, and down his fingers went, following the fishnet stockings, down, down, down, to the bottom of Westy's feet. And then he let his hand linger on its way up again, touching, wondering, stopping, stroking, tickling, and all the time Westy was silent, her head high on her pillow, the covers drawn up around her and only Rufus moving like a dark little animal down in the bed.

When he came up he was shaking. His body was wet with his own sweat. It felt puny and small up against Westy.

'I'm boiling, Westy, I'm boiling.'

'What am I then?' she whispered from her very safe, cool place high on the pillow.

'You are one of the bad ladies who dance!' said Rufus earnestly.

And Westy, loving that, had giggled softly, smiled a slow, wet smile and said: 'Well, fancy you knowing that, Master Rufus. And where have you picked up that information from?'

And for a delicious moment Rufus was frightened, frightened that she might guess he had looked at the pictures in the book in Hugo's library, frightened of being found out and stopped from doing it again. Smacked even, by Westy, as he lay here beside her so vulnerable and so small, so needy, as always beside her huge self.

But she didn't chastise him, for that was not the way of the whore. No, instead she stroked him, played with him, fondled him, turned him over and tickled him . . . pretended to change his nappy as if he were a baby. Just like he'd watched her jealously and seen her handle Joel. And Rufus gasped and Rufus muttered, and Rufus squirmed and struggled but Rufus did not want to get away, oh no. 'Did I guess right, Westy?'

'Most certainly you did, my charmer. You got it quite right. For there are women who dress like this and they will do these things to you one day. But they are like me, remember, they do things but they do not feel anything. What they do is for you, because they love you. You can touch them but you cannot make them feel. Why, you don't think your little hands are really touching Westy, do you?'

'I did touch you,' whispered Rufus.

'But did I move? Did I writhe? Did I call out for more?' asked Westy modestly.

'No, Westy, you did not.'

'And neither will I, dressed in this way. For that you must find somebody else.'

'You will dress up as somebody else?'

'That's up to you, my little prince.'

Rufus was breathless in the dark. 'How do I get you to do it again?'

'Well, you must be very good . . .'

'Yes . . .'

'And you must never tell anyone . . .'

'No . . .'

'And you must earn your ten stars . . .'

'How?'

238

'By only ever attaining perfection. By never accept-
ing second best. Do you think I am only worthy of
second best?'

'No, Westy, everything I bring you, everything I do
from now on is going to be perfect.'

'Like your own little body is perfect,' said Westy,
touching him again.

'It's quite dry, Westy, now.'

And Westy laughed. 'Sometimes we will make it wet
together. There's great fun in that.'

And Rufus imagined himself slipping and sliding, up
and down in the darkness of this soundless bed, and his
teeth gritted and he clenched his fists and Westy felt this
in the darkness and Westy sighed.

'We can have some fun together, my charmer, like I
used to have fun with your father. If you just obey
the rules.'

A broadening smile crossed Rufus' face. 'I will always
obey you, Westy. I am going to marry you when I
grow up.'

'Of course you are,' said Westy, turning over. And was
she really going to sleep with her costume on? And would
she allow Rufus to explore her again? Even though she
was asleep and wouldn't know where his little hands
went? *We'll gather lilacs in the spring again . . .*' Rufus
could just hear Westy singing.

There were other uniforms then . . . and Rufus guessed
them all . . . the policewoman . . . the schoolgirl . . . the
kitchen maid . . . the nurse. They were all kind to Rufus
. . . they all made him happy.

Except for the terrible times. The times when Westy
chose to dress as the nun. For the nun was the cruellest
of all. When Westy became the nun she was hard and she
was forbidding. She was frigid and cold. She lay beside
Rufus and he had to be still. Sometimes she made him
watch her as she lifted the habit to reveal her own, vast

239

nakedness and whipped herself raw with her strap. She raised welts on her back and Rufus got out of bed and begged her to stop.

'You will never touch a nun,' Westy used to taunt him. 'She won't let you near her! She is innocent and pure and has no need of men! That, my little charmer, would be the perfect specimen . . . an innocent woman without wicked thoughts. But is there such a creature? Is there such a one? Find her and bring her to me and I might let you touch her . . . touch where nobody else has ever been . . . where nobody else will ever go.'

And Rufus had tossed and turned on the bed in a sweat of wild frustration . . . for he had got his stars and been denied . . . everything he had brought to Westy had been perfect, he had kept his part of the bargain but was forced to lie there, powerless. While Westy stripped in front of him, showing him her all, but never cuddling close and not allowing his hands to stray.

Sometimes, in the darkness, they lay and they wept together. And then, in order to make him better, Westy would sing to him.

There are so many terrible imperfections, Nanny. Rufus groans as he strides along beside the whispering sea, treading deep in the wet sand, his footprints leaving a dragging shape behind them. For when Nanny was the nurse Nanny was willing and gentle; when Nanny was the policewoman she was willing but strict; when Nanny was the maid she was willing but coy; when Nanny was the schoolgirl she was willing but innocent; but nurses are not always gentle and certainly they are not willing – same with all those others – they were not as Nanny said they were. Terribly flawed, they had to be punished. They had to be broken and thrown away.

When Nanny was the whore she was willing but untouchable . . . Chelsea, she gave pleasure to herself secretly and so she had to die! Tricked! After all these years . . . how could he have been so hopelessly blind? Never knowing until he found that infernal machine hidden in her drawer! A vibrator! Dear God! And he had brought her to Westy, presented her, proud of her! Anguish! Defeat! Humiliation!

He had quickly changed his priorities. He had gone to the shrine and changed the costumes from nun to whore. Chelsea must be destroyed!

And Helen? Well Helen's fate has long been decided. When Nanny was the nun Nanny was unwilling. As Helen should be unwilling, as Rufus, quite naturally, assumed she always would be. Helen has to die, for Helen *is* willing and Helen is lusting . . . Rufus has seen that mesmerised stare in her eye . . . and he has assumed that stare to be a loving one.

As they all have.

Wrong! Wrong! Everything is so wrong! There is sheer horror in Rufus' eyes.

And Mother? Well, Mother deserves to be punished for it was Mother who sent Westy away.

'*Pitter patter pitter patter on my shoulder I will be your master. In and out the dusty bluebells . . .*' and Rufus strides, head lowered, on across the dunes.

241

25

When she came out Helen Weston dropped the end of her name because it felt too heavy. She could hardly drag along the West which was left.

She had felt life stirring uneasily within her soon after Mumma died. And the life she felt was a restless kind, turbulent, uncomfortable, not to be contained behind convent walls. And it grew, like a thing that had been unborn for too long.

As a child Helen had never dreamed of being approached by a famous actress, a diplomat, a member of the aristocracy, approached and claimed for long lost as many of her peers had done. Well, Helen, not quite orphaned, had not had that option. Mumma visited regularly as clockwork on the last Sunday of every month, and it was Mumma Helen dreamed of, it was Mumma who would one day come to claim her and take her away, it was Mumma's voice which, one day, would call her in from the garden.

Oh those fevered opening moments and those unresolved departures. Never quite abandoned, yet Helen lived with the permanent ache of abandonment. She would kneel on the high-backed wooden chair in the refectory, parting the curtains and staring out down the street. 'There is violence in such impatience, Helen. You do violence to yourself and to your mother,' said Sister Miriam. 'Sit with your hands together and contemplate the fact that a restless heart can only find rest in Him. You would do well to ponder upon the words of Gregory of Nyssa who said that the soul's desire is fulfilled by the very fact of remaining unsatisfied.'

But Helen looked out and waited for the first moment when she would see Mumma's face. And she knew she would feel like the Israelites when they saw the face of

Moses, needing to cover it up because the feelings it gave them were too much to bear.

If it was spring or summer Helen would pick bunches of flowers to put in the refectory on the days Mumma came. She wanted Mumma to see the flowers, know they'd been picked for her and admire them. But the room was so big they were hard to see. They got lost amidst all the tables.

Mumma brought a cosy wonder into the room from the outside world. The fire would burn more brightly. They would pull up their chairs and Mumma would rest her stockinged feet on the guard. Out of her bag she would bring presents . . . some rainbow wool, and she would teach Helen to crochet with her finger, on and on and round and round until she made a tea cosy; oil paints and pieces of crisp, white card that they would fold together and make wondrous butterfly patterns out of mindless squirts; yellow and orange raffia which they would sew into cork with big needles and make table mats. When you sucked the raffia to thread it, the colour came off on your tongue, and Mumma did it on purpose to make stripes.

And very often Mumma would tell Helen stories. She would tell them by heart in a crooning voice, or would bring well-thumbed books from the nursery at Burford. The books had a scenty smell about them, and smooth pages, and some, with rougher pages, had tissue paper between the colour plates, and Helen knew she must handle these with great care. She wiped her fingers on her apron, always, before she picked up one of Mumma's books.

When Mumma went away she collected the books, the paints, the raffia, the rainbow-coloured wool, put them tidily into her bag and took them off with her. She never left anything behind, not anything.

So once Helen had hidden the story of *One Eye, Two Eyes and Three Eyes*, one of the books with tissue between the pages. She hadn't been able to bear to let it go. She

243

saw herself as Two Eyes, the scorned one, the abandoned one, and knew that one day Mumma would see, like the handsome knight did, that, in spite of her ordinariness, Two Eyes was the best and the kindest, and Mumma would come and carry her away to the place that haunted Helen's dreams.

And this place was no grove or grotto. This place was the nursery at Burford, every detail of which Helen knew intimately from corner to corner. Well, Mumma never spoke of anything else.

'Rufus has learned to tie his own tie, standing on a chair in front of the mirror over the nursery fire.'

'What if he fell off and got burned?' Helen would ask, half hopeful.

'Oh bless you, he'd never do that! What, with his stocky little legs? And if he did he'd only fall on the meshing. The nursery guard is always up. You should see the concentration on his little face, how he scrunches it up and sticks out the end of his tongue. Like this, look!'

And then it was: 'When I told the story of Little Brother and Little Sister, guess what? That silly boy Simon began to cry!'

'Tell it to me, Mumma. I won't cry!'

'I'm sure you won't! You're far too sensible a girl for that.'

And also there was: 'Guess what Rufus likes best to eat? Best of all . . . even better than sweets?'

Helen sucked the slab of stick-jaw toffee which Rufus and Simon had made on the hot plate next to the laundry room, and felt a warm, wet trickle of it browning her chin. 'What?'

'Well it isn't cake and it isn't toast and it isn't muffins and it isn't rock from the seaside.'

The rigid toffee bumped the soft bits in Helen's mouth. She held it aside with her tongue and asked: 'What is it?'

'It's mussels! Straight from the rocks! They put them in a pan of boiling water . . . poor mussels . . . they say you can hear them scream but I've listened and I never hear them.'

'Why must you go back?'

'Oh now bless you, dear! Why must I go back? Well, where else would I go? I haven't a home like you have! I must live where my work takes me! And what would my little boys do without me, I ask you? I'm needed there . . . I've always been needed by all my little boys. How would they learn to do up their laces without me? Who would cut their toenails and make sure that their hair was brushed? Who would make sure they put out their lights at night and who would rub Vick on their chests when they got their snuffly colds?'

'I can do all those things myself.'

'Some of us can and some of us can't. You are a girl and therefore more sensible! Well . . . look at you! Look how you're growing! I can be proud of my Helen without having to worry if she's washed behind her ears or taken the nasty tangles out of her hair . . .'

But all the time they spoke like this, Helen saw that Mumma's eyes were not quite on her. Her mind not quite on the subject. Her thoughts were wandering back to Burford, taken on the wings of angel's heels. Helen could see them take Mumma there behind those quick little smiles.

'What if I had been born a boy?'

'What a silly question! What if . . . what if . . . now do you know, Joel is always asking me things like that.'

And then, in a year when they all got chilblains, Helen had knitted a pair of red, fingerless gloves which she gave to Mumma to take to Rufus. She hadn't dropped one stitch and the ribbing was neat and even. She'd even managed to work a band of white at the rim. 'If Rufus gets chilblains,' she said, 'he'll feel better with these on.' She'd done this because she'd been told if you do

245

things for people you don't like you feel better about them. 'Love!' sang out the choir deafeningly. 'Love can conquer all!'

Mumma had looked at the gloves, folded them and put them into her bag. 'Chilblains, my dear, need all the fresh air they can get. And lots of diversions for overactive little fingers!'

Helen never heard if Rufus liked them. Even if he got them. She hadn't known, then, that at Burford nobody knew she existed.

One day Mumma brought photographs. There was herself and Rufus and Simon standing under a big beech tree, and Joel leaning forward in a floppy bonnet, covered in lace like a girl, with a fringed canopy over his pram. It was the first time Helen had seen Mumma's little boys, and she was struck by how alike they all were, and how tightly the two oldest boys clung to her for the photograph. Simon was standing up straight like a soldier, holding Mumma's hand, and Rufus, not touching, yet clutched with his worshipping smile. Mumma looked very solid, like the tree, and her shadow spread further across the grass than all the tree's branches . . . right to the feet of the photographer.

'Who took the picture, Mumma?'

'Master Hugo of course. Now he was a lovely little boy. Let me tell you about the day he rode on his first donkey. We had gone to Southend with a picnic . . .'

'Most little girls have a father, Mumma. But I've never heard of mine.'

'Have they been asking you questions in here?'

Helen shook her head, bewildered by the change in Mumma's tone. 'No. They never ask questions.'

'You can forget your father, Helen, as I have. He was no better than he ought to have been . . . a wastrel and a scoundrel. I only saw him the once and that was enough. I ought to have known better, I was old to be a mother, into my forties before I had you. You were born the year

246

before Rufus was born . . . you are just one year older. Your father was a painter, a friend of Master Hugo's. He promised to marry me after, but he got killed right at the end of the war. In a Spitfire.' Mumma looked off into the distance, and said with a sigh: 'He died mucking about playing games in a Spitfire. Caruthers was his name, but that has nothing to do with you. You take my name, Weston, which is a fine, solid name and good enough for anyone. We wouldn't want you to grow up with ideas above your station. I don't know what I'd have done in those days if the nuns hadn't taken me in!' Mumma glanced at the watercolour Helen was painting. 'But I think you've inherited his talent for art,' she said reprovingly, as if there was something not quite nice about that. And Helen gathered that there was something not quite nice about her father, also. She left the circumstances of her birth well alone. She licked the tip of her brush and stared, thoughtfully, at Mumma.

Helen's tongue moved cautiously round her mouth before she asked: 'Mumma, what when your little boys have all grown up?'

'There are always little boys somewhere, Helen, waiting for dear old Westy.'

And then Helen said, in a flippant voice, looking away: 'But what about me?'

'Oh you'll be big and grown up yourself then! You won't want cod liver oil or malt! You won't want your chest rubbed!' Mumma's reply was an energetic, and a positive one.

Prior to the first ceremony, Helen happily handed over the photograph of Mumma and the boys, but the book she had stolen was different. There hadn't been many things to give in, only old birthday presents from Mumma, and they had always been sensible ones for the nuns wouldn't let her accept anything frivolous or immodest. There was a Mason Pearson hairbrush –

they let her keep that; the guitar she had asked for one year but never learned to play; her oil painting set; her pyjama-case dog and her fluffy blue dressing gown. The toys she had played with as a small child had all been communally owned. She had never missed any of those. Even the doll with the woolly hair, although she had nursed it for hours, Helen had not really loved. So she sat in her cell throughout her retreat in the days before the ceremony, and it wasn't the Bible she read at all, it was the story of little Two Eyes.

So Mumma had never recognised . . . the one-eyed children and the three-eyed children who lived in all those big houses had won. Helen looked at Mumma when, clad in her new habit, her white veil, and wearing her novice's cross, she was led, in procession, back to the chapel while the organ pealed out in glory to God. Mumma was there with all the others, wearing her uniform and her 'strict' hat (Helen had always been so proud of her when she came in it), and as the sun streamed through the plate-glass window, casting the colours of joy, Helen screamed out inside: 'I'm going, Mumma, I'm going. My name is little Two Eyes, and aren't you coming to get me?'

But, to her dismay, Mumma said afterwards: 'Helen, my dear, you look wonderful! You look as if you were born to wear that habit. You look quite radiant!'

And that was the year that Mumma was leaving Burford.

Quiet, self-effacing, Helen asked: 'Where will you go now, Mumma?'

'I already have a position lined up, with two little boys in Somerset. Their own mother is dead, poor lambs, so they are needing a shoulder to cry on.'

'And won't you miss your old little boys?'

Mumma sniffed, in the way that the other relatives did as they contemplated their newly robed daughters. But she did not hold a handkerchief to her nose and her eyes were not misted. 'In a way, yes I will. But it is my life, Helen, and I am used to partings. You do get used to them, you know.'

And Helen wondered in what sort of way her mother loved.

Helen would have liked a parting, a definite, final parting. But that was not to be. Mumma came less, but Mumma still visited, still brought along her bag full of memories, now just momentoes. For Helen felt, very strongly, that Mumma was past her prime, that Mumma had never felt for those poor little motherless Somerset boys in the way that she felt for the Pilkingtons. And Mumma clung, even then, to the careers of what she called her 'special ones'. Much later she used to bring Helen newspaper clippings of Simon playing golf all over the world; articles about Joel and his amazing orchestral success – she even brought publicity photographs, thinking, perhaps, that Helen wanted to, or would be allowed to stick them up all over her cell wall.

And as for dear Rufus. 'Well all I can say is that it's a pity you don't get to watch television,' said Mumma. 'For he weaves magic! Before you turn on you know that if it's a programme involving Rufus, it's going to be good. You know you're going to be enthralled from start to finish.'

But Helen did not have a television. She merely read the criticisms that Mumma insisted on sending.

Helen became twenty-four. 'I am thinking of taking my final vows,' she said to Mumma. It was a bright summer day and they strolled round the convent garden.

'Well, I thought that one day you would,' said Mumma. 'I hope you have given it a great deal of thought.'

'Of course I have,' said Helen.

'Won't you miss the outside world? Won't you miss all the people?'

They stopped and sat down on a bench, for Mumma was out of breath and puffing. Over the years she had grown fatter, so that now, even though she had always been big, to Helen Mumma appeared much larger and seemed to need a great deal of strength to get her body along as briskly as she wanted. And, Helen noticed with shock, Mumma was getting old.

'Well, Mumma, did you miss the outside world? Did you miss the people?'

Mumma looked puzzled. 'I never cut myself off,' she said. 'I never shut myself away. My life has always been full of people and happenings, comings and goings.'

'But all from high up behind the nursery door,' said Helen, 'with your little boys.'

'You cannot compare it at all, Helen,' said Mumma, seemingly insulted. And Helen felt an involuntary pang of sadness, for Mumma, for Mumma's life, for what they had missed and what might have been. Here they were, the two of them, sitting in a convent garden with their lives closing in on them and nothing bright beckoning anywhere except for the silver-finned goldfish that now and then nudged the lily leaves in the pond by their feet. Both of them wore sensible brogues, tied with black laces. Helen stared at the sun on the water and wondered what would have happened if either of them had ever danced, if either of them had worn dancing shoes. Helen would have chosen shoes of the brightest gold. But Helen would be afraid to dance now . . . in case she fell over. And Mumma, she guessed, would have felt the same.

Helen saw it would be pointless to go on making comparisons, pointless and unkind. So . . . two frightened women, sitting together, frightened to love . . . afraid of it, sat silent for a while. So they had both chosen a communal love, learned, and based on the foundation of indifference.

' . . . And then I suppose I will retire,' Mumma was saying. Helen held her breath. Was Mumma asking? At last . . . was she asking? 'To a little house by the sea where all my children can come to visit me and bring me various little comforts.'

'And won't you be lonely, Mumma?'

Mumma laughed. She crossed her black-stockinged legs, her heavy shoes came one over the other, and she laughed. 'Lonely? Lord! I have a piano-top full of photographs to look at. I have scrapbooks so full I can hardly lift them. And some of my boys have children of their own now. I will always be wanted,' said Mumma. 'I will always be needed.'

Helen clutched her candle very firmly as she moved towards the crucifix. '*My beloved speaks and says to me, arise my love, my fair one, and come away.*'

'*What do you desire?*'

'*Thou, oh Lord God, are the thing that I long for.*'

'Have you ever known a deeper joy than this?' asked Sister Augustus. And pale, serious Helen could only shake her head.

She prostrated herself on the ground to embrace the stone-cold love, the love that would hold her.

Mumma had a stroke, and she lived in a home paid for by the Pilkingtons. Helen was not needed, she could not have gone anyway. Every now and then a card would arrive, written in a spidery hand. Still, the little bursts of news would be telling of Rufus' doings, of Rufus' visits and presents, of the outing he had taken her on.

Helen genuflected in front of the altar, day after day, year after year, as spring gave way to summer and winter came again. When the letter came to tell her that Mumma was dead, life burst through to Helen, starting as merely a trickle before it came roaring and ripping, tearing and spinning right through her like

251

a mighty, crashing, majestic chord of thunder from the sky.

And there, so simple, taking the place of the crucifix, had been Rufus, beckoning to her with a signature smiling in green.

26

It is evening. And Harry, who hasn't been in this pub for years, has come across to the Merry Fiddler in order to find Desmond and have the whole thing out with him. If he's involved in this desperate mess – Chelsea is dead, Harriet is in the hands of the law, a self-confessed murderess, a martyr to her children and to her cause – as this is all going on the least that Harry can do is talk to Desmond and find out if Harriet's terrible assumptions are true. Man to man.

But, never a man who has been able to pass a menu without putting his specs on, Harry pauses to look up at the blackboard on the yellowy pillar. As he runs his eyes up and down he begins to feel sweat prickle under his arms. It spreads up his body until it stands out on his brow just as it does when he tries to play tennis. He takes out his gaudy handkerchief to wipe it. For there, standing out starkly in chalk among the letters that make up 'platter of mushrooms', 'fisherman's pie' and 'freshly made pasties' . . . there stand three Fs . . . three Fs that Harry has only ever seen once written like that before! For who else draws an F with its back almost to the floor, the top branch pointing up to the sky, the lower one down to the ground, so it resembles more of a broken R? *'Payment For the maid . . .'* all the Fs in the blackmail notes had been written like that.

Feeling faint, Harry staggers to the bar. Harry clutches it. Desmond, sitting on the nearest stool, sees Harry's agitation and edges himself away. He can't wait to get away from these people but they seem to be dogging his footsteps. Because of Chelsea's death, Desmond has been able to hold on to his dreams. She might have loved him. She might have agreed to go away with him. He might have become the most important person in Chelsea's life and no one can now tell him otherwise. He hugs this knowledge to himself and no one can take it away. He looks back on his old self with a mixture of pity and scorn. He is a man, he has been lusted after by the most beautiful woman he has ever seen, the most fascinating person to whom he has ever spoken. She wanted him . . . he saw that in her eyes. She wanted him. And she was not lying.

He might go to Renfrew with Roger, but then again he might not. Whatever happens now he is no longer prepared to stay at home and be blackmailed by guilt. He can do no more for Enid . . . all her misery and sadness she brings upon herself. He can no longer be blamed. He is no longer prepared to have anything more to do with it.

Harry looks as if he is having an epileptic fit. Desmond calls warily from his new position: 'Are you all right? Can I get you something?'

'Just the landlord,' gasps Harry hoarsely, loosening his collar. 'Just fetch me the landlord!'

Desmond calls and Cope comes over.

'My God! Cope! It was you! Why, for God's sake man, why?' Harry is almost beside himself. He can hardly speak.

Cope nods towards the hatch through which Nellie's head is just coming. Her shoulders are hunched with the weight from a trayful of vegetable stews. 'Nellie the wife. You remember all about her, don't you, Mr fancy Featherstonehough!'

Nellie comes out then, seeing that something is up. She comes out rolling slightly from side to side, her mouth just a livid scar of a smile but Harry recognises her eyes. Her eyes, after all these years, are still that palest of watery blues, and fishy, they are still just the same. With that tired air of resignation in them . . . exactly the same.

254

Harry flushes and says: 'Nellie? Good grief. Little Nellie Mundy?'

'What's this?' asks Nellie, picking off dough from between her fingers. Sensing the tension she looks up at Cope and she looks across the bar at Harry, eyeing him directly. 'I said what's this?'

Harry shakes his head, for this is a terribly private matter and there are people all round, ears bent, eyes glancing. But he can't help whispering to Nellie: 'And you? Are you part of it, too?'

Cope is as uneasy as Harry. Because Cope loves Nellie, in spite of her hip and her fat and her roll. Cope has always loved Nellie. But Nellie is a simple creature, afraid of the law, afraid of scandal, afraid of a bad reputation and of losing her money and of her mother and of the recent bad cough she's developed. Oh, Nellie is frightened of so many things. And Nellie has her nasty side. If Nellie knew what Cope had got up to, then Nellie would be furious. Nellie might never forgive him, she'd certainly not understand.

'Nellie does not know what you are talking about,' says Cope meaningfully, polishing a glass.

'But you do, don't you?' says Harry, feeling a fraction less fraught on sensing Cope's obvious discomfort.

Cope nods and closes one eye. 'Aye, that I do. I know.'

'What is he talking about?' asks Nellie. 'There is something going on here about which I ought to know.'

'Is there?' Harry asks Cope. 'Is there something going on about which your wife ought to know?'

Cope clenches his teeth together and the smile he drives across the bar is not pleasant. There is none of the lovable brigand about him now. Cope is under pressure, and Cope's stare is a warning.

So is Harry's. They take stock of each other as they stand there, taut as arm wrestlers, but all that they try to bend are each other's eyes. While Nellie tugs on Cope's sleeve, saying: 'Kitch! Kitch! I want to know what's going on!'

'You know my wife, I believe,' says Cope, venturing into dangerous territory with one eye betraying him, twitching slightly.

'Everyone knows me,' says Nellie, interrupting. 'I've known Harry since we were children here at Tremity together. Everyone knows me and everyone knows Harry. You know that quite well, Kitch, so for goodness' sake what are you getting at?'

In the one-minute pause that is granted them, while Nellie takes a tray out to some waiting customers, Harry spits across the bar: 'You know that your damned fool notes have driven Harriet to murder?'

Cope casts his eyes around him and answers: 'How could they do that?'

'She was told at the time,' whispers Harry. 'At the time Hugo approached you. She's been brooding on it for years and she finally settled upon poor Chelsea . . . as I almost did, and daft Desmond over there . . . this is what this sort of thing leads to! This is an example of cause and effect . . . You're damn lucky it's not you lying dead in the morgue with a broken skull. If Harriet had known the truth, no doubt she'd have dealt with you in the same way!'

'Oh?' Cope gives a belligerent shrug. 'Oh, so it's all my fault! So some old woman goes mad and it's my fault!'

'The police might think it was your fault . . .'

'If the police ever got to know.'

'Precisely, the police, or even your wife,' he says as, stiffly but with trembling legs, Harry stalks away from the bar.

Harry knows the point has been taken. Harry is safe. His children are safe. His friends are safe. And all because of the crime committed by the mad, noble, self-sacrificing Harriet – who has killed and taken upon herself the mantle of martyrdom. They will survive this little scandal. Oh, Jessica might well be adversely affected, but Harry can deal with that.

And murder . . . done by a deranged old woman . . . murder does not compare with the rape of a child. For nobody can be blamed for Harriet's sudden, extraordinary flight into madness, or for the strange tales she tells. And Hugo is dead and wouldn't give a damn about a posthumous reputation. Harry knows there will be no more notes. That that dreadful weight has for ever lifted, and all because of a badly formed F.

The nun knows it must be tonight for there is no time left. And yet there is no hurry. Let it happen naturally and with some dignity. After all, ritual is important to both of them.

Helen's is, and always was, a simple vision.

She knows that Rufus does not have long, and that he must know that, too. Soon they will make the connections. Soon they will find out who killed Chelsea . . . there is no proof against Harriet. No one believes her rantings. And they will come . . . with all the other dead women like ghosts pointing accusing fingers . . . and they will come and take Rufus away and he will never be properly punished.

Helen has waited a very long time for her vengeance.

She is prepared to wait no longer.

She has to prepare herself, as a bride would prepare for her first night with her groom, or as a nun would prepare for her God. First she bathes. She must be spotless. She scrubs her arms and legs with a nail brush until they are quite sore. Then she lies in a bath of white bubbles and covers her body with foam. She washes her hair and she brushes it, staring into the mirror. It was years before she saw herself in a mirror, she still finds herself hard to recognise.

Not here, Rufus, oh no, not here in this house.

She listens as she goes, dressing-gowned, towards the

attic steps and up to the art room and through the door in the roof. Bent half double she half crawls, following the passages under the rafters, keeping her feet on the struts for fear she will fall through the plaster. At the place where she knows the trunk to be, she pauses, switches on the torch, and lets it rest on the school trunk, opens the lid, lets the light rest on the clothes.

The habit and veil are there on top. She gathers them into her arms and looks no further. There will be nothing of the whore there now . . . Rufus lost those to the police. But the nun has only to go into Chelsea's room to find what she wants. And then, for something else, for something important, she will make her way into Desmond's where the African souvenirs are. But now, in the pathways around the roof she blows the cobwebs away from her as she half stumbles, feeling her way back towards the light and the safer place. For that which she leaves behind her is fetid and black and crawling with evil.

As night comes to Tremity, as the White Waves lights go on, the nun dresses slowly and with care. She waits until she hears the family going to bed, and she's used to waiting and being quiet. No one will ask her what she's doing, or how she is, or if she wants any supper. Nobody ever does in this house. And she is Rufus' guest. She is Rufus' responsibility. And Rufus is out of his mind . . . with grief? They think!

When silence comes to White Waves Helen knows it is time. Quietly, as is the way of a nun, she glides across the garden, a figure in black, passing the wrought-iron chairs – they gleam in the darkness – down past the bower where Wendy, the brigadier's daughter, lay catching the sun the previous day.

No one else is in sight. It is still as midnight and warm as midday and only the trees flutter beneath the stars. The water whispers in ghostly time with the pine cones. The water whispers and Helen's sandals whisper their way down the silent rabbit track, down the steep, sloping side of the bank which is the only approach to the cave.

The empty cave. Now that the skeleton is no longer there.

Rufus will come because he has to. Rufus cannot stay away, he is not able to do that. Helen waits. Helen stares. Helen is hardly breathing. She takes the place of the bones on the rock . . . and there, quite still, she poses.

He comes now, she knows that he comes. Helen can hear his breathing, the breathing of a bright-eyed animal coming late to its lair through the dark. He creeps. He pauses. He comes on. Crouched like a man hiding, she knows, because of the many occasions she's seen him, because of the times she has watched him.

But never before from inside.

Rufus steps softly into the cave. Slowly he comes to his full height, arms at his sides, his regal head proud in the air. He sees the nun. His teeth glint as he brings to his face a kind of smile. Such a smile, the smile of the Devil, the crooked smile of the torturer, the ravaged smile of the damned.

'Helen.' Rufus speaks softly as in a caress. 'You've come then.'

Helen licks her lips with her tongue. She watches him through narrowed eyes, her head lowered.

'Helen? Why don't you answer me?'

Rufus steps forward. His fists clench. For this is the one and now is the time, he and his victim both know that. Westy always knew that . . . and Rufus always knew the nights when Westy would choose the nun . . . cold, closed, dry nun. Rigid. Loveless. Pure?

No, this nun is not pure. This one cannot be collected. This one must be disposed of, like all the others, like all the other filth and dirt and offal that he has disposed of along the way . . . the policewoman who would not love him . . . the nurse who laughed at him . . . the schoolgirl who tried to tantalise him . . . the waitress who would not play with him . . . his wife . . .

Yes, even his wife. Chelsea. Damn you Chelsea! With your dirty ways and filthy habits.

And now. This woman. This nun! Who is not a nun! Who lusts. Who has to be his before he can throw her away!

Rufus' eyes burn brilliantly in the darkness. The nun watches him carefully, aware of every movement and noticing how he takes a deep breath every time he moves forward. His hands reach out to touch her. The nun stays still, she does not flinch. Instead she allows him to feel her robe, to take it between his fingers, to lift it to his lips, to hold it to his nose, to savour and relish and remember . . . with childlike fingers to remember Westy.

His words hiss out between his lips. 'Yes . . . oh yes . . .' says Rufus, stepping closer. 'Oh yes . . . Helen, how long have you wanted me? How long have you lusted? For how many nights have you lain in your lonely bed, arms across your chest, yearning and dreaming and sweating and steaming, imagining my body on yours, myself in yourself . . . dominating, taking possession of you . . .'

Rufus grips her shoulders, he brings his mouth to her face ready to cover her lips and her screams. Helen lets her veil fall back and Rufus retreats, his eyes form a silent scream. For that is no nun's face . . . black eyes smeared with purple, the mascara on the lids is so thick the eyes will hardly part. Rouge across her cheekbones makes them bloody . . . the scarlet gash which is the lipstick is wet like a freshly cut wound. And the hair that is normally so simple and pure, the hair is frizzed and stiff with the cheapest lacquer . . . sour hair . . . sinful hair . . .

Helen laughs. She has never laughed like this in her life. She lets her habit fall. Her breasts are hardly covered . . . the bra that she wears is cut in half, revealing the nipples daubed with thickest lipstick. She wears suspenders and fishnet stockings and nothing else, and those high heels must be Chelsea's, but most of all she wears the laugh that he hears . . . and her flesh is white and blank and piercing as any scream.

Rufus cries into the silent night. His hands fall to his sides. He retches, steps back, falls down on to the sand. He lifts up the sand and covers his face, pours it over his head like water, lets it flow over him . . . he must be cleansed he must cleanse himself of this . . . of this . . . WHAT IS THIS?

'Who am I, Rufus, who am I?'

Rufus cowers like an animal, his eyes red-rimmed and full of sand. His mouth falls open, slackly howling. Helen stands up, she walks like a prostitute, brazenly defiant, flaunting the awfulness, proud of it, and her face is loose and abandoned.

He stares. He tries to scream again but cannot.

'All those women,' says Helen, in Westy's strictest voice. 'All those women you killed and nobody knew it was you. Except me. And maybe Westy. Did she know, Rufus, did she?'

Rufus shakes his head. He tries to speak but he has no voice.

'What did she do, Rufus, what did she do? Did she dress up like this? Is that why you keep coming here night after night as if to a shrine with your hopeless little offerings? Was it Westy's praise you were after during those long lonely nights? Did you think you would please her with your gifts, even after she was dead? But they were flawed, weren't they, Rufus? You could never find anything that was perfect, or that matched your idea of perfection. You never could, and so you killed. How many were there, Rufus – five, six, seven? Over and over again you killed. And now you want to kill me, don't you, Rufus?'

Rufus, down on all fours like a dog, presses back to the wall, letting the coldness cool him.

'You thought that Westy was perfect, didn't you, Rufus? You thought she was yours. Is that what she told you? Did she reassure you, tell you she'd love you only, and then did she go away and love some other little boys? But at least she was yours, wasn't she? She never gave her body to another man. That's what you thought, Rufus, isn't it? ANSWER ME! That is what you thought!'

Rufus nods, vacant eyed. His mouth opens as if, from somewhere deeper than that, he is howling.

'Now listen to me, Rufus.' Helen brings her head down to contemplate the scum on the ground in a grandly imperial manner. 'Westy was my mother.' She smiles when she sees the effect of her words. For Rufus is shivering now, and drooling, his gold is very tarnished and to Helen he has never been so small, nor so far away, nor so undeserving of her attentions.

There is no point in prolonging the agony. There is only one thing Helen can do so she hardens her face in order to do it. With eyes as opaque as frosted glass, Helen goes to the back of the cave and retrieves the black habit lying there. She throws the billowing black material over her head and lets it fall. Easily she clips the veil into place, adjusts the wimple and straightens the folds. She picks up the lethally sharp assegai she has removed from Desmond's wall, steps back towards Rufus, steadying herself, and as he stares up at her she thrusts the blade forcefully into his throat.

'When I was little all I wanted to do was hold your hand while we fed the birds.'

Dumb like an offering on his knees he stares, as if he's known this day must finally come. His eyes plead for death as his crimson blood covers the hem of her habit, as the bubbles froth from his wound, as the spear breaks flesh again and again. And when he coughs and falls on his side she straddles him, steadies her weapon and thrusts again. There is no mercy here, or pity.

As there was none when she stared into the eyes of Christ all those years ago. Just a stone-cold stare, offering nothing.

Helen does not resist when they come for her. Well, she is an institutional person, always has been. She is dignified when they take her away and she stays dignified to the end.

Helen won't speak to anyone. She says nothing. She has no one to speak for any more and she doesn't even deny it.

The children tell their tale. 'It was Helen,' they say, every one. Not even the wily Inspector Ainsworth can break their story. 'Not Harriet. We saw Helen take the golf club . . . we saw her sneak off with it . . . she was gone for over half an hour and when she came back there was blood on her hands. She went to the sea to wash it. It was Helen who killed Chelsea.

'It was our fault,' they add, 'for making her drunk. Because soon after she came back she went to sleep. She lay down behind the dunes. It was Helen,' they say. 'We saw her. She was always in love with Rufus. Everyone knew that. She never hid it. She killed Chelsea, and when Rufus still turned her overtures down she decided to kill him too.'

There are no other clues. The river washed away any footprints and the shaft of the ancient golf club had been slopped by too many waves.

Harriet goes into a home, voluntarily. The same home, incidentally, where Westy was sent. Her family visit her often. She is allowed total freedom – to knock her balls, to go on her walks, to drink gin and tonics just the same. And there is always someone there to make up a hand at bridge. She is not mad, just a little eccentric. No one can find anything wrong with her, but they just think she'd be better not left alone for so much of the time. After a straight, private talk with Harry,

Harriet quickly came to her senses, retracted her silly confession.

And poor little parentless Gregor? How terribly sad it all is! Well, Gregor is doing very nicely, being spoilt and made a great deal of fuss of in the home of his uncle, Simon the golfer, his royal wife Wendy and their petite daughter, the pretty, coquettish Amelia.

He seems to get over the violent deaths of his two parents quite quickly. 'Let us hope the trauma does not wait until later in life to rear its head,' says the family doctor uneasily.

'Gregor,' calls Amelia prettily. 'Come out into the garden! Come for a swim! We're all waiting.'

But Gregor is putting the last rib on a skeleton of a model dinosaur. He clenches his teeth when he hears her . . . he wishes she'd leave him alone.

'Come on, Gregor! Come on!' Amelia bursts into the room, disturbing the boy's concentration. 'You can do that later,' she says, pulling his sleeve.

'I'll be there in a minute,' says Gregor softly, half to her and half to himself. 'I cannot leave this until I've got it just perfect.' He turns to face her. 'Well don't you understand that?' he asks, and his strange expression is covered by the very sweetest of smiles.

also available from

THE ORION PUBLISHING GROUP

☐ Mothers and
Other Lovers £5.99
JOANNA BRISCOE
1 85799 248 2

☐ Judicial Whispers £5.99
CARO FRASER
1 85799 377 2

☐ The Pupil £5.99
CARO FRASER
1 85799 063 3

☐ The Trustees £5.99
CARO FRASER
1 85799 059 5

☐ All My Friends are Going
to be Strangers £5.99
LARRY MCMURTRY
1 85799 141 0

☐ The Desert Rose £5.99
LARRY MCMURTRY
1 85799 140 0

☐ Streets of Laredo £6.99
LARRY MCMURTRY
1 85799 139 7

☐ Terms of Endearment £5.99
LARRY MCMURTRY
1 85799 192 3

☐ While the Music Lasts £5.99
ALICE MCVEIGH
1 85799 342 X

☐ House of Splendid
Isolation £5.99
EDNA O'BRIEN
1 85799 209 1

☐ Astonishing the Gods £5.99
BEN OKRI
1 85799 374 8

☐ Absolution £5.99
OLAF OLAFSSON
1 85799 227 X

☐ Beastly Tales £4.99
VIKRAM SETH
1 85799 305 5

☐ A Suitable Boy £9.99
VIKRAM SETH
1 85799 088 9

☐ The Crow Biddy £5.99
GILLIAN WHITE
1 85799 204 0

☐ Grandfather's Footsteps £5.99
GILLIAN WHITE
1 85799 337 3

☐ Mothertime £5.99
GILLIAN WHITE
1 85799 208 3

☐ Nasty Habits £5.99
GILLIAN WHITE
1 85799 338 1

☐ Rich Deceiver £5.99
GILLIAN WHITE
1 85799 256 3

All Orion/Phoenix titles are available at your local bookshop or from the following address:

Littlehampton Book Services
Cash Sales Department L
14 Eldon Way, Lineside Industrial Estate
Littlehampton
West Sussex BN17 7HE

telephone 01903 721596, *facsimile* 01903 730914

Payment can either be made by credit card (Visa and Mastercard accepted) or by sending a cheque or postal order made payable to *Littlehampton Book Services*.

DO NOT SEND CASH OR CURRENCY.

Please add the following to cover postage and packing

UK and BFPO:
£1.50 for the first book, and 50P for each additional book to a maximum of £3.50

Overseas and Eire:
£2.50 for the first book plus £1.00 for the second book and 50p for each additional book ordered

----

BLOCK CAPITALS PLEASE

name of cardholder ....

address of cardholder ....

....

....

....

postcode ....

delivery address
(if different from cardholder)

....

....

....

....

postcode ....

☐ I enclose my remittance for £...............................

☐ please debit my Mastercard/Visa (delete as appropriate)

card number ☐☐☐☐☐☐☐☐☐☐☐☐☐☐☐☐

expiry date ☐☐☐☐

signature ....

prices and availability are subject to change without notice